Ana's Way

Ana's Way

A Novel

By

Manuela Draganova

Library of Congress Control Number:		2018904040
ISBN:	Hardcover	978-1-9845-1907-8
	Softcover	978-1-9845-1906-1
	eBook	978-1-9845-1905-4

Print information available on the last page.

Rev. date: 05/25/2018

To order additional copies of this book, contact:
Xlibris
1-888-795-4274
www.Xlibris.com
Orders@Xlibris.com
775901

CONTENTS

CHAPTER 1

ANA

An anadromous fish, such as salmon, is born in freshwater, and afterward migrates to the ocean in order to grow and to learn to subsist. When ready to spawn, it swims upriver to return home to freshwater streams. The etymology of the word *anadromous* comes from the Greek, meaning to run upward.

On the plane to California, a good-looking woman in her early forties was reading a book. She had dark hair, pale skin, brown eyes, peachy lips, and seemed nothing extraordinary. Beneath her groomed appearance, though, Ana was dearly sheltering a few big dreams and a certain amount of . . . well, she was hoping it was a kind of wisdom. Previously, as if testing her adaptability, *la vida* had presented her with many unconventional circumstances both in and beyond her control. Some of them gave her wings; others wracked her. Seemingly so far her life had been penciled in like a cardiogram—ups and downs, and ups and downs, with a complete lack of monotony. Perhaps some people would say it was a string of downfalls. Others, a series of achievements. Her father believed that life was what you made of it, so Ana tried to do the best she could.

Turbulence interrupted her reading, blurring the words.

Okay, enough for today, she thought, marking her place in *Atlas Shrugged* with a picture of her daughter, and closing the book. She then looked at the blue sky out the window, preoccupied with the power of progress and ambition, and recalled vividly her past emotions when she was on a mission and absolutely in love with horses. She missed those great times—dynamic, eventful, and bold. It was then, whilst following her own waves in the mighty ocean, that Ana felt it for the first time—that strong yearning to thrive.

Overlapping images in her mind, she leaned closer to the window and let her sight fly. Lately the corporate world had become too salty for her taste, especially after the conflict with the Collector. So she began dreaming of transparent relations and ultimate freedom. Integrity—that's what she was thirsty for—not vanity, not falsehood. Outside a few fluffy cumulus clouds were shaping into the image of a fish. Wait, it looked just like salmon! Ana smiled, assuming that to be a sign, marking the beginning of her journey back to the freshwater streams.

The hostess approached with breakfast, interrupting her thoughts. And once Ana resumed diving into her memories, the topic changed: *My dandelion is lovely,* she opined. Yet it was not a flower she was envisioning, but rather a girl, a sweetheart with a delicate, tender soul—her daughter. Ana smiled. It felt like yesterday when her girl was sneaking into her bed to sleep through Sunday mornings, and cuddling while watching cartoons. Now she was an eighteen-year-old missy, just out of college in Oxford. Her name was Lilly.

Oh my, she looked astonishing at the prom, remembered Ana. *My girl had grown. Should I feel old now? Maybe . . . someday forty more years away.*

"Excuse me, ma'am." It was the same hostess again. Apparently breakfast was over. When the platter had been removed, Ana ensconced herself in her thoughts again, sure she would remain undisturbed until the plane touched down. She reminisced.

Where was I? Ah, Lilly . . .

Due to many circumstances, Ana had raised her alone. And she accepted single parenting as a common situation, not a tragedy. Life was just the way it was. By good fortune Lilly was a healthy, simplehearted, and easygoing girl, tiptoeing very often. Ana loved her with all her heart. Jolly Lilly had her mom's eyes, and in general they looked so alike, people often joked that they were clones. "Oh no, we're sisters," Ana would reply with a smile.

All of a sudden, an echo from the recent past interrupted her pleasant meditation; the air hostess had nothing to do with it this time.

"I want to see her today!" When the Collector's voice thundered in her mind, Ana quickly shook her head.

Damn it, I should stop myself from thinking about him on my journey. I should enjoy my trip and leave him behind, she strongly intended.

The last thing that came to mind before landing was related to Lilly. For the past three years, Lilly had mostly resided in England studying—far from their snug little home in the capital of a small Eastern European country. That very endeavor had been both an expensive and heartbreaking one, as they had struggled to survive the premature separation—but it was worth it. Firstly, because Lilly became a very well educated girl; and secondly, but above all, the bond between mother and daughter strengthened to the level of closest friends. And that was priceless!

Meanwhile the plane landed. It was August 1, 2014.

At the arrivals area, a lady with a perfect white smile and a nice bouquet of garden flowers was expecting Ana.

"Welcome to America!" Stacy said cordially as they tightly embraced. Then, after a quick scan, she remarked, "You look surprisingly fresh after such a long flight."

"No way. As you know, airplane travel is a natural way of making you look like your passport photo," larked Ana. "And thanks. The flowers are wonderful."

On the way home, they talked animatedly in the car. Being close friends in their youth, they had lost each other for years, until destiny had decided to give their amity a second chance.

"You're gonna love Cali! The kids have made a long list of things to do and attractions to show you," said Stacy. "They're very excited. Tomorrow we'll visit Stanford, the next day San Francisco, then

Napa, and the rest of Silicon Valley. By the way, is there anywhere in particular you wanna go?"

"Sure, I want to visit Pebble Beach!" Ana blurted out. "The rest is up to you."

It was already dark when the car turned into a small roundabout nicely named Loveland Court and stopped in front of one of the charming white houses. The place was located in the middle of Silicon Valley, where Stacy's family had resided for fifteen years. Her husband was a successful software engineer, and they had two adorable kids and a deaf dog. The girl was ten years old, and the boy—seven.

"We're home," said Stacy, turning off the engine.

"Looks great, My Lady of Loveland," joked Ana. Then they grabbed the suitcases and walked in. The sound of running, merrily screaming kids overfilled the house. Ana had arrived, and was going to stay with them until her coaching training at Santa Cruz began.

*   *   *

When she woke up the next morning, Ana felt at home. It was that familiar sense of connection and belonging.

"Good morning, Anché!" she whispered. Anché was her childhood nickname that sounded sweet and even funny in her native language. She used it when talking to her inner self. According to the noise level downstairs, the kids were already awake and watching TV over breakfast. The tempting smell of fresh pancakes teased her appetite, so Ana quickly put on jeans and a white T-shirt and went downstairs.

"Morning, guys. Weather is killer!"

"It's like this almost every day," Stacy said, smiling.

As promised, the sightseeing tour began right after breakfast. First stop: Stanford, as it was nearby Loveland Court and easier on Ana's jet lag. So, the three adults walked, and the two kids rolled, along the beautiful path toward the 123-year-old buildings of the dignified Main Quad. As it was August, lots of tourists instead of students were circling around.

Naturally Ana compared it to Oxford, where she had spent many days over the past three years visiting Lilly. The town in central England was notably a worldwide hub of knowledge, imprinted with academic spirit. However, compared to rainy England, California was blessed with an abundance of sunshine naturally brightening its colors. And there was something more... Searching her phone for additional information, Ana found a phrase that instantly hooked her mind:

"The wind of freedom blows!" she softly pronounced. That unofficial motto perfectly described the spirit here.

"Hey guys, listen to this." Ana turned to the Lovelands, looking at her phone and reading from the official website: "California Senator Leland Stanford and his wife founded the university in 1885 on an 8,000-acre Palo Alto Stock Farm for breeding and training horses. The campus still carries the nickname 'the Farm.'" There she paused for a while. "'The Farm' has an equestrian meaning similar to the word *hippodrome*." She was sensitive to anything reminding her of the hippodrome back home that she dearly called "the burg."

"Hurry up, let's go!" urged Stacy. Her friends did not seem very impressed by that piece of information. They headed toward the archway leading into the Quad courtyard and walked through. Ana took some pictures and texted them to Lilly.

"We're in Stanford. It's kind of magnetic. I wanna take you here someday," she wrote.

"Awesome," her daughter replied almost instantly.

"Don't forget to feed the cat, or I'll kill you!" reminded Ana. They had a Persian pet in the colors of the sand.

"Relax, have fun!" Lilly added a smiley.

Exactly. *Fun* was the best word to describe the kids' attitude. If California hadn't been suffering a dry spell and the main campus's fountains had been properly functioning, the kids would've probably been hopping in the water.

They parked at Loveland Court at dusk. That evening all the rituals happened a little differently. The kids had dinner at half past seven instead of half past six, the husband had two glasses of wine instead of one, the plates were left on the table 'til morning, and the Lovelands were asleep by eleven, not ten. The lights went off. The house became peaceful. Yet Ana was awake—the jet lag was hiding somewhere in her pillow, jumbling her thoughts.

The Farm for breeding and training horses . . .

The wind of freedom blows . . .

A Collector-free zone . . . Shush, don't mention his name, Anché. Not on your trip, remember?

This journey will change my life . . .

Finally, she fell asleep with a smile.

CHAPTER 2

THE COLLECTOR

The Collector was . . . he was . . . himself.

Primarily he was a very clever person, way above average. His brain processed information faster than others', giving him the advantage of seeing many moves ahead, as if his mind were a next-generation bio computer. No wonder he had a master's degree in advanced mathematics. For ordinary people, it was difficult to keep pace with him. Moreover, as if his being a fast thinker was not enough, he spoke quietly and rapidly, requiring the whole of his interlocutor's attention. Yes, communicating with the Collector was consuming.

Another important particularity of his was that he used to be and still was a brilliant poker player—one of the best. So, consequently, he was an expert in handling emotions, controlling the odds, manipulating, and, of course, bluffing. Meeting him for the first time was like watching a Formula One race so up close that the racing cars resemble colorful flashes. And right after the interaction was over, a creeping feeling would rankle one's mind, signaling that imperceptibly he had extracted any information conceivably beneficial to himself. *Con maestría!*

Dominating would be the most accurate word to describe the Collector's appearance. In general, he dressed casually in jeans and a shirt, but all his manly accessories were rare and very expensive, such as the exquisite, limited-edition watch or white-gold ring with a big yellow diamond. He had a slightly expressive face, as if he wore a mask. Because of his bone structure his eyes were placed deeper, so it seemed that the Collector was observing the world from inside. His hair was cropped short, and he was in good shape. When walking he kind of glided over the floor, probably a skill related to his Sambo martial arts background.

In summary, no matter where he was or what he was doing, he was fit and centered, aware of the surrounding environment and his particular position in it. In other words, he was always alert—alert and prepared to act up to his full potential. Due to security reasons in his country, the Collector was 24/7 protected by at least four professional bodyguards, members of his personal SWAT team. He was only able to calm down and relax when abroad, far away from his office and obligations.

He notoriously had three great passions: money, art, and women (in that order). For him it was not only about the possessing, but also the whole ritual of searching, locating, and conquering. And he was always looking for more. Day and night his bio computer was constructing strategies for expanding his wealth. When the Collector was after a particular object or goal, it was absorbing to watch his moves—precise, adroit, and ruthless. No limits, no scruples, no mercy, no loyalty, no compassion, no feelings involved. He was a person of his own morals.

Money was the sun in the Collector's solar system, the supreme source of light and energy, the center of all gravitating planets and satellites, the cause of being and existing, and the greatest value of all values. He was convinced money could do everything. And with his brains and mind-set, it was only a matter of time until he had acquired a huge amount of cash in his accounts and vault. Making money in a newborn democracy with no laws and regulations was like playing poker, and habitually the Collector practiced the same strategies in his business affairs. He took short-term deals with high profits and assumed bluffing to be a part of the game.

There was one organization in which he invested consistently, and for more than twenty years he was its majority shareholder—the only bookmaking company in the country. Established right after the end of socialist rule, soon it became one of the largest franchises. It was known worldwide that the betting business was providing considerably high profits to its owners, and of course the Collector was no exception. That was his inexhaustible source of money, constantly supplied from millions of people seeking easy and fast fortune.

Over the years, it became his primary goal to protect the status quo, and to remain the monopolist in the domain of betting. And so far, he had been victorious. By ably using his financial power and political influence, in two decades no other foreign or local company had been able to compete with him by acquiring a bookmaking license. The Collector was devoted to pulling the weeds before any of them managed to harm his favorite plant or poison its golden fruits. No other company he had ever been involved in had lasted longer or been more important to him than this one. In his other ventures, his exclusive aim usually was to maximize personal benefits. And sometimes many of the "served-the-cause" companies declared insolvency or bankrupt after his furious exploitation. The Collector considered that to be collateral damage.

Meanwhile, the Collector's personal collection of paintings and especially antiques expanded tremendously. Some of the artifacts he bought from antique dealers, others from bargaining with black market traders and looters. Unfortunately, most of the sellers' antiques were in poor and even terrible condition. The Collector was not satisfied. Having certain requirements, he assembled his own team of experts and renovators. They were located close to his office and were strictly supervised by him personally. His lab was supplied with advanced technical equipment for conservation and restoration. A huge amount of work was done with remarkable professionalism, and the outcome was formidable at the end.

Now he had a collection of astonishing, shining pieces of high value, unconventional beauty, and perfect condition. Among the

Collector's treasures were many splendid artifacts, mostly from the Thracian period—his favorite era. He owned at least three of the Thracian rulers' golden crowns from the fifth century BC, which were declared to be among the most fabulous and rare pieces of Archaic culture. Only a few of them were ever found. If sold at auction, the price of each crown could easily race up to millions.

Furthermore, he owned the largest number of rhytons (horns) in the world from the sixth, fifth, and fourth centuries BC. The Collector also possessed a gold funerary mask from the fifth century BC, all kinds of vessels, and many Thracian jewelry specimens. He had five almost complete warrior sets from the same time period, and was a proud owner of the Emperor Trajan Decius's marble bust and two bronze statuettes of Mars and Venus from the third and second century. In sum, it was said that his exceptional collection of ancient artworks was valued between 100 and 200 million dollars, and was bigger than the one at the National Historical Museum.

Once most of the pieces had been successfully restored, the Collector decided it was time to show off his treasures. And so, one day, his office was turned into a museum. A special air-conditioning system was installed to keep the room's temperature appropriate for the paintings and other exhibits. Then the exemplars were selected and moved to his chamber. If the exponents were smaller, such as the crowns, for instance, they were showcased individually under crystal glass. The rest were arranged all around the room.

For sure the Collector was celebrating: firstly, because from now on he would spend his days surrounded by his precious belongings; and secondly, because every single visitor invited or allowed in his premises-museum was going to be duly impressed and respectful. Mission accomplished.

Certainly, the satisfaction of possessing all the paintings and statues in the world couldn't compare to the bliss the Collector was receiving from his other passion—women. Females who erected his lust were everywhere, and luckily the Collector enjoyed a vast range of qualities that could attract them. He was not picking and choosing fastidiously; no, it was all about the joy of collecting. And the pussycats were ready to purr for him.

"Who said limitations? Burn them at the stake!" he liked to say with a proper gesture, clearly showing where the stake was located.

So, the Collector could find attractors in many forms and colors—blonde or brunette, skinny or shapely, single or taken, celebrity or ordinary, and even underage. His desire was congenital and endless, and for him pairing was both an anti-stress therapy and a self-esteem booster. Presumably in his late fifties, the Collector had had numerous affairs and had tried almost everything in bed (or wherever else). Now he was finding it most thrilling to be with unsophisticated young girls. Occasionally, among the many chicks tasted he would find some special ones that particularly tickled his taste buds. With them he would be generous—supplying them with cash, cars, or even careers. And because the Collector was capable of paying many bills, the number of these chosen girls was very high. After all, "having enough" was not among his virtues.

As a lover, the Collector was a conqueror type. Wooing or flattering was not part of his approach, as he found such behavior to be a waste of time. If fond of somebody he went straight to the point, at the same time craftily supporting his sexual offer with something tempting and irresistible to each lady's particular needs or values. This strategy had been proven in time, and it worked with almost absolute reliability. Only a few exceptions were ever recorded.

As for many years the Collector lived a tense and stressful life that kept him awake at night, he got used to spending the dark hours out, going around the nightclubs with his mates or alone. He hopped from one location to another to get a broader perspective on the city's nightlife fusion. And if for most people clubbing was drinking and dancing, he was not much of a drinker or a dancer at all. For him it was a parade. The Collector would examine all the women in the bars in search of some new intriguing ones, while at the same time flattering his ego by counting the number of those he saw that were already trophies. At night he went out to update his female collection.

CHAPTER 3

THE RED FOLDER

Sixteen years ago, on a typically rainy November day in 1998, the Collector received a phone call from an unknown number. That day was busy. Many people were waiting in front of his office to meet him. His secretary was overwhelmed by the rush, but as a proven professional she kept politely helping the visitors to feel as comfortable as possible. When at first his personal mobile phone rang, he disregarded the unfamiliar number and put the gadget aside. Who knew what kind of crap might come from such a call? Maybe it was some jerk trying to waste his time.

The phone rang again. This time, on a whim, the Collector changed his mind.

"Hello," he said as he picked up.

A melodious female voice greeted him. She introduced herself as his buddy's wife and asked the Collector for help.

Hmm, very interesting, he thought, and suggested she come to his office as soon as possible.

She confirmed. It was a short conversation.

Then the Collector leaned back in his comfortable leather chair, exhaled the smoke of his fine Cuban cigar, and retrieved the memory of the girl he had just talked to. He had seen her only once, during dinner a few months ago in a fancy Chinese restaurant. She and her husband had come late and accidentally joined the Collector and his companions without an invitation. While sharing one table, the Collector had done his usual perusal. She was charming, had a pretty face and expressive eyes radiating joy. He appraised her at twentysomething, still more of a girl than a woman.

Wait, what was her name? He tried to remember. It didn't come up. Instead he recalled the levity in her appearance, which he found very appealing. She was acting kind to her husband, showing intimacy and love. They both were in a funny mood that night, making jokes with the waiter or each other. Well, behavior like this was something the Collector couldn't afford in public.

I wonder how she would look naked with those bamboo chopsticks in her fingers, he thought, and the lust rang his bells.

Ugh, but what was her name? Shortly after that evening he was told that mysteriously her husband, his buddy, had disappeared, leaving his wife with a two-year-old baby girl.

What an idiot! The Collector saw he had reacted spontaneously. However, during the gloomy years of transition, everything was possible in their small post-totalitarian country, where awkwardness was beyond belief. So, if somebody had gone missing or dead, all he had to do was to erase his number from the contact list. Realizing he needed to do so, the Collector grabbed his phone and pressed the delete button on the buddy's name. Afterward he shifted his attention back to the lady of his recollection. "Help," she had said. Was she in trouble? He wanted to know the true reason of her call. And also, was she still looking good? But above all he wanted to know her bloody name!

*   *   *

Within an hour, the secretary came through on the intercom to discreetly inform him that some girl called Ana was waiting outside.

"Yeah, right! Ana! Bring her into my office right away!"

Then the door opened and the girl from his memories slowly entered. She looked almost the same as he remembered her, only with one significant distinction—all the joy was gone. Ana had become very skinny in her grief, which was equal to elegant from his perspective. She was stylishly dressed in a formal black-and-white skirt suit. The sheen, classic, black high heels emphasized the delicate shape of her ankles. In her arms Ana embraced a big red folder as if it was a baby.

"Come in, Ana. Relax, have a seat. Do you want something—coffee, water, anything else?" He hoped to comfort her, seeing as she was standing next to the door ready to run away like a deer. With her big brown eyes, she explored the environment.

The Collector sat on the opposite side of the room behind the imperial wooden desk with a crystal skull on it. Ana looked at his many paintings decorating the walls, apparently recognizing a few famous pieces in beautiful frames tightly positioned close to his nest.

"Well, there will be more space in the new office for my art," he bragged, as if he had just read her thoughts. Then he pointed to one of the guest's chairs.

"Come, sit here."

Ana followed his instructions, firmly holding the red folder in her arms. She sat on the edge of the chair. "Coffee and water will be fine, thank you."

Obviously she was scared, the Collector acknowledged, but at the same time she did not act like a victim. When the cups were served, he looked at her questioningly.

"Well, what's going on?"

"I'm sorry for the rush," she said, "but my husband trusted you. He told me to ask for your protection if I was in trouble, and here I am. A man is brutally forcing me to pass him the shares of something precious to me. He's threatening to use alternative convincing methods."

"Ana, who's after you?" the Collector asked without demanding any further details. She answered straightaway, then he dialed a number. The wanted man picked up. The Collector's voice became cold and even.

"I just want you to know that Ana is here with me! And from now on, whatever you want from her, you will have to take it from *me*!"

He spoke imperatively, with short pauses between phrases. The other man didn't argue at all. The negotiations were over.

"See?" He put the phone aside and smiled. "Everything will be all right. Now tell me, what was all this about?"

Ana placed the red folder on the desk between them and opened it to page one.

"Well, it's a property with a hippodrome. A huge property near the capital city. . ."

With every turn of the page and every following note, the Collector became more and more engrossed. For a while he focused on Ana's face, wondering if she was aware of the red folder's true value. He determined she definitely wasn't.

"Wait!" He stopped her and called his secretary. "Cancel the rest of my meetings and bring me another coffee!"

Last night's clubbing meant he had barely slept, and consequently he needed a boost. This intriguing turn of events would require his full attention.

The Collector caught the opportunity immediately. Ana had brought to his office all the permission papers, basic agreements, and majority shares of a multimillion-dollar project: the hippodrome. Since her husband was missing, she would need a reliable partner to help complete it. First, he calculated the price of the land and was pleased by the figures. Second, as a representative of the only licensed bookmaking company in the country, he considered the potential for this eventual joint venture. As a bonus, he appreciated that Ana was clever and attractive, and he wanted to see more shades of her . . . skin color.

Sure, I already have her number, the Collector thought, noting for later. But at present he concentrated on work.

They talked for an hour and a half, maybe two, or maybe more. Ana was pretty well informed, rational, and down-to-earth. He liked that she was a feisty kind of a person. What he didn't like was that now the land had been seized by the state—a tiny obstacle. Ana's husband's disappearance had triggered a legal case, and now the court was keeping the land under its jurisdiction. Even for a well-connected person like the Collector, with proven protégés in every orbit including the civil court, it would be a challenge. He'd have to manipulate the system and turn the odds in their favor. Was he capable of that? Certainly his influence was wide enough. Was the hippodrome worth it? Absolutely. The land on its own was worth millions.

"So you'll provide the land, and I'll support the project, right?" summarized the Collector.

"Yes," answered Ana. "From my side, I'll participate with the in-kind contribution of the land, and you will assure the general protections of the venture, including dealing with the legal case's twine. Oh, and of course, you should bind the hippodrome with the bookmaking company one day. Could we go fifty-fifty?"

"Nah, I'll take at least 51 percent of the shares. I never split down the middle," he said firmly.

"Okay, fine," agreed Ana.

She was such a naïve chick, he thought, and clearly a desperate one. It seemed that project was the only lifeboat she had for her lost finances, certainty, and hope.

Afterward they created a precise plan to save the hippodrome that yielded Ana a long to-do list of personal tasks and further steps to be taken. When the land could be regained, they would establish the first authentic horseracing operation in their country. The Collector suggested they initially should focus on the legal case, and she should bring the rest of the documents to his office so his lawyers could revise them and build up a strategy. Then he suggested they call it "The National Hippodrome" project. She would be in charge of it, reporting directly to him—which, to be honest, was exactly what Ana wanted. Before leaving his chamber, Ana stopped for a moment, turned to the Collector, and frankly asked, "How can I be sure that you'll remain loyal?"

He looked straight into her eyes and answered, "You have my word, Ana!"

CHAPTER 4

THE STORY BEHIND
THE RED FOLDER

Ana was raised as an only child in a district named "Juvenility" in the capital. As a chemist, her mom, Mrs. K, was punctual and scheduled, but at the same time always a ready-to-help kind of person. Mr. G, on the contrary, was spontaneous, adventurous, and creative. Both of Ana's parents were reliable people, cherishing the virtues of loyalty, dignity, and respect for others' needs. Subsequently Ana became a self-confident girl, with good manners and a proper education. At the age of twenty-three, during the last year of her studies in the technical university, she started working as a journalist at the economics desk of a national daily newspaper, one of the popular prints at that time.

One summer Sunday afternoon, Ana was at work writing an article for the Monday paper when her colleague Tina called to invite her for a drink that evening.

"Sure, why not? Where shall we go?"

"I'll pick you up with a friend of mine, if you don't mind," suggested Tina, without any additional information about her companion.

"Of course I don't mind," replied Ana, and they settled on a meeting point.

At the arranged hour, Ana was waiting on the boulevard in front of the newspaper's offices when a shining red BMW 8 Series pulled up. *Vroom-vroom . . .*

First time I've had a chance to ride in a beast like this one, Ana thought delightedly, though her enthusiasm vanished the moment she found out that she had to shove herself into the tiny backseat of the sports car.

"Seriously, it's a dog's seat back here," she complained, yet she had no choice but to fit inside.

The driver turned around and said, "Hi, Ana. Have you been to the American restaurant at the hippodrome?"

"Hello, nice to meet you . . ." she hinted, but no name was forthcoming. "No, I haven't been there. Frankly, I've never heard of it," she added as politely as she could.

"Perfect, let's go there."

The stranger's exquisite vehicle sped off in an unfamiliar direction.

Loosen, Anché, it's just a test, she thought to herself as they drove all the way out of the capital. The ride was a noisy and most uncomfortable one, so when the car stopped in front of a wooden arch with a signboard saying Saloon, she crept out in relief.

"Gee, when we have self-driving cars in the future, will BMWs be programmed to drive like jackasses?!" Ana turned to the wheelman.

He didn't answer . . . again.

They just walked into a dandy, country-style American restaurant with a nice garden. The evening was warm, and it was crowded. There was a party going on. The young waitresses were dressed in cowgirl outfits with authentic hats, jean shorts, and leather boots. They ran around with big salvers overwhelmed by ribs, potatoes, salads, and lots of beer. Under the sounds of the rhythmic country music, the party was like a Wild West jamboree.

In the middle of the restaurant only one table with a Reserved sign on it was available, so the three of them were settled there. Ana noticed that all the staff members were somehow exceptionally welcoming and friendly—perhaps to an odd degree.

"What's your opinion? Do you like it here?" the driver asked.

Maybe I shouldn't answer since he won't, she thought, but then she reconsidered her manners.

"Yes, as a matter of fact I do. It has that authentic American feel from the movies. Oh, and I also like that everybody's so chummy."

"Good, very good. It's a part of my new enterprise," he said proudly.

"He is the big boss here," interjected Tina. Well, that explained a lot, from the super polite crew to his James Bond kind of attitude. Yet so far, she still didn't know his name.

The surroundings were pleasing; the food was good; and Ana felt no discomfort when Tina asked her in a whisper to not draw attention to herself in the guy's presence.

"Sure," agreed Ana, who ceased being active in the conversation. She assumed Tina was probably fond of him. And why not? He was an intriguing, nice man in his midthirties, with a "Brings Me Women" car. So, following Tina's instructions, Ana quietly left her to be the prima donna of the evening.

That conspiracy didn't work as expected. When driving them home, the man discreetly revealed his preference for Ana. It became complicated. Ana worried about hurting Tina's feelings, and therefore tried to avoid seeing him for days. But he was very persistent in his phone calls, and they ended up having dinner together.

However, this time, Ana talked a lot. She also asked many questions, and he properly answered most of them. It turned out to be a pleasant date, and the chemistry between them grew.

"Hey, you tricked me, little missy, leaving me with the impression that you are not much of a talker."

"Well, it's not my fault. It was Tina's idea," explained Ana, putting all the blame on her colleague, as "loyal" friends do.

Well, after their first date, the mystery surrounding his persona started to thin—his first name, his second name, his third name, his age, his background . . . Ana's date was twelve years older and wealthy, mainly involved in bank affairs and the media. He had facilitated the establishment of the first private TV channel in the country, which had recently started airing. Moreover, he had various local and foreign business investments in trading, tourism, and other concerns. Operating with a big swing, he had the strong belief that everything was possible for him.

Their romance blossomed fast. As a boyfriend he was reliable, loyal, and caring, totally satisfied with their relationship. He used to say, "There is only one woman for me," and Ana had no occasion to doubt his faithfulness. As a person he was quite generous, supporting many worthwhile start-ups, as well as helpful to his relatives. For Ana, his good heart was virtue number one.

Despite his individuality of character, Ana's date was not outstandingly clever, but he compensated with hard work, boldness, and largesse. To take care of his businesses he was usually the first person to enter his office, and many times, the last one to leave it. So far, he was still expanding. Elated by his fortune, sometimes he was arrogant and even haughty, acting like a rooster. Ana excused him by saying, "Nobody's perfect," since toward her and her parents he showed only kindness and respect. It could be summed up that her boyfriend had two main addictions—work and Coca-Cola, as he did not smoke or drink alcohol.

One day she couldn't help but to ask him, "Why do you have to work so much?"

"Because it brings me joy. An organization is like a tree full of monkeys, all at different branches and different levels. When the monkey at the top—i.e., me—looks down, it sees a tree full of smiling faces. But do you know what the monkeys from the bottom see looking up?"

"No." Ana shrugged.

"Assholes," he joked.

"And . . . you like the view from the top?"

"Quite," he answered, then changed the subject. "Hey, listen, I want you to come with me next week."

Due to his superior position, he had to travel a lot. And he preferred going abroad escorted by his cherished lady, as she was both his best companion and personal translator. On those trips from Brazil to Germany and beyond, Ana began discovering the abundance and the diversity of the world. She saw marvelous places, experienced different cultures, established outlandish acquaintances, and naturally expanded her horizons way above average.

"Since you met him you have become a snob, Ana," Mrs. K concluded a bit critically one day. But Ana had another explanation for her change: getting out of the box. During socialism people had been restricted from traveling abroad, and Ana had been nowhere else except the motherland. Now, the universe was blooming with vibrant colors, carrying endless opportunities and ultimate progress. Just like that Ana had been able to freely open her eyes and mind to all this creative variety, and no matter what happened in her future life she planned to keep them open 'til her last breath.

At that time, the Internet entered the public consciousness with no limitations. Humanity took a big step into the Information Age, providing worldwide connection between computers via telecommunications. Ana quit the newspaper and started working as personal assistant to a Sprint Communications Company representative. Sprint owned half of the second fiber cable spanning the seafloor of the Atlantic, and in the same year announced the completion of the first coast-to-coast telecommunications route ensuring voice, data, image, and video service without interruption.

Ana was still getting used to her new duties when a few months later, she discovered something fundamental—she was expecting! Checkmate! Now what?

Within a couple of days, and with a fresh dose of courage, the future father decided, "We'll do it in the best way!"

"Awesome!" cheered Ana, who started addressing him Papsy.

She would always remember that sunny morning in Paris when Papsy, kneeling with an elegant diamond ring in his hands, officially proposed to her. And that wasn't all: Her fiancé announced that the wedding would be there in Paris in October! *Mon Dieu*, she was deeply touched and elated—and as she had every morning lately, she quickly threw up. Despite that short-term inconvenience, her joy was great. The marvel that she was going to be a mother, and the thrill of marrying the man she loved, felt like growing big white-feathered wings! It seemed that heaven was missing an angel.

The Marriage

On October 1, 1995, in the Hôtel de Aigles with its breathtaking view over Paris, Ana's wedding ceremony was about to take place. The room's exquisite ceiling was ornamented with gold-leaf eagles. It was the same hall where, in 1919, the League of Nations was founded. Built in 1758 during King Louis XV's reign, Hôtel de Aigles itself was one of the world's most majestic hotels. It was long owned by the illustrious family of the Counts of Aigles, until the mansion was transformed into a luxury hotel in 1909. And as a nouveau riche, Papsy chose that imposing edifice for his modest occasion.

That day white flowers complemented the ambience of the main salon. Mendelsohn was performed on harp and viola. It was a small black-tie wedding—only the parents and a few friends were invited—but at the same time it was glamorous and unforgettable. Ana was as beautiful as a princess in a long white satin dress with high gloves and a stylish hat and veil. The bodice of the dress was designed like a corset, underlining her currently generous breasts. When exposed to the chilly air outside, she covered up her shoulders with a refined white marabou mantle. The diamond ring glittered on her finger, along with a matching necklace on her décolletage.

After the ceremony, three white Rolls-Royce motorcars were waiting in front of the hotel's main entrance with drivers at their opened rear doors. Then the newlyweds and their parents went on a romantic drive all over flamboyant Paris, followed by a formal dinner at the historic Michelin-rated La Tour d'Platine. Commanding an incredible view over the Seine and Notre Dame, the restaurant founded in 1582 had been frequented by Henry IV and kept one of the first known forks in the small museum on the ground floor. The wedding party had the signature pressed duck and sampled from the restaurant's collection of over 450,000 wines, estimated to be valued at twenty-five million euros. Ana's husband was permitted a Coke, with the condition that he drink it from a nontransparent glass.

The next day, after all the parents had flown home, the newlyweds rented a car to drive down to the French Riviera for their honeymoon. It was a scenic journey—Monte Carlo, Cannes, Nice, and Saint-Tropez. Luckily Ana's pregnancy was going smoothly, and she was full of energy. The last morning, at a snazzy bistro on the Promenade de la Croisette, they were having warm croissants with fresh orange juice when an important subject came up: the delivery. Where? How? Which doctor? It was quite the subject because at that time medical care in their country was lightyears behind that of Western Europe. For sure, they both wanted the best treatment and arrival, and since Papsy could afford it, by the last bite of croissant they had decided that Ana would deliver in Paris with Dr. Naisse.

Chapter 5

The Baby

Within a month of the honeymoon, Papsy rented a lovely apartment for Ana to move into. It was in the safest neighborhood, less than two hundred meters from the Eiffel Tower. Conveniently, the new residence would last for a year, and Ana could wait there for the stork to make the delivery of a lifetime. Afterward she could nurture the baby for six months. And of course, she wouldn't stay alone; somebody had to accompany her around-the-clock, just in case.

A long absence from his business affairs could lead to unpredictable consequences for Papsy in their country, so he only flew over every one or two weeks for a couple of days each trip. Next on Ana's list of preferred caregivers was her mother, but Mrs. K was working full-time. So Papsy's mom, Luisa, subsequently volunteered.

"Fine," said Ana. "Anyone capable of taking me to the hospital on time will do."

In the beginning, Ana's stay in Paris was calm and even, mostly boring. When it was not raining, Ana took long walks along the picturesque avenues, then spent hours in the baby sections of department stores. Unforeseen and for the first time in her life she felt isolated without her parents or friends around. Though she was properly settled in the Capital of Love, Ana missed her home. She always kept her phone at hand, eager to chat and hear the voices of her loved ones.

She also had trouble sleeping and spent many lonely nights writing letters to her mom and grandparents in the motherland. She wrote to her father in Belarus, where he recently worked with ABB Susa on a project regarding SALT II, and to her friends everywhere, relating trivial moments from her trivial life:

"Today I had a Perrier with mint near the Galeries Lafayette. On the wall a sign said, 'In case of fire, keep calm and don't yell, "Fire!" Attack the center of the blaze with a fire extinguisher without exposing yourself to flames.'"

Most of her letters ended with "I miss you very much. Love, Ana."

Only when Papsy visited were her routines a bit more amusing— but afterward, she would return to her friendless roving. And so, by nature, the little kick-the-boss baby became her dear soul mate. Ana was told it was a girl. She had even seen her tiny button nose on the ultrasound. It was so cute!

"Please tell me—when will my baby move?" she remembered asking the doctor.

"With any luck, right after she finishes college," he had joked.

One day, while walking down the Champs-Élysées for what felt like the seventy-fifth time, Ana turned into the Disney Store . . . again. Christmas was coming, and the store was packed. Screens all over the place were streaming *The Little Mermaid*. With a seven-months-big belly, she was already tired—and resting on a nearby sofa seemed a brilliant idea.

Just for a while. We must go home soon, she thought, leaning back and gently caressing her tummy. A little foot kicked in response. Dr. Naisse was positive the baby was going to meet the world in the beginning of March.

"Calm down, love," Ana whispered, sending her vibes to the being in her body. "March will come soon . . ."

Then she looked at the screen nearby. The red-haired Ariel was so charming . . .

Wait. If the baby is born in March, then its astrological sign will likely be Pisces. She'll be my precious Little Mermaid, Ana concluded with fondness. Thereafter, full of energy, she toured the store and bought all kinds of plush toys depicting the main characters, along with various branded accessories. Later, she arranged them all over the living room, and just like that, she no longer felt lonely.

New Year's Eve came soon. There was no buzz, no party. Ana, Papsy, and his mother rang in 1996 at the exclusive restaurant, on the second floor of the Eiffel Tower. The setting offered a wonderful panorama over the Field of Mars.

"Snails? Why the hell do French people eat snails?" Ana asked, looking at her appetizer with confusion.

"Because we don't like fast food, madame," answered the waiter with a smirk. "You should try it. It's very delicious."

He didn't lie; the snails were tasty. At midnight fireworks illuminated Paris. Under the bright splashes in the sky, Ana made a wish.

My guardian angel, please bless me with a healthy baby and a fortunate delivery when the moment comes.

And the moment came one night in the beginning of March. After the first contractions, Luisa helped Ana get to the hospital in time.

"Should I stay with you?" asked Luisa. It was late, after midnight.

"Not necessary. I'll be fine. Go get some sleep."

"Okay," said the old lady, who then set off.

If Mom were here, she would never leave me, thought Ana. But there she was alone, lying in the dark room with her labor pains and hopes, trying to repress the ache and to swallow her screams in the middle of the quiet, sleeping hospital.

Encore, encore, encore . . . Early in the morning, Ana followed Dr. Naisse's instructions until half past eight, when she heard her daughter's voice for the first time.

"Congratulations, Mrs. Ana. It's a girl," said the doctor. Ana saw his eyes beaming above the surgical mask. Then he said, "We have a tradition here. When the baby is born, we rest it on the mother's heart so her heartbeat can calm it down. At the same time, the eternal connection between them can begin." Then Dr. Naisse gently placed the baby on her chest.

While embracing her daughter close to her heart, Ana felt an incredible felicity such as she had never experienced before. She shed tears of joy. Her love was cosmic.

"Hello, my lovely Lilly," whispered Ana, "Shush, shush . . ."

The baby relaxed and fell asleep. For a while, Ana remained like this, willing to hold that memory forever. Afterward she searched for her phone. Now it was her privilege to spread the splendid news. She called three people—her husband, her mom, and her dad. To each she said, "Lilly was born. We are both fine!" Just a few words that meant the world to them.

Papsy took the first possible flight to meet her in the hospital that same afternoon. He showed up with a glowing face, a huge bouquet of 101 red roses, and the words: "This is the happiest day of my life!"

*　*　*

After two long weeks, the green twenty-four-year-old mummy made an emergency call late at night.

"Mom, I need you. Please come over."

"Oh, Ana. I work, you know. Calm down. It's just a symptom of postpartum depression," Mrs. K said.

"No, please! I need you! Luisa said she is afraid to touch Lilly because she might do something clumsy. Can you imagine? I'm taking care of the baby on my own, and it's stressful. I worry my milk might stop. Seriously, Mom, please!"

Things were not going well in Paris. Ana was desperate and completely out of her comfort zone. Thankfully, her mother could sense that backup was really needed, so Mrs. K decided to quit her job and to pack.

Two weeks later, Ana met her at Charles de Gaulle Airport with glee.

"I'm so glad you're here. I haven't slept in days," said Ana. Due to breastfeeding she had to be awake every third hour, around-the-clock.

"Everything's gonna be all right now! Granny is here. I can't wait to hug the Little Mermaid!" said Mrs. K. She was a *belle madame* in her midfifties wearing a chic beige ensemble. One could tell she used to be a beauty in her youth.

At last everything fell into place. Ana and her mom got along very well, and Lilly—who was simply adorable—was always smiling, showing off her big brown eyes and long black eyelashes.

"I have the most beautiful baby in the world!" Like any other mom, Ana was positive it was so. But she had evidence proving her point, as strangers were always exclaiming, *"Quelle jolie bébé!"* (What a pretty baby!) With Mrs. K's support, Ana was able to enjoy the rest of her stay in Paris, and even to study some French, until before long, their baby girl was five months old.

CHAPTER 6

THE RETURN OF ANA

At the end of August, once the French mission had been accomplished, the new paramount member of Ana's family and her relatives took a plane back to their hometown. Unfortunately, the environment there was quite contrary to the opulence and exuberance of Paris.

"Mom, I'd forgotten how gray everything in our capital is," Ana confessed at the airport. She had to admit that now her small country seemed like a moor—and not only because the environment was grim. This moor they inhabited by necessity had come to infect the mind-set and behavior of the people.

Ana believed that after the end of the socialistic regime, a mighty titan had stirred the ooze, creating chaos. And in the chaos some weeds grew much larger than the others—the weeds of crime. Out of control gangster activity spread all over, and the mafia became stronger than the government. The entire population suffered. Every citizen could become a victim of racketeering or personal harassment, armed burglary, or even public assault. Horrible things were happening almost every day. During those complicated years of transition from a socialist system to something foggy called democracy, the society was forced to witness various acts of violence. Now, more than a decade after the stir, the situation was still ill-defined.

One evening, less than a week after her return, Ana and her husband were watching the news when he said in a strange tone,

"Well, so far everything is going great, and I'm the luckiest man to have you and the Little Mermaid in my life." He kissed her head. "But I have to tell you something, my dear."

"What's up, Papsy?" She was listening to him with one ear only, as she was following the broadcast with the other.

"See, lately I have these creepy nightmares . . . As if they've come to warn me something bad might happen. Honestly, I am afraid our life might change dramatically."

"Oh, please, just flip the pillow. Everything will be fine!"

"No, listen. I feel this bloody anxiety in me. How can I describe it . . . It's like receiving messages warning, 'Danger, danger.'"

Ana broke away from cuddling and looked at him, inspecting whether he was serious or not.

"Or maybe it's just that I'm simply going nuts," he backpedaled.

A few days later, in the beginning of September, Ana was waiting for her husband's driver to take her and Lilly to their monthly visit to the pediatrician, but the driver was running unusually late.

"Hmm, that's odd." She looked at her watch. They were almost fifteen minutes late.

Then the phone rang. It was Papsy.

"I didn't want to bother you, but the driver is late. The pediatrician—"

"Yes, I know he's late. Something happened," he said. Without giving her a moment to respond, he added, "But guess what? Today, I'll be your personal pilot. Just give me five minutes."

Soon, speeding down to the doctor's appointment Ana asked about the reason for this awkward switch.

"Well, it's just a random coincidence. On his way to pick you up, the driver was attacked at a red light by two masked gangsters with guns. They threatened his life, punched him in the face, threw him out of the car, and stole it. That's it."

"That's it?! My goodness, is he okay?"

"Yes, yes, he's injured but will be fine. I gave him three days off. Then I canceled the rest of my meetings to come take care of my girls."

"Where did it happen?" Ana wanted to know.

Papsy specified the spot: at a traffic light in the central area. But she could tell he was trying to belittle the attack as a random event.

"Really? Where were the police?" she asked, even though she knew it was a rhetorical question because the police were working with the criminals. Suddenly, Ana comprehended that she and Lilly could've been in the car during the burglary, and a terrifying thought came to her mind: Would the baby's presence have stopped the criminals? Then a volcano of wrath erupted from within her.

"What's wrong with this country? Where is the government? Where are the laws and regulations? Where are the police officers? How can we live here normally? How can we raise our kids here?"

"Calm down, Ana. I told you, it was just a coincidence. You have forgotten the reality here."

"Damn it, there is so much violence here it's getting harder to breathe," Ana said as they parked in front of the doctor's office.

"Let's go upstairs!" commanded Papsy with even tone.

And as their baby's welfare and health was the immediate priority, the discussion was put aside.

CHAPTER 7

THE NIGHTMARE

Ana had been abroad for only a year, but now everything in her country seemed so different, cluttered, and hostile. She wondered what had happened to the reforms the politicians had promised to implement in the state during her absence. Wasn't the system supposed to evolve, and the society to become more prosperous as it strived for the virtues of democracy?

Instead, Ana witnessed the most severe financial and political crisis over the next few months. It all started with a huge food shortage in autumn, and at the same time the National Bank revoked the licenses of not one or two but fourteen commercial banks, nine of them in one day. The socialist government's intention was probably not to create a massive panic in the country, but instead to reassure the finance sector's stability. But in the end, history proved that to be the wrong move. The decree dramatically affected people's savings and security, followed by the logical loss of trust in the bank system along with their leaders' proficiency. Under these circumstances, at the end of 1996, inflation launched up to 310 percent. For ordinary citizens, hyperinflation meant that by the time they were having a coffee, its price had doubled, while their salaries and pensions had plummeted by 60 percent.

At the same time, changes were also occurring in Ana's private life. This year, unlike her last peaceful fall near the Eiffel Tower, appeared to be restless and fidgety. Seat belts were fastened, turbulence was shaking her world . . . A storm was coming.

Unfortunately, Papsy was a majority shareholder of one of the fourteen foredoomed banks. Bad news! Officially all those finance institutions were to be seized under a receivership's supervision, until the auditors, inspectors, and the National Bank's management revised the monetary status quo. Nobody knew what would happen next.

"Damn it, probably some bureaucrat has judged hastily or somebody has deliberately included the bank in the list or . . . I don't know why or who, but I know one thing: Our portfolio is worthy! We have top properties with value many times more than our borrowings. I'm telling you, it's a healthy bank that they want to ruin, and I'll make them change their minds." Papsy was protesting, as would a boy wrongfully expelled from school.

"You think so?" asked Ana.

"Listen, I'll show them who I am! I'll ask my red friends for help." (He meant Socialists.) "No, I'll firmly insist upon their protection since I've done them so many favors." And he was right. In recent years, he had financially supported the red party not once or twice. So what the hell was his stockpile doing on the foredoomed list? He was bewildered.

"Who made the list initially, Papsy? Wasn't it the Socialist government?"

"Well yes, but . . . hey, you have been away for a long time. I still have my positions and contacts here. Just watch!" he said, with a hoity-toity expression on his face.

"Okay, go on, I'm with you," said Ana. Frankly, she was still finding it difficult to accept the reality at home, feeling a bit like a stranger in her own country.

"Oh, and one more thing," he added. "Until we get out of this mess, there'll be no time or big money for travel and leisure. Roger, soldier?"

"Roger. We'll stay in the bunker," she confirmed. "You know I'm not used to wastefully living anyway." Most important for Ana was the fact that they were whole and alive.

It was a hell of a winter. Misery and cold numbed the whole country. There were strikes everywhere. Rampageous citizens blocked the main roads. Nobody could tell how this crisis was going to end because the government was running out of grain, hyperinflation was out of control, and the average pay had dropped to twenty dollars per month.

Nationwide poverty transformed people into blackhearted wolves—furious and violent. In January, during a demonstration in the capital, many angry citizens invaded the parliament building demanding the prime minister's resignation. The situation became extremely explosive, and a civil war was right around the corner. The newspapers called it "The National Catastrophe!" Only by chance did it not turn into a bloodbath, and human casualties were avoided after the militaries and the police somehow managed to calm the rebels down. However, the coup was a fact. The red prime minister and his entourage resigned, making orphans of all their protégés, including Ana's husband. A caretaker government was immediately installed.

Papsy called it "bad luck"; Ana was speechless. No matter the label used, they both agreed the moment for complete mobilization had come, so he turned to his most powerful resource—the brotherhood. Ana's husband was a member of one of the Masonic Lodges in Berlin, and now he was hoping to favor from his good connections abroad. Luckily the brothers embraced the idea of rescuing his business and entire career. They accurately checked the numbers from the auditor's sheets, financial statements, accounting balance, etc. After all, "The eternal truth was a very serious search for perfection," and thus the search was done properly. Subsequently, the brothers initiated negotiations with the government to acquire. After they sent the official letter of intentions to "whom it may concern," the Masons equipped their accounts with the amounts needed for a same-day bargain with German punctuality. And they waited for a green light to proceed.

Meanwhile the seasons had changed, bringing warm summer sunshine and fresh strawberries. The caretaker government assigned in January had served its purpose, nationwide elections had been conducted, and a new cabinet was voted in—the democrats. Now everybody was hoping for national prosperity, especially Ana. As a mom, she dreamed of a better environment for Lilly to grow.

"I'll have dinner with the brothers tonight, to discuss the bank's development strategy, and tomorrow evening I'll stay with you girls," said Papsy as he picked up the phone. He silently mouthed, "It's them."

Later, at two or three o'clock in the morning, he came home overexcited and woke Ana with a kiss.

"Gee, we had such a constructive dialogue tonight! I'm sure everything's gonna be tip-top! Tomorrow I'll have to wake up early in the morning to run straight to the office. I'll call you at noon. Love you," he whispered in her ear.

"Aloha, Papsy," Ana replied sleepily. She had been dreaming of a romantic holiday in Hawaii.

*   *   *

It was Friday, June 13.

As usual Ana was in the park with Lilly. She was in a good mood after her husband's optimism. It was lovely to have dreams again. At last everything was going to get back to normal! And so, enjoying the beautiful sunny day, she commenced planning her upcoming twenty-sixth birthday party. Meanwhile a jolly girl was playing in the sand on the playground nearby. Now Lilly was a bit more than a year old, already walking and talking in this funniest of baby ages. She was such a sweetie!

The phone jangled, and Papsy instructed her that his security expert was going to meet her there.

"Sure, send him over," Ana said cheerfully. "I'm sitting on the same bench in the same park with the same baby making sand figures."

Suddenly his voice became more demanding and formal: "Do exactly what he tells you to do!"

Within twenty minutes the security guy walked along the benches in the park toward Ana. She noticed his tense face even before he spoke.

"Mrs. Ana, please remain calm!"

Something was wrong. She held her breath as he silently handed over Papsy's belongings –his watch, wallet, and some pieces of paper. It was an ominous act—freaking eerie, as if he had died.

"Oh my God, what's going on?"

"He's alive, but he was arrested today."

"Arrested? Today? Why?"

"I don't know, Mrs. Ana. I'm so sorry. They say it's related to the bank's affairs, but in my opinion, it's a witch hunt. The new democratic cabinet is after the Socialists' supporters, and apparently your husband was one of the targets. I'll find out more as soon as possible and will contact you."

Ana still couldn't believe the news. Her head was spinning. Her hands were as cold as ice. Her mind blanked.

Please, Anché, don't panic! Think! She commanded herself. Then she asked the security guard, "What should I do now?"

"Go to your parents' place and stay there. I'll reach out to you," he said. He then rushed away.

And that was exactly what Ana did. Her parents' house was the only place in the world where she could survive the toughest moment in her life so far. From then on her childhood home became the sanctuary where she could feel safe, unconditionally loved and supported, and it served as the only confessional where she could freely share her fears, hopes, big things, and little things. It was her shelter in which to cry or hide from the rest of the world when in grief. Under the circumstances Ana hated being alone, and moreover she was not tranquil enough to focus on Lilly as before. Now she felt like a bird with one wing—a muddy, filthy, and low bird with one damn wing.

Fortunately, Mrs. K was there to help. At once she established a solemn principle: No matter what, Lilly's sweet childhood was not going to be to infected by the bitterness of the present mess. Granny's rule number one was to protect the kid's soul! Everybody agreed.

The warmth and affection her parents provided during that episode of her life was crucial to Ana. In the next months, she was fighting to survive emotionally, financially, and even biologically. She lost weight, becoming skinnier than ever before.

In the meantime, Papsy's name was all over the news. The authorities were blaming him for signing fake bank documents for huge amounts while working for another bank years ago. He said it was a setup, but nevertheless, his image had already been tarnished. Naturally, the German investors were troubled by the media's allegations, so they packed up the victory flags and flew back home. The bank's bargain was *kaput*!

Papsy was devastated. "Damn it, they wanted to stop the deal, and they did. I can't blame the Germans for stepping back . . ."

So did many of his friends, colleagues, and relatives. From their perspective, he was a criminal.

At that time the legal system in their country was far from providing justice, but at its core it was a moneymaking business. Massive corruption raged at all levels, regulated by the so-called "prosecutor's mafia." As expected, soon after the arrest, the messengers of the same ruthless faction contacted Ana, offering to "fix the problem" in return for some "donations." The messengers had only two questions on their checklist: first, if she was desperate enough, and second, if she had enough money. Ana's answer was yes to both. But in the meantime, one more accusation on Papsy conveniently arose that automatically tripled their price.

"Fine. If they want money, we shall give them money," Ana said when she conveyed their message to Papsy's parents. They would need to use their additional savings, as she would not be able to cover the outrageous costs on her own. Hoping that after meeting the payments this harassment would finally end, the whole family pooled their finances and paid both the bribe and bail—an amount that broke the record of highest in history ever claimed by the civil court for bailment. No murderer, no rapist, no drug dealer had ever paid more than Ana's husband for his freedom.

At last, after five months of public humiliation, personal threats, and racketeering, one man walked out of prison. He had lost more than thirty pounds; his clothes were kind of fluttering on his body; his hair was long; but his spirit was still high. He was going home to his beloved wife, his adorable grown-up girl, and his own bed. What more could a man dream of?

The family celebrated, believing misfortune was finally behind. They would be able to build up their life again. And slowly, day by day, the matters kind of returned to normal—but the nightmare was not over yet.

One black night with dense fog, Ana saw a little red dot on the terrace wall. What was it? She turned the lights off and yelled, "Papsy, get down! Something's going on!"

Her pulse was drumming. Was that a sniper's dot?

Hiding in the dark, Papsy explained his theory. Apparently, in addition to their problems with the prosecutor's mafia, now his ex-business partner was after him too . . .

"Why didn't you tell me?" Ana asked.

"I didn't want to bother you."

"What does he want? Money again? Shall we start printing our own to survive?" She was mad. Everything was upside down and getting worse.

"He wants my shares, and for this purpose he has hired assassins to do the job. My informant told me so."

"You guys are outrageous, playing all these stupid games!"

"But I—"

"You! You let all this happen!" She blamed him for not being careful enough to prepare a plan B and to protect his family. Ana's personal verdict: guilty of lack of acumen!

"What shall we do now?" she asked after a while.

On one thing they agreed: The situation was dangerous and demanded an immediate reaction. Because of that, early in the morning they left home and stayed at their friend's house for a few days. But that solution couldn't last long. After they rationally analyzed the circumstances, two possible conclusions remained: Either Papsy would get trapped in the prosecutors' net again (as they wanted more money), or he would get killed by his partner's assassins. It seemed the opportunity for a proper living in their country didn't exist for him anymore. He was totally ill-fated. In order to be free and alive, Papsy would have to run—to run far and away from their country.

Therefore, in the beginning of May, he packed his essential belongings in a small case, kissed Ana, and said, "You have to be strong, my dear! Don't lose your faith, and take good care of Lilly. Trust me; everything will be all right in the end. When I settle down somewhere in the world, you'll move in with me and we'll be happy together again. Until then, you can travel to me in secret." That was the original plan.

"Of course I'll take care of her," said Ana. "She deserves a decent life no matter what. And for her sake, one of us has to be legitimate. Thus, I'll never break the law! I want her and me both to always be welcome in our homeland, anytime, and with no legal obstructions."

"Fine, fine," he agreed. "We'll do it your way. I'll contact you shortly. So long, my brave girl!"

Soon, Papsy went missing. Understandably the authorities were enraged, and confiscated the bail straightaway. But that was not enough. A third accusation was announced in absentia, whereby the land of the hippodrome was seized. Ana was interrogated about her husband's actions, though she had nothing more to say.

"I don't know where he is, and I don't know who helped him. Nor am I familiar with his bank affairs."

"And did he leave something behind?"

"Yes, he left a bad reputation!"

She was telling the truth, though not the naked truth. The red folder was resting at home—a tiny piece of information that Ana kept for herself. After all, nobody asked about it.

Later on strange transformations happened to Papsy's business affairs. After he vanished, most of his partners conveniently came up with outdated protocols saying he had transferred his shares to them. And since he was busy hiding, litigating the documents was impossible. So the country courts, and even the ones abroad, assumed the protocols were authentic. And just like that he lost everything. He became a refugee with no business, no family, no home, and no identity.

At the same time Ana had to move on. After all, she had a little child to support on her own. Therefore she pulled herself together and managed to stay centered when in public. Santa Ana was guiding her. If people had known what a gigantic storm of feelings she hid inside, they probably would have named the next hurricane Ana. Being a very emotional woman, she suffered a lot. Her dreams were crushed into pieces. Her heart was broken too. When alone, Ana doubted herself.

Why the hell is this happening to me?

I haven't done anything wrong, so why do I have to squirm?

What is wrong with this world?

During one of her many sleepless nights, a concept came to her: With or without answers to her questions, she had to forge ahead. Somehow she had to find a way to reassemble the parts of her broken heart, so she and Lilly could enjoy the prodigy called "life" together—disregarding the past and embracing the future. And for starters, she had to hone her focus on the things she wanted to stand and fight for, putting aside all those bad memories. The nightmare had to end! Ana had already learned the universal lesson of wisdom: "Sometimes bad things happen to good people. Just like that."

Soon she had initiated the divorce procedure, sorted out the documents in the red folder, and called the Collector.

CHAPTER 8

THE SEDUCTION

Due to the dramatic events in her life, Ana had to reconsider her friends, as some had disappeared without a trace. What a pity, she thought, and wrote it off as "non-natural selection" in order to appreciate the ones still present. She knew she would need them more than ever, as she considered honest friendship to be the best cure for her wounded soul.

Ana met her in the middle of the nightmare. She was almost the same age, almost the same size, almost the same skin tone, and had a baby only four months younger than Lilly. They instantly liked each other. Neither one of them had a sister, so soon they started addressing one another as "Sis." The babies also got along, so a multilateral friendship sprung between them, bringing warmth and intimacy to everyone. The four of them gathered almost every day—for evenings during the workweek and as long as possible on the weekends. Sis had a good husband, and he also embraced their friendship with an open heart.

"Where should I come for dinner?" he would ask when he called after work, and according to the answer, he would head either home or to Ana's place. During those evenings the adults had lots of fun planning weekends, national holidays, summers, or winters, while their kids' mischief made them smile . . . or twitch. Side by side the babies were learning to talk, walk, run, count, and read. Furthermore they were learning to take care of each other, to make compromises, and to share toys. Harmony settled into that peculiar tiny community, and among their friends the husband was soon nicknamed "the man with the two women."

Ana was deeply grateful for this sincere friendship, as it helped her overcome the disappointment, loneliness, and grief left behind from her unlucky marriage. Hallelujah, Sis was around!

* * *

One day it was Ana's turn to cook dinner, and she was in the supermarket when her mobile phone rang. Surprise surprise, the Collector was calling out of the blue.

"Hey, how are you doin'?" His voice sounded friendly.

"Hello, nice to hear from you. I'm shopping. My friends are coming over for dinner. What's up? Do you have some news about the project?"

"Nah, nothing in particular. Are you still on the right track?"

"Of course. I'm following the strict plan we made."

"Hey, why don't you come over to talk about it?" said the Collector, but in an insistent tone.

Something's probably going on that he's not willing to talk about on the phone, thought Ana.

"Sure, when's convenient?"

"How about now?"

"Now?!" she repeated, assuming this was probably a test. She added without delay, "Okay, coming right away."

"Fine. Come to my new office," he said, then gave her the address.

* * *

"Please park over there in front of the main entrance, ma'am," directed one of the guards. Following his instructions, she maneuvered into the empty spot, turned off the car, and—chop-chop—was immersed in thought about the project when . . . she saw the building she was facing was remarkable! Ana stood in front of one of the capital's cultural monuments, perfectly located right beside parliament and the cathedral with the biggest golden domes. The aristocratic edifice once belonged to a former prime minister, who served the country in that post for three years, had previously been the minister of finance twice, was elected eleven times to parliament, was Chairman of the National Bank and Chairman of the Academy of Science (not simultaneously, of course), and also participated in an international peace negotiations delegate. According to the annals of his youth, this noble man had studied at Owens College known as Victoria University in Manchester. During that time he won the British Spelling Contest (unusual for a foreigner), earning him the honor of teatime with Her Majesty Queen Victoria.

Later on during Socialism, the building was confiscated and turned into a policlinic for the university's needs, and now . . . well, now the monument was in the Collector's hands.

Once inside, Ana walked up a set of marble stairs to a restricted area on the second floor. The beautiful stained-glass doors opened automatically. A young woman saluted her with a fake smile, and both ladies exchanged compliments before the receptionist pointed at the dark wooden door on the right.

"The boss is expecting you."

Behind that door . . . was another. Presumably past this second one was the Collector's new chamber. Ana delicately walked in to find an office even more luxurious than the rest of the building; everything was first-class down to the smallest details: shiny, chocolate-colored wood flooring, elegant royal blue furniture with corresponding curtains, and bright crystal illuminants. The walls were decorated with unique, beautiful paintings. All around the place various artifacts were showcased as if in a museum. One exceptional golden crown sparkled on the room's right side. Across the room the Collector sat behind his new imperial desk and talked on the phone—obviously with a woman. The crystal skull was invariably placed next to him.

"I'll see you later. Ignore the underwear!" He hung up with those words, looked at Ana, and smiled. "Hey, you're looking good. Take a seat. Let's have whiskey!"

"Whiskey? Isn't it a bit early?"

"No, no, no, it's the perfect time. I had a fortunate day today, so we have to celebrate."

The bottle was already waiting on the desk alongside two crystal glasses, so he ably poured a rare kind of scotch, passed a glass to Ana, and lifted his drink.

"Cheers to our success!"

"Okay, cheers to our success," Ana repeated, still wondering what the hell was going on.

The Collector took a sip and asked, "What's the occasion for the dinner party?"

Hmm, he was acting very unusual . . . so merry and friendly. "Oh, it's informal. Just friends. We raise our kids together," answered Ana.

"You have a girl, right?"

"Yes—Lilly. She's in kindergarten."

"Is she as pretty as her mom?" he asked with a smirk.

"Yes, in fact we are very alike. One friend even calls her my mini-me."

"Wonderful. Maybe one day I'll meet her," he said, then proceeded without pause to tell a joke. "A sheikh writes a farewell letter to his harem: 'My dear wives, you have taken excellent care of my person and my life. I appreciate it a lot. Unfortunately, I have to inform you with tears in my eyes that I'm leaving you today. I've fallen in love.'"—he paused—"'with another harem!'"

Ana was still laughing when the Collector stood up, full of energy, and approached her from around the desk. Without a word he reached for her hand, and with a gesture he invited her to stand. She did this with no clear idea why she should. Then he pulled her closer and embraced her with authority.

Blimey! The dizzying tricks of the whiskey along with her mixed emotions became too much for Ana on this late afternoon. She ran through her choices in her head—to make an ugly scene, to run away and forget about the project, or to stay and become a part of his collection . . . His lips on her neck felt like something in between a gentle buzz and a vampire's kiss. Next, firmly holding her hand, the Collector opened another door behind her chair into a twilight vestibule.

"Come here," he commanded, leading her to his private suite.

*   *   *

Nothing changed in Ana's life after that afternoon. She kept it a secret—except from Sis. To her Ana confessed to being embarrassed, confused, and unwilling to expose this strange new subversion of their "partnership" to others.

One Saturday morning he called with an offer.

"Hey, what've you been doin' lately? Long time no see . . ." His voice sounded hollow from a distance.

"I'm busy decorating my new apartment."

"So boring . . . Meanwhile, I'm lying in a huge round bed at the Ritz thinking about you. Why don't you come over to Paris for a weekend?"

"Oh, a weekend in Paris—how thrilling!" Ana hadn't been there since Lilly was born, and she was dying to go.

"Well?" He waited for an answer.

"Thank you, but unfortunately, I have no one to watch my daughter. I can't come."

"Really?"

"Yes, I'm sorry. I'm alone with her," apologized Ana, knowing full well Mrs. K was always around to care for Lilly. Ana was simply not willing to go.

"Fine, call me next week," he said indifferently. Then he asked if she had any attractive friends in town, and she denied that she did.

CHAPTER 9

THE ENDORSEMENT

As the project was still on and a matter of a vital importance to Ana, she had to find a way to diplomatically smuggle her private life out of the bargain. The next time they met, she tried to clarify her point of view.

"I'll be honest: Even if it may sound naïve or stupid to you, I believe in love and happiness, and I want to have a fully intimate relationship with a loyal man. No games, no cheating, no crap."

"Okay . . ." He wore a quizzical look. "Though until then, you could experiment with being more broad-minded, if you know what I mean . . ."

Ana didn't answer; she was looking at her nails.

"Never mind," he said, then changed the subject. "What's going on with your husband?"

"Hmm, nothing new. He's still away. I've started a divorce procedure in absentia. Afterward I'll have to file for exclusive custody so Lilly will be able to travel and study abroad without his notary-signed permission."

"Right, right. And what's going on with the hippodrome? How long will it take to unveil the project?"

"Well, you tell me," Ana said, reminding him of their agreement. He was the one obligated to deal with the authorities.

"Correct, but first the shares have to be endorsed to the offshore company of mine . . . for the venture's sake. We can only overcome the existing legal case and get the property back if both the judges and the public are convinced it's no longer your ex's but mine. Otherwise they will procrastinate for years. Once I stand behind the hippodrome, my mediators will do the rest. They're well-connected in the city court, so the process could happen pretty quickly."

Whoa, isn't that way too risky? thought Ana. "But what about my royalty? How can I be sure I'll stay on board?"

"It will be on paper only," the Collector answered, looking at her mildly. Then he came up with an offer: "We could name your father chairman of the board, and you could be an executive when the time comes. That way, you would be aware of all the decisions being made. How about that?"

"Well, that makes sense . . ."

"So when will I meet him?"

"Who?"

"Your father, of course."

"My father!?"

"I won't be asking for your hand. Bring him over. The future chairman and I need to meet each other."

"Ok, I'll arrange it, but . . ."

"My secretary will give you the papers. You'll have to sign the endorsement on the back. Do it soon."

"But . . ."

"What?" asked the Collector, glancing at his watch. For him, this meeting was over.

"But still there's no guarantee for my shares . . . I mean, other than your word."

"More guarantees?" He seemed to getting touchy. "Well, if we leave it this way, I can give you certain guarantees that you'll lose the land. Look at you: You're just a chick with a hippodrome, and the foxes outside are waiting to tear you apart. Think, Ana! I'm your best bet. Don't you get it?"

The ugly truth was that he was right! Alone she was doomed. At that moment and under those circumstances, he was the best choice. But could she trust him? Ana was aware of his bad reputation as a dishonest, cheating person, so in dealing with him she expected an element of hazard. At the same time, hope and a great opportunity lay ahead. So she took the papers from the secretary on her way out.

*   *   *

That same evening, Papsy called.

"I've rented a lovely house, and I'm waiting for you and Lilly to come here according to the original plan," he said.

"But we're not ready. The custody case has yet to go through. Only afterward will Lilly be able to travel abroad. As I told you, I want us to be absolutely legitimate. For her well-being we have to be rational."

"Yes, yes, I just want it to happen sooner," he agreed with regret.

"So the Collector wants me to sign over the hippodrome's shares. In return he would manipulate your legal case," Ana told him.

"Why not?" From his point of view, that meant one less accusation.

Later, Ana reconsidered the odds.

Worst case, the Collector misappropriates the land that I don't possess anyway because of the legal case. Best case, he keeps his word, and we proceed with the project as settled. But what happens if I don't sign the endorsement? I lose the possibility of working with him for good. Even if I found a new partner, which would be pretty difficult, we'd end up back at his headquarters since he represents the only company with a betting license.

Now the direction was clear: It was a one-way street. Then Ana called her father and asked him to come over. When he came, she told him about the endorsement's details.

"It seems the Collector is not a compromising kind of person," concluded Mr. G.

"Yes, I'm afraid so. It's a 'his way or the highway' situation. Would you be willing to meet him?"

"Sure," her father said. As usual, he was there for her.

Mr. G

Shortly after the Collector confirmed the interview, which he referred to as "the tryst," Ana and Mr. G arrived sharp, ready and steady. The Collector knew that Ana's father was a former basketball player, so he was not surprised to find before him a tall, handsome man. His silver hair naturally complemented his profound appearance, and he dressed tidily that day in a dark suit, white shirt, and necktie. The Collector, by contrast, wore a T-shirt with a printed skull on it. Ana introduced them.

"Welcome. Please make yourself comfortable," the host said, pointing to the seats in front of his desk. Once coffee had been served, he continued, staring at Mr. G. "Well, tell me about yourself."

"Originally, I am an engineer. During Socialism I worked for the Central Laboratory of Automation for eighteen years under the Ministry of Chemical Industry's jurisdiction. I was the head of my division, and my team did research and implemented real-time control systems for diverse factories."

"I see . . . And what, for example, was your team's latest project?"

"It was the Peteravet plant, sir."

"The Peteravet?" The Collector was intrigued. "Really?"

Unlike Ana, he was aware that the plant was known to be a leading European manufacturer of nutritional food additives, bulk active substances, enzymes, and pharmaceuticals mostly for animals, though for humans also. Since its establishment in 1954, Peteravet was among the most prosperous factories in the country, exporting 90 percent of its output worldwide. Just recently it was privatized, and now it sat among the other local oligarch's assets. The Collector wanted to know more.

"Hmm, very interesting. And what in particular did you do there?"

Mr. G replied. "Back then the minister assigned me personally the task of drawing up a project for a modern factory generating high-quality bio stimulators. We conducted massive amounts of research.

One state factory was located south in the mountains, and it was just perfect for the occasion. There we worked with a unique strain . . .

The microflora of the local river's crystal water was the only place in the whole world where this particular bacillus would grow—and nowhere else. That exceptional strain was and actually still is among the national treasures. Examples of it are preserved in a cryogenic bio camera in the National Refrigeration Institute . . ."

"Do you mind if I light up a cigar?" asked the Collector, reaching for one.

"No, it's okay. My wife's a smoker," answered Mr. G.

Exhaling, the host said, "Please continue."

"As I said, Peteravet was exactly what we needed. Par excellence it could become a futuristic factory, if a reliable real-time control system was properly applied, and of course a complete modernization was executed. So after long, exhausting negotiations with two major US companies and one Japanese, and after many extended reports had been written, the minister accepted Rosemount Inc. They had a proven reputation, technical equipment, and the know-how to be the dependable partner for this enterprise. And so the project was approved."

Sitting next to her father, Ana listened with full attention and respect. In her childhood, she had never understood what this man, her father, had done for work.

The phone rang. Hastily the Collector picked up, answered, "Hmm . . . yes . . . no," then emphasized that he was busy and did not want to be disturbed anymore.

"And . . . ?" He invited Mr. G to continue.

"Let me briefly explain the biotechnology's essence. It's a repeatable batch process. The strain grows for a hundred days in huge tanks, where the exact control of the process inside is of crucial importance. The temperature, the pressure, the airflow, and the pH in the reactors have to be monitored and sustained as prescribed. When the process is over, the substance is dried and powdered, and the regrowth starts again after a hundred days—again and again, and so on.

That's why we wanted Rosemount's equipment. They manufacture and sell one of the most precise sensors in the world. When the first humans landed on the moon, the astronauts' space suits were supplied with their systems for oxygen flow control. Remarkable, right? Working closely with NASA equates to punctuality, reliability, and innovative ideas. And there's more: Nearly all US spaceflights use Rosemount's appliances. Even the spacecraft *Voyager* carries many of their sensors to the outer limits of the solar system and beyond."

The phone was ringing for the third time.

"What?!" the Collector answered.

The secretary apologized and informed him that the CEO of a significant state company had arrived.

"Take him to the boardroom," instructed the Collector before turning back to Mr. G. "Such a pity. If I had this information about Peteravet a year ago I would have probably gone for it. So you're saying the modernization was successfully accomplished?"

"Absolutely. During the installation I was consulting American experts. When the new system was launched on schedule, they asked me to represent Rosemount Inc. for the country and the region . . . including Russia. With that privilege, my team and I arranged Rosemount's presentation in Moscow for five hundred people. And after working in the same field for nearly ten years with the Russian Institute of Automation's director, I was able to ask him to support our event. His name was Yury Luzhkov."

"Yury Luzhkov? As in, the mayor of Moscow?" The Collector leaned forward and shook his cigar.

"Yes, same Yury. Now his second mandate is marshaling the Russian capital." Mr. G smiled.

"Yeah, it's a small world! And what happened next?" The Collector was completely out of time, but he was eager to hear the rest of the story.

"Next . . . next everything collapsed. The nation bankrupted after the coup, the government declared a severe electricity ration, many factories were closed, many were looted . . ."

"That part I already know, thanks." The Collector stood up, indicating the meeting was over. Ana gave her father a sign, and after a courteous thank-you, Ana stopped.

"Well?" she said to the Collector.

"What?" He pretended to have forgotten the reason for their visit, looking at his PC. Then finally, he spit out, "Okay, fine. Let's stick to the plan."

Ana had interpreted the Collector's last phrase as an okay to elect her father for the position. On the way home in the car, she turned to Mr. G.

"What's your opinion of the Collector, Dad?"

"I think he's a hard man. You'll have to be mindful, flexible, and very, very diplomatic. Remember, a smart woman could achieve her goals by using cotton, not a spear."

"Well, should I sign the endorsement?" she asked, looking for his advice.

"That's up to you. Though if I were you, I would do it. The coolest people I've ever met—they live through challenges, sometimes making bad choices, but always learning their lessons. The most important thing is that they are not afraid of being real!"

"Cool. Thanks, Dad. Thanks for everything. You know what I'll do? It's very simple. I'll ask myself which choice will make me feel better when I look in the mirror tomorrow morning."

"Sure. Ask your inner buddy," encouraged Mr. G.

And she did that. The buddy said, *Jump!*

CHAPTER 10

THE OMEN

Summer came. Ana's mom and daughter were at the family's seaside cottage, and Ana was as carefree as a damsel. With her father already chairman of the National Hippodrome board, she was allowed to loosen up a little bit—and why not go wild for a change? The business forecast was optimistic; even though the land was still seized, the dark clouds were melting away from the sky above the hippodrome as the Collector's winds commenced blowing.

One late afternoon Ana was working out at the gym when her high school friend Natalie called.

"Hi! How about an African party tonight? Would you join us?"

Wasn't it perfect timing for a jamboree? Ana didn't blink an eye. "Awesome. Count me in. Is there a dress code?"

"Nope, though you might need a cardigan. It will be outdoors."

At the set hour, a green Jaguar turned on Ana's street and stopped in front of her building. Natalie and her husband waved her to jump in. With Adriano Celentano's music blaring from the speakers, the car headed northeast outside the capital.

Among Ana's friends Natalie was the one always in a good mood—a little elevated and a little introverted. She had a photogenic face with a fluffy curly hair and agile eyes. She was smart and sophisticated. In her youth, Natalie used to be a TV presenter, popular for interviewing worldwide celebrities such as Julio Iglesias, Plácido Domingo, the lead guitarist of Queen, Brian May, Diego

Maradona, Björn Borg, and many others. Now she and her husband ran a successful company selling professional media equipment to TV studios, and due to the recent broadcasting expansion in their country, they were doing pretty well.

In between Italian songs, Ana was informed that their destination was one of the best beauty and plastic surgery clinics in the suburbs. Soon the car arrived at a private parking area with many posh cars.

"Okay, ladies, let's have some fun," said Natalie's husband, switching off "Il Tempo Se Ne Va."

Past the parking lot, an alley with burning torches was wedged between two properties.

"Wow, that looks mystical!" said Ana.

"Even spiritual," added Natalie as they paced into the twilight.

Like in the fairy tales an impressive, enigmatically illuminated aristocratic mansion unveiled itself at the end of the alley. A circle the size of a small circus arena, covered with sand and surrounded by burning torches, was arranged in the courtyard in front of the main entrance. All around it stood tents with tables and assigned seating for the carefully selected guests. Exotic rhythms pounded from hidden speakers. The setting was totally outlandish, and awe-inspiring.

"Please, follow me," the hostess said, kindly inviting them to one of the central tables, where three others were already settled.

"Hi, guys. You're late, the show's over," said one smiling man from across the table. At that time he owned the local rights for publishing *Playboy* magazine. His wife escorted him, and the other person was a foreigner. He, a Greek, introduced himself as the CEO of a popular TV channel—the one Ana's ex-husband was once involved in.

Yeah, that's life, thought Ana. "Well, I'm just a Natalie's high school friend," she said.

Meantime Natalie's husband rubbed his hands together and said, "Right, let's make it a night to remember. Champagne, please!"

A bottle of Moët & Chandon quickly materialized at their table.

"Dear friends, let's drink to the hedonism!" he proposed as the first toast.

"And to the beautiful women," added the publisher, winking at the ladies present.

"Cheers!" And the sound of crystal glasses sounded from their tent.

*   *   *

After introductions Ana managed to have a look around. In the dark she couldn't distinguish very well the faces under the other tents, tinted as they were by the torches' light. Under all these moving penumbras the whole place looked kind of surreal, even bizarre. Suddenly the music stopped and it became quiet—the show was about to begin.

One, two, three, dum dum—and the air exploded. Musicians with djembe drums, shell maracas, and rain sticks performed with such intensity it was electrifying. The basses' vibrations penetrated everyone's bodies, as if attempting to change the rhythm of their heartbeats.

"Gee, I've got goose bumps," whispered Ana.

"Jambo, jamboo," the musicians started singing after a while.

Natalie's husband leaned toward Ana and said quietly, "'Jambo' is a greeting that means 'hello.'"

Well, hello, dancers! In the glow of the night lit by fire, a dozen beautiful, nearly naked girls with dark chocolate skin performed the Zulu wedding dance. Their bodies were supple and expressive, full of energy and even lust. Ana could detect a pinch of madness in their eyes. It was a very powerful performance, yet spooky— completely absorbing the whole audience's attention until the show ended sometime past midnight. For the last dance guests were invited into the circle. Their shoes were off—the genie, out of the bottle.

"What a night! Thank you guys for taking me with you," commented Ana while taking her high heels off. Then her back disappeared among the crowd on the dance floor made of sand. It was killa' dancing barefoot.

In the meantime the second bottle of champagne was emptied, and the third one was on the way. Soon the foreigner vanished after saying, "Folks, I'll be back in a while." Fifteen minutes later he returned with a cock-a-hoop expression and three handmade wooden canes.

"There's an improvised market near the entrance. Africans are selling their crafts," he explained before turning to the ladies. "For our beautiful companions: souvenirs to remember a wild African night."

He then handed each one a cane. Ana was awarded a unique stick with an elephant's head on the top. Natalie received an eagle, and the last one had a lion's head carved atop it. After a couple more hours the night was no longer young, and everybody was pretty exhausted.

"Let's go home," whined Natalie. Her offer was promptly and unanimously accepted. It was almost dawn when the green Jaguar turned onto Ana's street and dropped her off at home.

CHAPTER 11

THE FALSE START

Time was passing. Lilly was nearly six and a half years old, and in autumn she would have to find her groove for school. But where? The divorce proceedings were over, and Ana had won exclusive custody of her daughter. Finally they were able to travel. So should they emigrate to Papsy or should they stay home? He had declared he was eagerly waiting for them somewhere in Latin America. Meanwhile, in the name of naturalization, Ana's ex-husband had remarried. "Pro forma," he said. "For better status." That was all well and good for him, but what about Ana and Lilly's status if they came?

"We'll figure it out somehow," Papsy said, yet this kind of answer did not please Ana. His previous actions had proved his lack of proficiency, and now Lilly would be involved as well. Ana had doubts. With the money she had previously sent him he had started a few small businesses, but he had invested most of their savings in a dubious financial company.

"That's way too risky. Interest rates are exaggerated," she warned him. Over the last few years Ana had grown a lot, and from her point of view his actions seemed irrational.

"Nah, it's okay. They just provide good interest to the chosen ones," Papsy replied. He was as stubborn as a donkey.

Should she entrust her and Lilly's future to him? Ana had asked herself that question a thousand times. But if they rejected his offer, then her girl would grow up without a father! Would that be fair?

Would that damage Lilly's personality somehow? And also, if the reunion were to ever happen, did it have to be now?

We'll go before she starts school, Ana finally decided.

The plan was to fly to Paris, where Papsy would send them vouchers for the rest of their journey. Mr. G and Mrs. K were wrecked, knowing it would be such a heartbreaking good-bye. However, they supported the mission for Lilly's welfare. Ana booked the tickets and told her daughter about the voyage to her birthplace, not stressing her with the "leaving-for-good" concept. Lilly was exited, especially when Disneyland was mentioned.

One day before their flight, Papsy's buddy called Ana out of the blue.

"Something's happened. He said you should not go to him now! I repeat, you should wait!" The guy sounded worried.

"Wait? Why? What's going on?"

"I don't know. He just asked me to call you and to tell you to wait."

"But … I've promised my daughter a trip to Paris. The tickets are prepaid. Please, tell him we'll proceed as arranged," replied Ana. She was very confused. Fortunately she had kept the true purpose of that trip from Lilly; otherwise her girl might be deeply disappointed.

Ana followed the original plan as if nothing had happened. She and Lilly went to Paris and stayed for ten days. Nobody called. Nobody sent vouchers. Ana took it as a sign they didn't belong in Latin America.

When they came back home, Ana enrolled Lilly straightaway in a prestigious private school in the capital. No more doubts, no more unknowns. The "moving to her father" chapter was closed. And he . . . well, in due time, he reappeared with an apology.

"I'm very sorry, I was in trouble, a huge mess . . . I couldn't make it work this time, though I promise next time everything will go smoothly."

"Are you kidding me? It's over. We aren't coming," Ana answered firmly.

"But why not? You have to!"

"I don't think so. Lilly's classes have already started and she's happy at school. We'll pass."

Her intuition had been alerted, and rightly. Soon the financial company collapsed along with their savings, and Papsy lost the house. Two years later he was arrested after the motherland agents claum. To his good fortune, the local court denied the extradition but still confiscated his passport. And that was how Papsy got trapped somewhere in Latin America.

*   *   *

Back to the first-grade routine. Lilly's classes were extended this year, and the school bus brought her home each day in the afternoon. Afterward, two options remained for the rest of the day: extra studying with mom, or chilling out with Sis and her daughter. Of course, Lilly highly preferred the second one, yet Ana went along only sometimes.

"Education is more important. It's your obligation, love," she would say.

And so, day after day, Lilly worked to learn to read and write, counting the days until winter came, and then—Christmas. As usual their small family gathered at the grandparents' house, where Lilly stayed through New Year's Eve as well. However, Ana had something else on her mind this year: to celebrate at a countryside ski resort with her new boyfriend and another nice couple.

CHAPTER 12

THE ACCIDENT

They say accidents happen for a reason. Maybe Ana's accident happened to her for a reason as well, or at least she would later be willing to think so.

She had recently been dating a conceited but hunky local diplomat, and he had invited her to ring in the upcoming year with him. The holiday's schedule was short—partying and skiing. She accepted.

The gala dinner was well orchestrated in the luxurious hotel where they were staying. Ana clicked with the lovely Michelle—his friend's wife—at once. They had lots of fun dancing for hours. Subsequently they skipped the next morning's skiing; however on the second day, everybody was fresh and sober enough to hit the slopes. According to the forecast, the weather was supposed to be absolutely splendid—sunny and not very cold. Was the extremely long lift queue going to stop them? Of course not.

Well, it took much longer than Ana thought it would to get to the top of the mountain, but the endeavor awarded them with spectacular scenery. At 2,200 meters there was a view of the little town below, the whole valley beyond it, and the other mountain across from them. It looked as though Mother Nature had left her kiss here. The snow glittered in the sunlight like white sugar, and the air was pure and fresh. Even the slopes were perfectly shaped—not too sharp, not too flat, simply heavenly. There was only one tiny little problem: It was too crowded. Even though this wasn't stressful for Ana's friends, them being experienced and passionate skiers, it was for her.

"Ana, don't look back. Others coming from behind should protect you. Don't worry," they encouraged her.

"Oh come on, guys. It's only my second season. Please don't wait for me. We'll meet up at the bottom of the lift," she replied—still nervous for a reason. The slope was an anthill, and Ana stopped repeatedly to check the traffic behind her.

"No, no, we'll pace you and consider it a warm-up. You just have to hurry up a little," said Michelle.

"Ugh, I'm sorry. I'll do my best. It's just . . . my instincts are on alert."

Then, trying not to be such a freaking beginner, Ana headed down without stopping or looking back. Until . . .

Bang! Something hit her with incredible force. *What was that? A human?* Next thing she knew, she was rolling down the slope, trying to protect her head and face. Blimey, everything was happening so fast! The scrubbing noise of her dragging jacket, those screams, and the snow . . . it was everywhere—in her eyes, mouth, nose. So much snow—she couldn't breathe!

When she stopped moving, the pain came—an intense, killing, satanic pain in her left leg. At least her spine was not injured. Somehow Ana managed to lift her head and chest from the snow so as to look down. What she saw was horrifying: Her leg lay at an unnatural angle on the snow, with the ski still on it. The bindings hadn't released. She panicked.

"My leg is backward, my leg is backward—it's broken!"

Ana saw her friends running toward her. Suddenly all her muscles simultaneously contracted, and she squeezed her fingers inward so hard that her hands became fists. She couldn't control her body, and the hardest thing on earth now was to breathe. It was a staggering moment! For the first time Ana was fighting for her life.

"Breathe, Ana, breathe, for Christ's sake!" she could hear the Diplomat yelling as he shoveled snow on her face.

She had to breathe to stay awake despite the pain, the panic, the fear . . . Falling into a drowse, she heard somebody calling the Mountain Rescue Service and asking for an ambulance.

"Breathe, Ana! Stay awake!"

As her boyfriend shook her head, she tried hard to stay awake. But her eyelids were so heavy. Her last efforts to survive had consumed all of the energy left inside of her.

"We have to reset her leg," Michelle said, her voice sounding distant.

"Yes, sure, but which way?" replied her boyfriend. Was it that bad?

"Okay, let's try this way . . ."

"Ouch," Ana cried, sinking deeper and deeper into sleep. It was getting darker.

What will happen to my Lilly? was the last thought on her mind . . .

Then Ana fainted in the snow.

Later she learned that the one who had hit her was a reckless snowboarding instructor on his day off. Showing off his irrational speed, he had crashed into her from behind. At first his board broke her leg right below the knee, which was the reason why the bindings never opened to release her ski. Then the impact of his strong athletic body against her thin one had the effect of crumbling crackers—resulting in a few more fractures.

*　　*　　*

"Hey, lady, wake up!" she heard a voice say, wrenching her back to reality.

Instantly, Ana felt the pain again. Her left leg was killing her.

"We have to move you to the stretcher. Then we'll ski you down the slope."

"Are you nuts? Don't you have a chopper?" the Diplomat asked. "We're on the top of the mountain! She could faint again."

Such unpreparedness was unacceptable, as the accident happened on January 2, 2003—the height of ski season in Europe. Since the state Mountain Rescue Service had been established seventy before, thousands of brave, decent men had contributed their time and saved many lives despite primitive resources. The guards were there when people needed them, but where was the state support for them?

"No, sir, I'm sorry. That's all we've got," apologized the rescuer.

"At least give her some strong painkillers. She is suffering a lot," said the Diplomat, trying to stay centered.

"I've got only analgesics, sir."

"This is madness!" Now he couldn't help but lose his temper, and he kicked the snow with all the anger that had accumulated within him. Then he turned with a crazed face and commanded, "Let's do it as fast as possible. Come on—move her to the stretcher!"

Ana cried all the way down the slope, aching through every bump. It was a long ride. The severe cold froze her limbs, and she shivered like a dog. When they reached the bottom of the lift, an old ambulance was waiting for them with the heat turned up all the way. Of course, the warmth dramatically increased the pain's intensity.

"Please, turn off the heat! Take me to the hospital!" begged Ana.

"Of course, but first we have to wait for another skier with a broken leg," said the driver.

"No way. Please take me to the hospital *now*." Ana was desperate.

By the time the other skier was settled, the Diplomat had already begun organizing the rest of the evacuation plan. For sure the best medical assistance she could get was at the emergency hospital in the capital, where he would drive her himself. However, before that, a local therapist would have to examine Ana and splint her leg for the ride. For this reason the ambulance would drop them at the hotel, where the doctor could wait in the lobby. When they arrived, they found Michelle and her husband there too. On three, the men moved Ana to her room.

"Jesus! Why the hell is the ski boot still on?" said the doctor.

Nobody had an answer to that question.

"We have to take the boot off immediately. Her foot is swelling more with every second."

"What do you mean, Doc? We have to do it right here?" Michelle asked with pure dread in her voice.

"Yes. Right here, right now!"

"But Doc, she has some fractures, maybe even near the ankle."

"I'm aware it's broken, lady, but there's no other choice. We have to remove the boot before it's too late." The doctor turned to the men in the room. "Ready, boys?"

Michelle sat on the floor next to Ana. With her golden curly hair and beautiful blue eyes, she looked like an angel.

"Don't worry, Ana. I'll be right here with you. Give me your hand," she said with kindness and compassion. Ana was so exhausted she couldn't move her hand, so Michelle reached out and held her tight.

First the doctor loosened the buckles as much as possible. Then the Diplomat grabbed her soundly under the shoulders as the others pulled on the boot. Ana's screams sounded all around the luxurious hotel. She was barely alive.

Finally it was off, and the doctor put the splint properly in place. Next they had to fit her in the car. Obviously the Mercedes coupe was not designed for the emergency transportation of passengers with broken legs, so it proved quite the challenge to shove Ana into the tiny backseat. When that was accomplished, they drove to the capital straightaway. Though it was uncomfortable, the sports car was fast enough to reach the hospital within two hours.

"Mr. G, I have to tell you something . . ." Ana heard the Diplomat say over the phone as they sped away.

The Emergency Hospital

Ana's father was waiting at the hospital doorway when they arrived, alongside a close friend of his, a former doctor for the same institution. That evening his friend's son was on duty as the anesthesiologist in the emergency room.

"Don't worry, Ana, everything will be all right," Mr. G said soothingly.

"Please, tell them to give me general anesthesia, no matter how much it costs. I can't take any more pain. I just can't."

Already she had suffered too much, but after a quick exam and brief consultation, the doctors' decision was to do the surgery with localized anesthesia on the spine. Great, more turmoil—Ana would be awake and aware during the whole operation.

Leaving her with no other choice, she was swiftly prepared and moved to the surgical room. With a needle in her spine, Ana was trying to calm down when the nurse put up a green curtain to hide the surgeon's team from her line of sight—but the curtain was transparent enough for Ana to witness most of their actions. Aghast, she noted that the operation looked similar to someone fixing a car engine rather than someone operating on her leg behind a green transparent screen. They used drills, pneumatic hammers, and screwdrivers on her gentle body. As if the misery were not enough.

The next morning Ana woke up in the hospital with a metal rod in her bone canal from the knee to the ankle. The rod was properly screwed in and secured on both sides with bolts. As the doctor explained, they threaded pieces from the larger shank onto the rod, as there were fractures up in the knee area and below it to the foot. The shank bone was broken too. The experts demanded Ana go through a comprehensive examination and concluded that despite the extensive bruising and the condition of her leg, everything else was fine. Therefore, the doctors were positive—luck was on her side, and she would recover soon.

"How soon?" asked Ana.

"Most likely a year. We will remove the metal rod a year from now."

"Holy crap, are you kidding me?"

"The worst is over," said the doctor.

And, of course, he was right.

*   *   *

That same day, Ana's closest friend and family came to visit and cheer her up. She was happy to see them all, yet her heart melted when her daughter entered the room.

"She was begging me to take her with me," Mrs. K said by way of apology.

"Oh, it's okay. Thanks, Mom."

Lilly came running toward Ana for a loving embrace. "I was so scared, Mummy," sobbed the kid.

"Don't worry, love. The worst is over," Ana said, tearfully kissing her daughter's head.

Lilly was a curious child who simply couldn't resist lifting the cover and looking at her mother's injured leg. But what she saw there was gruesome: Due to continued drainage, there was blood on the bed.

"Ew!" She was about to faint when luckily her grandma reached for her and placed her on the next bed.

"Poor kid, she's scared of blood," Mrs. K said, rubbing Lilly's head.

"You have to leave, Mom," said Ana. "The hospital is not a playground."

"Right. Then we'll wait for you at home," said Mrs. K, and they left immediately.

Ana was falling asleep when Sis came late in the afternoon.

"Hey, hey, hey . . . What happened to you, sister? How do you feel?"

"I feel like I've been chewed up and spat out. Seriously, it's hell," said Ana.

"Is there anything I can do for you?" asked Sis.

"Yes, actually, you can. I'm sick of these bedpans, and I want to go to the restroom like a normal person. Will you help me, please?"

"Of course. Let's do it."

And so very slowly, inch by inch, Ana managed to sit up on the bed with Sis's help. She took deep breaths, trying to overcome the pain. After taking some time to rest, the next part of the "restroom" operation included stepping on the healthy leg. Again, very slowly with huge efforts, she did it.

"Be careful, Ana. Please be careful," Sis repeated, almost as if reciting a mantra.

"I'm okay, I'm okay, go on," Ana said through her teeth.

Now, while holding the crutch in her right hand, she put her left hand on Sis's shoulders. Tightly holding each other, they were ready for the next part: stepping.

"Okay, Sis, let's do it!"

They worked as one. Finally they took the first step. And then the second one . . .

A nurse was walking by in the corridor when she saw a soul-stirring scene through the hospital room's open door—two young women slowly moving along toward the restroom. Apparently one was a patient, and the other, a visitor. After every step they stopped and breathed together.

"They must be sisters," concluded the nurse, who turned back to her duties.

CHAPTER 13

THE REVIVIFYING

Within a few days it was time for Ana to leave the hospital—which was easier said than done. Every motion caused her pain, but unhurried she could "walk" with crutches so long as she was cautious with the fresh stitches.

Back home the living situation required some changes. The Diplomat moved into the house to be in charge of walking Lilly to the school bus every morning before work, and also of keeping both girls company during the evenings and weekends. Just a simple task; however, tolerance was of crucial importance. The doctors were clear that Ana needed to rest; no stress, no drama! Moreover, for the next three months, she was restricted to staying indoors until her immune system recovered enough to be able to fight the colds and viruses lurking outside. The physiotherapist inspected her at home, treating her muscles, joints, and tissue so as to heal more efficiently.

"You're doing pretty well, Ana. If I have to send you for an MRI afterward, it'll be because of your magnetic personality—not any health concerns," he joked. He was pleased with his patient's recovery. And so was she.

*   *   *

In the meantime her circumstances transformed the sofa into her nook, and the living room turned into a colorful garden. All those flowers meant a lot; each one was brought by a dear friend. The January snow blizzard may have been severe outside, but Ana's home was warm, filled with kindness and concern. Of course, she was deeply grateful for the genuine support she never asked for. It was simply heart-melting.

For instance, those with the orange-colored blossoms were a get-well gift from Natalie and her husband. When presenting them, the man seriously scolded her.

"How could you mess up those beautiful legs, missy? You should be banned from skiing for good, as I forbade my wife after she scared me to death with her concussion last year in Saint Moritz."

"True," Natalie confirmed. "He doesn't ski at all, so I was alone that day. Something happened and I fell. However, the Swiss Mountain Rescue Service was sharp—they immediately transported me via chopper to the local hospital, never giving me a chance to panic. Actually that ride was quite comfortable. I could have taken a nap if we hadn't landed so quickly."

"Hey, this is not a game. Skiing is dangerous! I mean it! You should both forget about the slopes." Natalie's husband was annoyed by their superficiality.

"Fine, fine, no more skiing," Natalie said with a smile.

A few days later Ana was reading a Russian psychology book when the doorbell rang.

"Come in," she shouted.

Michelle opened the unlocked door.

"You shouldn't leave the door open like that. Someone dangerous could come in, and you're helpless in your condition!" she said with concern, though Ana had her reasons too.

"It's more convenient this way, because then I don't have to stand and hop along every single time someone comes to the door. It's so hard!"

"Ugh, you should at least get a panic button and keep it close so the security company can come at once if something happens."

"Awesome idea, Blondie. I'll do it. Now stop patronizing me and get yourself a beverage from the fridge . . . please."

Michelle chose tonic water. With a fizzy glass she sat close to Ana and changed the subject.

"Hey, how's your cohabitation going so far? Is he behaving?"

Well, that touched a sore spot, because lately the Diplomat had been acting kind of hostile.

"I think he's jealous," Ana said. "He's jealous even of my mom and Sis. Can you believe that?"

"Sure. It's in his nature to embezzle women. I've seen it myself since I've known him much longer than you have. You should be really watchful," cautioned Michelle. After all, she had been married to the Diplomat's friend for many years and could confide in Ana. Besides, Ana had already noticed that occasionally he could become a very mean person, especially when liquor was involved. Lately they had started to fight a lot.

"He's acting like a tomcat pissing to mark his territory. It's weird. A sophisticated diplomat? Yeah right, when pigs fly."

"Beware," warned Michelle one more time on her way out.

Ana agreed and dialed the security company.

*   *   *

In early February, a little more than a month after the accident, Ana was still a prisoner at home. Now the pain was dissipating, and each day she was getting better, stronger, faster . . . but her left leg was now much thinner than the right one. Apparently many more hours of physiotherapy and exercise lay ahead.

Ana had just finished with her daily gymnastics when a dear friend called.

"Hey, how're you doin'? Can I come over?" asked Natalie.

"Sure, whenever." Good company was always welcome.

Shortly Natalie was sitting in the living room, pointing at the unidentified substance on Ana's spoon.

"What's that mess you're eating?"

"Oh, this is baked and powdered eggshells. Yummy!" But it wasn't yummy at all; it was shitty.

"Seriously? Shells?"

"Yup, I have to eat them since I need extra calcium for my bones," Ana said before putting the teaspoon in her mouth and swallowing. A look of pure disgust crossed her face.

Natalie blinked three times, and then stuck out her tongue. "Yuck, I can't stand this. Please have mercy. I'm pregnant."

"Pregnant? Really? Congratulations! I think it's the best thing that can happen in a woman's life. Probably in a man's, too, but I'm only speaking from my experience. Whoopee, we're going to have a baby! Come over here! I wanna hug you at once."

A beaming Natalie didn't hesitate. A hearty hug for the splendid news was a pretty good trade.

"I'm sure you will be a great mother," said Ana as she tightly embraced her friend.

"I'll do my best. We've been dreaming of a baby for a long time."

It was such a wonderful day, and Ana felt elated and full of energy until its end. Nothing could muddle her sprightly mood, not even the stupid quarrel she had with her boyfriend after dinner about whether or not Lilly was getting spoiled. Luckily, the girl was asleep in her room.

The next day Sis came. Of course, she was the one who visited most often, and she was always welcome in Ana's apartment. While making coffee and putting things in order, Ana told her about the previous night's argument.

"Now he's trying to discipline Lilly? I don't like him. I don't like him at all."

Certainly Sis was not among the Diplomat's fans, as his brutality was interfering with the harmony of their friendship. His so-called help was turning out to be a more and more of a burden with each passing day.

"When I was little," Ana added with regret, "my parents used to argue a lot, sometimes waking me up in the middle of the night with their screams. I'll never let that happen to Lilly!"

"Absolutely, you shouldn't. She must be the priority!"

"Of course. She's my number one," Ana said, and she meant it.

"By the way, how's she doing at school?"

"I'm afraid I'll have to move her to a better one."

Ana had come to this conclusion one afternoon after studying with her daughter. The quality of the lessons from her recent classes appeared to fall short of the school's reputation, and as an ambitious mom, Ana wanted more for her daughter.

"Hey, the Russian school near parliament is known for its discipline and its skillful teachers. However, it's almost impossible for a random kid to get in there. If you want to enroll her, you're gonna need solid recommendations."

"Probably, though at first I'll try a sincere conversation. Sometimes that works better than any patronage, don't you think?" smiled Ana.

"Sometimes it works, sometimes it doesn't. Luck plays a role in everything. Anyway, you might as well conduct an experiment since you look so pathetic with those crutches."

"I hate them! I'd rather wait 'til it's time to use a cane."

The Canes

In April, three months after the surgery, Ana swapped out her crutches for a handmade wooden walking stick—her souvenir from the wild African night the previous summer. It was much easier this way. Luckily she had an automatic car, and her one good leg proved sufficient for driving—so it was her turn to visit Natalie. By now Natalie was tied up in bed for the baby's sake, as doctors warned she was an inch away from . . . that bad thing she was not even willing to pronounce.

When she stopped in front of the building, Ana remembered she had missed a tiny detail: Her friend's apartment was on the fourth floor of a building with no elevator. Brilliant! It was too late to go back, though, as Natalie was waiting. *Hop hop hop* . . . It took Ana approximately seventeen minutes to climb up the stairs, taking short breaks each half floor. Finally she reached the top, and the housemaid invited her in.

"Please forgive my delay. It was due to unforeseen circumstances," she apologized to Natalie.

"I see . . ." answered her friend. Even though Natalie was smiling a little, Ana sensed her fear of losing the baby and tried to cheer her up.

"Today I received the weirdest compliment ever. A guy on the street looked at me and said, 'Hey, nice cane, ma'am.' It was so clumsy."

However, Natalie was not laughing. She was sad.

"Hey, what's up, Mummy? How're you feeling?"

"I don't know." Natalie's eyes were full of tears.

"Shush. Don't worry, everything will be just fine. Talk to it, create a bond, and never let it go. By the way, is it a boy or a girl?"

"They say it's a girl. I'm so scared . . ." moaned Natalie as she reached for her empty glass. "Can you please fetch me a new glass of water from the kitchen?"

"Sure, water's coming." Ana took the cane and made one step, then another. Wait, something was wrong. She looked at her cane: An eagle's head was where the elephant's head should have been. What?!

She was beyond confused. "Dear Lord, this must be yours!"

"It appears so. I'm only allowed to walk with it," Natalie answered calmly. She was not getting it yet.

"But that means the one over there is mine," Ana said, indicating the other stick still standing near the sofa.

"Huh?"

Now they were both puzzled. Was it pure coincidence that they both had circumstances that forced them to use their souvenirs?

"Hey, who has the third cane?" asked Ana.

"The third one . . . the third one . . ." Natalie paused for a few seconds. "The lady with the third cane broke her leg in her eighth month of pregnancy and uses it as well!"

Unbelievable! How was that possible? Was it a coincidence? Or was it a hex? A logical answer was missing. They could only guess.

"Those must be some cursed voodoo canes," Natalie finally concluded. Even though it sounded completely irrational, that was the most plausible explanation, wasn't it?

Fortunately, there must have been angels above watching over them. Despite the voodoo canes, the worries and fears, Natalie gave birth to a wonderful baby girl in September on the holy day of faith, hope, and love—and they named the baby Hope.

But on the day in question, all Ana could think about was getting rid of that damn stick as soon as possible . . . at least, after it served her for two more tasks.

Task one. Due to her handicap, Ana's parents decided to move closer to her place to help both their daughter and granddaughter. The area was nice, so everybody happily agreed to the idea of living closer to each other. Ana's job was to place advertisements around the neighborhood that said, "We're looking to buy an apartment here." The flyers listed her personal phone number. Limping down the streets, holding the cane in her right hand and the flyers in her left, she left them on a few chosen buildings close by. Starting that same day, a few offers came in, and within a month her parents had moved into a small condo on the next street. Just perfect. Task one—accomplished.

Task two—and the last one before the cane found its destiny in the trash—had been planted in Ana's head by Sis: She wanted to secure a new school for Lilly. So at the end of the school year, Ana dressed properly and headed to the Russian school.

"Good morning. I would like to talk to the principal, please," she said to the doorman.

She explained the purpose of her visit, and after he made a short call, she was invited in. The principal appeared to be a kind, middle-aged woman, clearly kept occupied by her duties.

"Good morning, madam. What's the occasion?" she politely asked.

"My daughter's well-being, ma'am," Ana answered, getting straight to the point. Then she explained how due to the accident she had plenty of time to help her child with homework, and how she had become unsatisfied with the low standards and the lack of discipline shown at her daughter's school. Ana was looking for a better education for her.

After mentioning that she had graduated from Russian high school herself and respected that system a lot, Ana simply asked, "I would highly appreciate it if by any chance my girl could be relocated here. Is there any?"

The principal measured the woman with the cane from head to toe, and replied, "Actually, it is possible, but first she has to pass a Russian language test in August."

"Oh, that's wonderful! Thank you so much! With some tutoring she'll catch up over the summer. I assure you she's a clever girl, and a nice one too. You won't regret your decision."

"I hope so. And I also hope that next time we see each other in September this stick will no longer be in your hand," said the principal, smiling.

And when the second task was also accomplished, the wooden stick with the elephant head was worn-out, outdated, forgotten. At last!

CHAPTER 14

THE DIPLOMAT

Running counter to Ana's successful recovery process was the Diplomat's increasingly despotic behavior. If presumably diplomacy was the ability to tell a person to go to hell in such a way that he would look forward to the trip, this time our Diplomat was about to personally experience solely the part concerning hell. Ana had already decided to break up with him; it was now just a matter of when. The restoration of her domestic independence would occur at the beginning of the summer—after Lilly finished school and escorted Mrs. K to the countryside. Ana definitely did not want her daughter to witness that chapter, with all the potentially nasty scenes. Until then, Ana had to reconcile her discomfort by humming the popular song's lyrics: "And soon shall come the happiest day, when you're gonna be for good away . . ."

The truth was that the Diplomat's ego had been too big to fit in Ana's home from the very beginning, and over time it had come to consume most of her privacy.

"There are way too many visitors at home," he would complain. "Your mom is always here, Lilly is a spoiled girl, I have lots of stress at work lately, and nobody understands." His favorite part was to judge what was "normal" and what was not, which of course was tied to the maintenance of his particular well-being. Thus "normal" was any point of view equivalent to his opinion, and "not normal" was everybody else's diverging points of view or behaviors. He thought a proper quarrel was the only way to avoid further deviations, on Ana's part, from normalcy. In short, the Diplomat appeared to be a classic example of the dominating alpha male, slightly different from the polished dinner companion Ana was familiar with. Woohoo, what fun for a woman tied up at home and recovering from surgery!

On Valentine's Day, instead of celebrating, he chose the evening to be their relationship's Rubicon. Why? Because he proposed—for the third time—and was met with the same answer as before: "I'm not ready yet."

"But why? Now we're living together . . ."

"It's me," she said. "I don't feel right making such an important decision in my condition. First I want to be able to walk again. Then afterward I could probably think about a long-term commitment . . . Only time will tell."

"Why? What's the problem? Marriage should be the next natural step in every mature relationship, don't you think?" He was trying to renegotiate her decision.

"Yes, in general it should be, and maybe it will be one day for us as well, but not now. Please don't push me. Let's leave this matter aside for a while and have dinner with some wine."

"Fine then, I won't ask again. You tell me when you're ready," he conceded, but he was plainly not happy with the outcome. His eyes darkened. Even the delicious meal her mom had cooked earlier couldn't fix the refusal's bad taste in his mouth. "Your mom's here every day, isn't she?"

"Almost. She's helping me a lot, like with washing my hair, for example. Whew, it was such a tough month, but I feel much better now. I'm thinking of helping Lilly with her studies again, so it won't be necessary for Mom to come over each day."

"Very good. Some serenity would be super," he said. That evening he was not in the mood for small talk—or profound talk, for that matter. His ego was badly hurt.

Soon quarrels became a daily habit, and peace remained only a dream, even though Mrs. K was not visiting so often. One night in the middle of "clarifying the normal relationship's parameters," the Diplomat brought up the topic of the proposal's refusal.

"You know what? I at least deserve a clear answer. Do you or don't you want to be my wife?"

"Oh, come on, that's ridiculous. It's late and I'm tired," said Ana. She wanted to weasel out of this mess. However . . .

"What are you tired of? You do nothing all day."

Was that the alcohol talking, or did he mean it?

"I don't want to argue with you. I'm going to bed," she said, reaching for her crutches.

"No, I want to know!" He raised his voice. "I want to hear you say exactly what you have on your mind."

"Shush! Lilly's sleeping behind the door."

Ana started toward the bedroom, but he followed.

"So if you don't want to be my wife, say it." His tone and expression held not a single sign of affection. Rather, they suggested hate.

"Ugh, you're such a pain in the ass. Don't you see it? You're totally out of line. The doctor said I shouldn't endure stress in my condition, and what do you do? I can't stand this tension anymore!"

"Well, I don't wanna stress you. I just wanna hear it." He simply would not give up.

Ana was pissed. "I'm sick of this bullshit!" Then she turned to pronounce in his face, "I—don't—want—to be your wife!"

First, he was surprised. Then, offended. Lastly, he became aggressive.

His mouth foamed as he yelled. "You fucking bitch! How can you do this to me?" He was completely out of control, and he raised his hand and slapped her. "Go to hell!"

The ache didn't paralyze Ana; it was the fountain of emotions coming from within—the insult, the rage, and the disgust together as one. For the first time in her life somebody had dared to hit her. Adrenaline exploded in her veins, and she felt almost capable of killing him no matter her size, strength, or gender. Unwittingly she had turned into a mad, ugly beast, just like him. She knew her next reaction would be critical. Thanks to . . . whatever it was, she somehow managed to remain human.

"I want you out of my house and out of my life!" she hissed with all the restraint she could muster.

The next day the Diplomat returned from work with a huge bouquet of flowers—begging for forgiveness, claiming he'd never acted that way before, and solemnly promising never to let it happen again.

"I swear my life on it," he said, putting his right hand on his heart. "Please, forgive me. I love you and I can't live without you. I hate myself for doing it!"

As one might expect, the only promise actually kept from that evening was not his, but Ana's: to get rid of him no matter what. She had to keep that freak away from Lilly! However, in the middle of the current school year, their breakup was totally inconvenient. So she scheduled it for the beginning of the summer holidays, when her daughter was going to be away.

Until then she had to lie low. As aggression was integrated into the Diplomat's personality, she had to be very cautious not to awaken his demons prematurely in Lilly's presence. Yet deep inside she knew— tick-tock—that soon the happiest day would come.

*　　*　　*

Once Lilly was away, she couldn't wait any longer. She and the Diplomat were driving to a birthday party when she broke the news.

"I need some space!" she blurted out.

"What do you mean?" The Diplomat seemed startled, though he must have been kind of expecting it.

"Please move out!"

"Not now. You must be kidding me! The summer has just begun, and I'm organizing a seaside trip for us in July."

"Seriously! I'm not coming. I need to spend some time on my own."

"But why now, when we're alone? Instead we could travel, have some fun . . . Don't be such a selfish woman. You'll spoil the holidays!"

"Don't, don't, don't. That's so typically you. Enough restrictions. All I want is my liberty!"

"Liberty? It's not normal to ask for liberty after all I've done for you. Let's talk about this tomorrow."

They reached their destination, which turned out to be an average party. The next day she made the same firm statement, and the day after that as well. Finally he understood she was adamant to break free; she was not willing to tango with him anymore. So he left the keys and moved out, but not without telling her he was convinced it would just be temporary.

Ana spent most of the summer at the seaside cottage absorbing vitamin D from the sunshine with her loved ones—Mom, Dad, and their English setter Larry, Sis, and of course, the two seven-year-old girls. Fun, fun, fun. The kids couldn't be happier than they were playing in the sea every day, and the warm evenings were marked by heart-to-heart dinners on the porch and profound conversations about various aspects of life.

The cottage was located on a hill near the biggest port town in the country, with a breathtaking view over the peninsula it populated. At nights, the dark canvas of the sea was delicately decorated with hundreds of lights coming from the anchored vessels. During the day it was also very beautiful—ships and boats crossing the big blue expanse ahead in an orderly line. For Ana it was a place of exceptional charisma, keeping the spirit of Mrs. K's parents—the captain and his wife—alive among the peach trees and vine trellises. Most of her childhood holidays she had spent there with her grandparents and cousin, and she treasured many wonderful memories of them.

There on the terrace, with a mesmerizing view, close to nature and feeling connected with her ancestors, Ana finally found what she was looking for: peace.

On August 29, she came back to the capital for an appointment at the Collector's office, as the saga of the hippodrome had taken an interesting turn. With some manipulation and good luck, it might be possible for the land to be excluded from the legal case soon.

After the others had left the meeting, the Collector gazed at Ana slyly and asked, "What's new? How's your summer going? Any affairs?"

"Well, it was eventful in the beginning and peaceful at the end. After I broke up with my boyfriend, I rested seaside with family. That's all—no affairs. But I do have something else for you." She got up and fetched him a wrapped DVD.

"What's that?" He was not used to these kinds of presents.

"*The Last Samurai*. It's a remarkable movie, worthwhile and spectacular—and an Academy Award nominee."

As the Collector looked at her in confusion, Ana explained more.

"It's such a great story! After I watched it the first time, I played it twice more in a row. The narrative is about the way of the last samurais," she said, turning to read from the disk: "Japan was made by a handful of brave men. Warriors, willing to give their life for what seems to have become a forgotten word: Honor."

With no comment yet and a skeptical expression on his face, the Collector thanked her and returned to his chamber.

Ana rushed home because she had a birthday party to attend that same evening. After chilling, drinking, and dancing, she came home around two a.m. pretty tired. She was brushing her teeth when the doorbell rang.

It's probably the doorman, thought Ana, half awake.

But when she unlocked the door, she was surprise to see in the low light of the stairs a different yet familiar figure. The tall and muscular Diplomat stood before her—furious, drunk, and acerbated. He pushed her and forced himself inside, then locked the door.

"Tonight I'm staying here, and you're gonna love me!"

"Jesus, look at you—drunk as a skunk. You need to leave now!"

"Ha, I'm drunk. So what? This time you won't easily get rid of me, after all we've been through."

"Don't you get it? It's over!"

"No, no, I'm not done with you yet."

Ana had a feeling that somebody else was looking at her through his addled eyes, as if he had a split personality disorder and now she was facing the other part—the crazy, violent maniac adamant on humiliating her.

"Thanks for welcoming me in. Now, let's go to bed," he said as he started unbuttoning his shirt.

How far could he go in his impudence?

"No! Stop! What are you doing? I don't want to go to bed with you! Get out of my home!"

"Oh, come on, darling, hurry up. I told you I'm staying here tonight." His intoxicated mind was totally out of control.

"But . . . but I don't want you to stay. Listen to me—I want you to leave! This is *my* home. Beat it!"

"Listen, bitch. I'm sick of your little games. Come here!"

"I don't want to!" screamed Ana.

"You have to!"

The next scene was brutal. He grabbed her arm and violently dragged her to the bed, then threw her down with malice. Ana was scared to death.

What should I do? How can I stop him? she thought, her mind racing. He was strong enough to do whatever he wanted. How . . . Then— salvation came: the remote security button. Yes! Ana calculated it was just within reach, in the first drawer of her bedside table.

Meanwhile, the Diplomat was sitting with his back to her, trying to undress, which appeared a highly complex routine given the amount of liquor he had consumed. He was busy removing his pants and cursing when—just a few seconds were all that Ana needed!— with a cheetah's quickness she reached and pushed the button. He heard nothing.

Two minutes later the doorbell rang.

"Hey, who's that? Probably your new boyfriend, huh?" The Diplomat hurried to open the door, eager for more action. And action he found in the form of two security guards and a policeman.

"Good night, sir."

"Huh? What the hell is going on?" His intoxicated brain was unable to make sense of the situation.

"We got an emergency call from this residence, sir. Is everything all right? May I . . ." The guard looked inside to find Ana standing in the middle of the corridor, frightened and trembling.

"Are you okay, ma'am?"

"No, I'm not okay. Please escort him out of my home!"

The Diplomat was startled. "Seriously? You want to lock me up?" Hate demonized his face, and for a second, Ana had the feeling that he would kill her with his bare hands.

The guard asked, "Who owns this apartment?"

"I do," answered Ana.

"Okay, in that case, sir, please follow us."

"This is a setup! I promise, you will regret this! I want my presents back, all of them—rings, coats, everything," the Diplomat yelled, enraged.

"Okay, you'll get them back—now get out of here forever!"

Enraged or not, he was out of moves. Cursing in the elevator, he followed the guards. The harassment was over. Finally, there was silence. Ana sat on the chair in the living room and buried her face in her hands. She cried and cried for hours, couldn't sleep at all.

In the morning, she packed the gifts he'd given her and delivered them to his friend's office early before work. Then she called Sis.

"Oh my God, you'll never believe what happened last night." Then she told her everything.

"That bastard is a total freak. You should be very careful. He might come back."

Sis had a reason to worry, and Ana knew it.

"You're right," she said. "I have to prevent it, for my good and for Lilly's. I know exactly what to do. Bye, Sis. I'll call you later."

She hung up. Then dialed a familiar number.

"Hello," answered the Collector.

*　　*　　*

At five o'clock Ana had a fever, but she was at the Radisson like they'd agreed. The Collector was running a little late, so a quick meeting was held in his car.

"Damn it, you should choose your boyfriends more wisely, Ana!" he said after hearing the brief narrative of her latest complications.

"Yes, I know," she said, her head down in shame.

"Okay, this is what we're gonna do: I'll send one of my bodyguards over to take care of that mess. He'll watch over you as long as necessary. Give me your address. He'll be there tomorrow at eight a.m."

"Thank you, thank you so much. You're a lifesaver—literally."

"Sometimes only." The Collector smiled before adding, "Go home and stay there. Get some medicine since you're burning up. Call me if he comes back."

"All right, I will. And once again . . ." She was about to thank him, but he was already looking at his watch.

"Gee, I have to run. Take care!" he said, then rapidly drove away.

The next morning the bodyguard informed her that he was waiting downstairs. He was a sporty, strong man, with navy blue eyes and quick reflexes—obviously a pro. From that day forward he became Ana's shadow.

In the meantime, the Diplomat tried to contact her in every possible way—calling, texting, waiting to ambush. She avoided him with disgust. After more than a month her bodyguard made a definitive case:

"This has to end, and you have to do it. My advice is for you to file a restraining order against him," he said to Ana.

"But that will ruin his career, and he'll hunt me down for the rest of his life. No, I'm sorry, but it isn't a good solution," she said.

"Then you might be right," he agreed.

Then they considered another plan.

Later that day Ana called the Diplomat and asked to meet for lunch the next day in an open, crowded restaurant near the Ministry of Foreign Affairs where he worked. He agreed.

"I told you so," he said by way of greeting. "I knew you'd come back sooner or later."

Ana was sitting at the opposite side of the table. "Did you get your presents back?"

"Yes. Should I send yours to the Collector's office?" he sarcastically said.

"If you wish," replied Ana. Then she got straight to the point. "Listen, there's a reason I called you, quite contrary to the one you presume. Actually, I'm here to tell you that we have to split ways forever. Today you go right, and I go left, because this harassment must end. This is *not normal!*"

The Diplomat was speechless. His face turned red, probably from high blood pressure. Ana continued.

"Look behind you. I'm not alone."

He turned—at the table behind him he recognized some of the Collector's best guys. She had trapped him!

"So, we are all waiting for your decision. Tell me: Will you leave me alone once and for all?"

"Fuckin' bitch," he growled. He was furious, but he had to behave. Some of his colleagues were eating in the same restaurant, and trampling on the Diplomat's code would not be applauded.

Stone-faced, Ana asked again, "Have we agreed—no meetings, no phone calls, nothing? It's over!"

"If that's what you want, then that's precisely what you'll get."

He threw some money on the table, for his part of the bill, and walked away red-hot. In silence, the Collector's men escorted him to the Ministry's main entrance.

Back in at the Collector's office, Ana was beaming. It was over, this time for real. So she thanked them all and wished them farewell. A personal guard was no longer needed. Finally, Ana was free to go back to her normal life.

CHAPTER 15

THE HIPPODROME

By the end of the year things were looking pretty optimistic: The diplomat was out of Ana's life for good, and so was the metal rod from her leg. So she met New Year's Eve with a basketful of hopes. By spring, after her long hours of physiotherapy ended, she was even able to wear high heels. Summer passed without anything extraordinary occurring. And then September came with two important occasions: Ana's daughter's first day in the Russian school, and the announcement that the land for the hippodrome was no longer under seizure. Finally, it was time for action!

When the "National Hippodrome" project had first been born a couple of years ago, the Collector authorized his experts to do comprehensive research on the status of thoroughbreds in the country and issue him a report. One day before the deadline, he picked up the phone.

"Bring me the report for horse betting—now!"

"Yes, sir," confirmed his secretary, and the expert in charge had to rapidly wrap up the report in order to deliver it a day early.

Unfortunately the situation was not good. During Socialism all forms of betting were forbidden in the country by law, and the main purpose of breeding thoroughbreds was to compete in extremely disciplined domestic races. Instead of money, jockeys ran for bowls and honorary diplomas. Apparently there were no betting traditions in the area, and thus an endeavor like this would have to break the ice of ignorance.

In brief:

Public sector: total mess. Most of the state stud farms had gone bankrupt after the end of the old political system. The few that had survived were not very active, so their capacity was not enough to support such an ambitious project.

Private sector: slightly better. The independent breeders were located all along the countryside, some of them with proper training facilities—though they were probably thought of as hobby expenses, not potential for profit.

Regulator: the Horse Breeding Association, which represented a weird symbiosis between the state and the entrepreneurs, occupied itself with preserving the national studbook, maintaining the relevant documentation, and facilitating certain events.

And that was all.

"It's too risky," decided the Collector. "The market is not ready yet. Let's wait and see what the future brings."

With the project on the back burner, it took six years to deal with the legal case concerning the property's ownership. The breakthrough happened only after a dozen postponements and by adding a pinch of additional methods, but the gloomy part of the saga was finally over.

*   *   *

One Friday in the autumn of 2004, Ana went on a drive toward the hippodrome, the American restaurant, and—why not?—the glittering future. The last time she had been there was with her ex-husband a decade ago.

I wonder how it looks now, she thought. Curious and thrilled, her imagination jumped from one memory to another when all of a sudden it came to her: *I have to learn to ride a horse!* What an electrifying idea!

A joke came to mind: *How did the cowboy ride into town on Friday, stay for three days, and ride out on Friday?*

Because his horse's name was Friday!

The punch line slipped out of her mouth, but nobody heard. Ana was alone in her car. The Collector's whole team of associates was following behind her; she could easily detect them in the rearview mirror. There was quite a gang—lawyers, accountants, security experts . . . Everything had to be overseen.

The doors of the property were wide-open, as if for the last few years it had been abandoned. Apparently not a single event had happened there since the land was seized. Ana slowly entered the main alley. Saloon, the American restaurant, was on her right. A memory of her first visit there with Papsy many years ago naturally came back. The outside of the place looked almost the same—a typical cowboy pub with a big porch. Only this time the impression was different, reminding her of a sad black-and-white photo. A few wooden tables with benches were arranged in the yard.

On her left was an old single-story administration building in terrible condition. The whole property was about fifty years old, and its facilities were obsolete. Further into the property she saw the stables, open paddocks, racetracks, and other premises, all of them outdated. The abandoned "burg" was surrounded not by walls, but by a thick chain of hundred-foot tall poplars. Ana held her breath at the momentous sight.

I'll gladly spend my days here, she thought, stopping her car at the end of the alley and saying aloud, "Hello, land!"

Thereafter, Ana and the Collector's new management team rushed into the administration office. Everything happened smoothly, with no complications or complaints. The embarrassed cashier lady with vermilion hair quietly cooperated. She was the only staff member on the spot. As she explained, only a few tenants kept their horses in the stables and occasionally paid their fees. With the modest incomes, the cashier was barely covering the hippodrome's utility bills, along with three humble paychecks—hers, the accountant's, and the maintenance man's.

At dusk, after a long inventory day, the hippodrome's front doors were locked under the surveillance of guards for the first time in years.

*   *   *

From that day forward Ana became a woman with a dual life. Some days she spent at the Collector's luxurious office in the heart of the capital, meeting him for weekly reports and further planning, or working with lawyers and councilors. Those days she dressed like a real lady—formal and elegant, always in high heels, with proper makeup and styled hair. People at the headquarters started addressing her as "the stable girl." She liked it.

Other days Ana spent occupied at the hippodrome—her burg. Casually dressed in jeans, shirts, and comfortable shoes, she took notes in a big black notebook. Starting from scratch, she had lots to catch up on, and used three main sources to do so: people, the Internet, and books. The more invested she became in the ranch's life and morale, the more fascinated she found it. Contrary to the complicated working relationships in the Collector's office, here dealings were simple: commanding and obeying, falling and standing up, going away and returning home, starving and having enough, helping and needing help, feeling primary sexual attraction, expecting inevitable death, and above all, having the deepest respect for nature. The hippodrome was like a living organism, following his own pace. Remarkably, all those people, steeds, ponies, dogs, cats, mice, birds, and even rabbits were living in harmony.

Humans here acted just like humans anywhere else on Earth—fighting and making up, talking behind each other's backs, all the usual crap. However, something universal illuminated their hearts and gathered them together at the hippodrome: their unconditional love for horses.

During the first year at the hippodrome Ana had to integrate herself into the existing system of relations between the locals, which was a pretty challenging task for a woman in a masculine world.

One day a stable boy asked her out of the blue, "Ms. Ana, do you know which side of a horse has more hair?"

"Huh?" She wondered why that info was not in her notes. Was it the neck, or the back, or . . . ?

"The outside, of course." he said with a friendly smile. Was it that obvious she was still an ignorant newcomer? It seemed it was.

She quickly discovered that horses were adorable creatures—just like any other pet, only bigger. Similar to kittens and puppies, colts were eager to play, always waiting for a good hand to rub them and someone to say the magic words—"Good boy!" From an old stableman, Ana learned a simple verse:

"He knows when you're happy, and he knows when you're not. Yet for sure he knows when you're bringing carrots."

Ergo, she kept carrots and sugar cubes within a hand's reach when walking around the stables. Regardless of the season, political events, changes in rates or national holidays, almost every single day at the hippodrome began at dawn and held the same sights, noises, and smells. And Ana loved everything about it.

With one stallion in particular she felt her first yearning to ride. He was a handsome brown one, with a suitable temper for a beginner like her. *Go on, Anché. Give it a try!* she told herself. And so she took some lessons and commenced learning to ride, yet with a tyro style far from that of the pros. And that attempt had been noticed. Instead of Ms. Ana, people started addressing her as "the patroness." She loved that nickname too.

Meantime, as she experienced it from the inside, the Collector was supervising from above.

"Well done, Ana. You have laced up the hippodrome!" Was he joking?

"How do you know?" she asked, as she had only ever seen him visit the site once.

"Very easy. I saw it from my plane when landing."

Well, judging by its acreage, the ranch was one of the three biggest plots in the capital's area, along with the huge metallurgical factory and the national film studios. Studying the old yellow papers in the administrative office, Ana had followed the hippodrome's fate through the decades. It was written that after a detailed survey of the climate and soil, the perfectly flat piece of land just three miles from the capital—with its independent mineral water sources, excellent winds, and railways passing by—was picked for development. Japanese architects designed it according to world-class standards. The hippodrome was meant to be the biggest racing facility in the whole area, and construction had started in earnest fifty years before. Unfortunately, it never was completed. The temporary grandstands provided a breathtaking, almost alien view of the site: five colorful, gigantic ellipses—yellow, green, and black—separated by white fences. Yes, there were five racetracks, each with a different function—flat, harness, and obstacles. The central area in between was crossed with steeplechase diagonals on the left, while on the right side there were the two adjoining lakes and a small pump house. Whenever she closed her eyes, Ana wondered, *What will the future bring to this adorable place?*

*   *   *

"Volunteers are needed to repaint the tribunes!" she notified the burg. As the hippodrome's income was still nominal, coming solely from the tenants' rents, flexibility and teamwork would save the day. Not only Ana, but everybody else there, was dreaming of prosperity, so her request quickly passed by word of mouth. Soon the most committed volunteers showed up to the office ready to contribute.

The following days, after morning practice, the trainers and jockeys could be found not in the restaurant as usual, but at the tribunes armed with paintbrushes and a portable radio. Ana was there, too, not only overseeing but participating in the renovation side by side with the others. That was a lovely unifying deed, one which would build the foundation of a promising future. Even little Lilly helped with a mop in her hands.

As a reward for her daughter's selfless volunteering, Ana bought two tickets to Lilly's birthplace for the winter holidays. It would be their third visit to Paris. And it was a great trip. Christmas day at Disneyland was like living the dream, and it brought Lilly immense pleasure. When Ana bought her a gorgeous yellow dress like the one from *Beauty and the Beast*, she was absolutely the happiest child. Her glee was simply sky-high. They rang in New Year's Eve on the Champs-Elysées—along with thousands of people from all over the world—with bottles of champagne with the words *"Bonne chance à tous!"* written on them. It was a memorable experience, after which Ana came back to the hippodrome full of vivacity and new ideas.

*   *   *

"We have to mark St. Theodore's Day at the hippodrome. It's unwritten law!" the cashier lady said assertively. After spending most of her life there, she was approaching retiring age. Ana treasured her, so she agreed to the celebration. "Okay, fine. We'll do it."

Traditionally on Saint Theodore's Day in late winter, the country celebrated the Horses' Easter. It was always the Saturday six weeks before Easter, and of course the most significant part of the holiday was its nationwide horse races. Folklore told that at dawn the men should braid the tails and manes of the animals, embellishing them with beads, tassels, and flowers; meanwhile the women should make the ritual breads for both riders and steeds. The races must happen before noon, followed by feasts 'til . . . well, it was not specified 'til when. On that day, attendants would be running around ensuring everyone's health and well-being; and the winners would be rewarded with new bridles, white shirts, or white towels.

"What do we need for the celebration?" Ana asked the cashier.

"A priest to say a prayer, traditional bread and honey, music, food, drinks, and of course, horses."

"Aha." Ana took notes in her notebook.

"Oh, and some kind of entertainment between the races."

"Sure, entertainment . . . What do you usually do?"

"Singers, dancers, something like that."

"Well I have another idea." Ana smiled. "A pinch of unconventional amusement."

As the years passed, that pinch varied from world-renowned circus artists from Kyrgyzstan and Monte Carlo Festival award winners on horseback, to camel shows and the one and only fashion race, where the riders were actually models dressed Lady Gaga–style with costumes made by a famous designer. No matter the year, St. Theodore's Day at the Hippodrome always made the evening news.

The first year of the event, the cashier hurried into the administrative office with a local newspaper in her hands.

"Look, look." She pointed at the title on the front page with delight: "The Hippodrome resurrected on Horses' Easter."

Ana laughed at the headline. It was so pathetic.

CHAPTER 16

DOC

It was Ana's second winter at the hippodrome, and everything was covered with snow. It was clean and quiet. Only the tractor's purring could be heard coming from a distance between the stables. Ana was working in her office, alone with her computer on, surrounded by papers and folders and her black notebook. Figures, figures, figures . . . So far the transition was going in her favor—everything in the company had been set up reasonably and legally. The tenants' contracts had been properly re-signed, providing reliable monthly cash flow into the accounts; the emergency construction work was done; the tribunes had been repainted; and above all, order had been permanently established on the property.

After a few hours, she put the pen down and walked to the French windows letting in cascading sunlight. Then she looked down: Her feet were just a step away from the sparkling white quilt behind the glass, where billions of seeds were sleeping under snow cover. Oh my, that awareness was beyond reality. It was universal, even divine.

Nature's miracles are the greatest ones. Simply perfect, she thought in contemplation. *And humans—those miracles should put them in awe!*

The mobile phone rang.

"Hello?"

"Good afternoon. May I speak with Ana?"

"Yes, speaking."

"This is an enforcement officer concerning your personal injury claim against the snowboard instructor."

Aha, an enforcement officer. His arrival brought the accident back to her mind, and she remembered how the instructor had disappeared and never offered his help, never called to check on her, never properly apologized. Ana had felt that this was wrong and decided to claim her rights in court.

"People have to learn to take responsibility for their actions in this country," she had said.

So soon after she recovered Ana hired a good lawyer and made the first steps against the instructor, but evidently he had escaped from the country and nobody knew where he was located at present.

"Did he vanish because of me?" she had asked her lawyer.

"Nobody knows. Maybe it's just a coincidence. The police report says he crossed the border shortly after the accident and never came back," answered the lawyer. "Nevertheless, we should continue with the case, and the court will decide how to proceed."

In the end, the court's judgment found the instructor guilty of personal bodily injury, and thus he had to pay for Ana's medical treatment and suffering in the amount of six thousand dollars.

"That's the price of a year of torment?"

"That's the law," said the lawyer. "Hey, at least it's something. Frankly I'm proud we won the case."

"Yes, we won, and so what? The instructor is still missing."

"Well, now you should find a proper enforcement officer and let him do the rest. He'll find ways to collect the compensation."

"More red tape? Lucky me," Ana remarked sarcastically. Suspiciousness crossed her mind. What if her civil rights crusade turned out to be a total waste of time and money?

However, following her lawyer's advice, she had contacted a well-known enforcement officer, given him the files, and begun waiting for his feedback. Waiting—'til now.

"Ma'am, the felon is still missing, but I have found his brother, who has agreed to compensate you with one hundred dollars per month."

"But that will take a lifetime!"

"I'm sorry, but that's all I can do for you. By the way, I've already got the first and the second payments. One of them we'll keep for company fees, and the other is yours."

"A hundred bucks? Why should I make that stranger pay a hundred bucks each month for his brother's mistakes? It's not his fault! What if I don't want him to pay it?"

"Why not? That's your money!"

"You don't get it. It's not about the money; it's about justice, and this is unfair . . . Please don't enforce it."

After a short pause the officer answered, "Whatever you want, ma'am."

"Thanks. Farewell." She hung up the phone without regret, her conscience clear.

Then Ana turned her attention back to the black notebook. The forthcoming summer would be important, as she was planning the first races during the sunniest months. The picture was becoming clearer now, though something or somebody significant was still missing. To ensure the success of such an ambitious plan, she would have to spend more time in the city dealing with the larger organization, and thus would need a loyal person to take care of the hippodrome's matters on the spot—somebody with passion and energy similar to hers, and also a person with special knowledge in the field. So far nobody was coming to mind, but her choice of employee definitely had to be reasonable enough to please the Collector.

*   *   *

A few weeks later, one cold windy morning, a man hurried through the office door, bringing a dozen snowflakes with him. He was one of the hippodrome's residents—a man of average height with a shaved head, a round face with a hint of Asiatic features, and electric green eyes. Instead of a simple greeting he started the conversation with a joke.

"Where are we—at the Siberian hippodrome? My balls are frozen!"

"Hi, Doc. Come in and warm up." The cashier lady smiled.

"Hey, I was told that due to the severe conditions, today you are giving a major discount to those who dare to risk their balls' welfare and chivalrously walk the blustery path to the administrative office, right?"

He was smiling right in the cashier lady's face. It seemed he was here to pay his rent.

"Oh, come on, Doc. Cut the crap and give me the money," she said, suddenly with an angry parent's tone.

"No discount?"

"I am afraid not."

"Fine, fine." Doc gave up and paid, then he looked around as slyly as a fox. "A small guy gets into an elevator, and suddenly notices a huge dude standing next to him. The big man looks down upon the small guy and says, 'Seven feet, three hundred and fifty pounds, twenty inches, Turner Brown.' Scared, the small guy faints, then the other starts slapping his face and shaking him. When the small guy opens his eyes, the dude asks, 'What's wrong with you?'

"The small guy says, 'Excuse me, but can you explain what you said previously?'

"The big dude looks down and says, 'Seven feet tall, three hundred fifty pounds heavy, twenty-inch penis, and my name is Turner Brown.'

"The small guy relaxes. 'Oh, thank God! I thought you said, "Turn around."'"

Ana was listening from her office, and his spirit amused her. Sure, he had a dirty mouth—typical of doctors—but at the same time, there was something about him . . . Intrigued, she invited him in for a cup of herbal tea.

"Please, tell me more about yourself," she said after the first sip.

The man briefly explained that he was the local veterinarian, with a small private practice somewhere in the capital. Also Doc had a wife and a teenage daughter a few years older than Lilly. He was renting one of the hippodrome's accommodations and saving money for his own great clinic. During their conversation she realized that they shared the same values, as he was holding the adorable hippodrome dear and calling it "home." That was interesting . . .

Once he had left, she started to make extensive inquiries into Doc's personality by talking to his colleagues and neighbors. Most of their statements were positive, and it seemed he was a decent person. She decided to meet him again in her office, and as he drank his second cup of tea, she extended him an offer.

"Yes, I agree with you," she said. "Everything has to be tip-top since my patron and I have big plans for the hippodrome. We are hoping to establish regular races along with betting as soon as possible, and in this role we'll need somebody who can take care of the local affairs while I'm running around. So, Doc, I'm asking: Do you want to participate by being in charge of the property management?"

Of course, he looked surprised, and also probably deeply honored, but . . . Doc leaned forward and looked straight into Ana's eyes, as if trying to find out whether she was sane or not. His usually beaming face became serious.

"Hmm . . ." he said after a short pause.

Ana smiled and waited for his answer. Doc was so hilarious in his actions.

At last he found his courage and solemnly said, "That's . . . that's . . . whoa, thank you, and yes—I would love to be a part of the team! Wait, can I keep my private practice after work and on weekends?"

"Sure, why not?"

"In that case, count me in. I'll give it my best, and for sure I won't let you down!"

He decided to take the hand offered him—and when he gave his word, he also gave his honesty, devotion, and loyalty. In moments like that, contracts are of no importance, notaries are not needed, and vows are silent.

"Perfect. Next I'll have to introduce you to the big boss," Ana said, shaking his hand.

*   *   *

A couple of days later Doc was sitting in the Collector's waiting area, dressed in a new suit as if he was going to prom. Meanwhile, Ana was cackling beside him at how his normally fidgety attitude had calmed. The merry Doc had disappeared.

"When we meet the boss, I'll tell him, 'Hello, sir, let me introduce to you to my colleague . . . Mr. Freeze."

"Oh, please, is it that bad? Is it that obvious I'm goosy?"

"Yes!" She found it very funny.

"Will he approve of me?"

"I doubt it. We'd better leave."

"Oh, come on, Ana. I'm worried."

"I'm not. Relax. You'll be fine."

If everything in there ran smoothly and the boss approved of Doc for the position, he and Ana would begin the challenging mission of awakening and uniting the whole horse breeding community.

CHAPTER 17

MEETING WITH THE ASSOCIATION

After they got the green light from the Collector, Ana and Doc committed to changing the harmony of the races' symphony. In order to do so they prepared a clever strategy for the upcoming meeting with the members of the Horse Breeding Association. It was to be the most important meeting of the year, when the new season's details would be discussed and voted on, so later the association could officially announce the dates and venues for the following racing calendar. Most of the members knew Doc personally, as he was a popular veterinarian in the field, however about Ana they had only heard of her great ambitions and superior support of the business. Already intrigued, they were eager to get more information.

Driving toward the convention, in a small town up north where everyone involved in the horse breeding industry was gathering from all over the country, Ana and Doc discussed their approach.

"Ana, I know these people. You have to be very precise when presenting our offer. Be short and sharp, then afterward immediately step back as if you're throwing a stone in a basket full of eggs!" He instructed her with passion. "Now let's summarize our position for the last time."

"Shoot."

"First, we have the best facilities in the country. We also have enough room to host both horses and people for up to two months. (Many of our tenants have racehorses, and they would gladly back

100

up our proposal.) Then, most importantly, we are offering a tempting prize fund. You will provide intensive PR and media support, something they haven't experienced before to such a degree. Believe me, Ana, this is something they have been dreaming of, and now they just need to hear it from you. There will probably be a vigorous discussion after your speech. However . . ." Here he stopped to make sure she was listening carefully.

She was. "However . . . ?"

"Mark my words, Ana: When the storm is over, everything will proceed nicely and smoothly. Keep calm. That's all you'll have to do."

So within the hour Ana was walking nobly into the big crowded hall wearing a long white fur coat that perfectly fit her elegant figure. She felt assertive and confident on the outside, but on the inside, she felt like an alien. The meeting was about to start when a middle-aged gentleman invited her to sit right next to the chairman. She followed his directions, took her place silently, then straightened her back against the chair and observed the audience in the room. Blimey, they were so many . . . and they were all men!

Okay, don't mess this up, Anché. Just throw the rock, she thought to herself, remembering Doc's words.

The chairman started the meeting by introducing Ana and Doc as special guests from the National Hippodrome, then he followed the agenda previously announced. Until the topic of the new season's calendar came to the floor, the discussion went pretty evenly. Then Ana was invited to speak. As Doc had suggested, she quickly ran through bullet points of the main advantages of the hippodrome's proposal.

Wow, Doc was right! She thought when she saw the gathering turning to an unholy mess after she finished. Some of the men stood, strongly gesturing at one another and occasionally at Ana. Others shouted from the furthermost corner of the room. The noise was earsplitting. Doc smiled at her from the first row with a smug expression that said, "I told you so!"

It took a while for the storm to pass and for the chairman to finally manage to calm down the most excited members. Once they had run out of steam, people started asking pragmatic questions, which Ana or Doc answered according to expertise until there were no questions left to ask. Though some of the members were still skeptical about the capabilities of the fur-clad young woman and a veterinarian in organizing such a big and important event, a prize fund was a prize fund. So they voted yea.

By the end of the meeting it was officially announced that eight of the most important racing days, including the Derby, would be held every weekend for two months at the National Hippodrome. And so the countdown began.

On the way back the vibes in the car were completely different—no stress, no tension . . . just chillness.

"Well done, Doc. We rock!"

"Well done, well done . . . 'Well-dones' we accept by cash or check."

"Ha ha, wait a second."

"Huh?"

"Once upon a time there was a man in search of the existential answers, who turned to God for help," she said.

"'God?' he asked. 'God? Are you there, God?'

"'What's up, my son?' responded a voice from above.

"'I have a few questions. May I ask?'

"'Yes.'

"'God, what is a million years to you?'

"'A million years is only a second to me, my son.'

"'Hmm,' the mortal wondered, then asked, 'God, and what is a million dollars worth to you?'

"'A million dollars to me is only worth a penny.'

"The man lifted his eyebrows. 'God, can I have a penny, by chance?'

"The voice from above cheerfully answered, 'Sure . . . just wait a second.'"

They were both laughing when Ana's phone dinged. It was a message from a date.

"Are you dating somebody?" asked the Doc soberly.

"No one special, just a guy."

"Why are you wasting your best years alone?"

"I'm not alone. I have Lilly. And after the complications with her father, it's my priority to protect her from bad, disrespectful people who could mold her personality."

"True, but there are many other decent men who would gladly share their lives with you both."

"I bet there are. But my last relationship was so consuming that I need time to recharge my emotional batteries and erase some of those memories from my mind. Honestly, I prefer to focus on work for a while."

And with that they turned from a personal page to a professional one. During the next few months, they divided their responsibilities as follows:

Doc and his team would groom the racetracks as close to perfect condition as possible, repaint the many miles of white fences between tracks, fix the pump station, renew the judges' tower, prepare the stables and accommodations for the newcomers, and organize the veterinarian control on the spot.

Ana's list was even longer, including the most important task: the financing. In the beginning the whole fiscal endeavor would hang on the Collector's neck, much to his displeasure, though she was adamant on expanding the sponsors net by every means possible. If the races became popular it would become much easier, so proper documentation on film and wide advertising were vitally important.

Both Ana and Doc were aware that they faced a mountain rather than a hill; and if they wanted to climb it, they would have to rely on each other unconditionally.

Chapter 18

THE DAWN OF THE FIRST SEASON

"Hello, where's Turner Brown?"

"Who?!" asked the cashier lady. It was early in the morning.

"I mean Doc. Where's Doc? He's not picking up," Ana replied.

"Oh, he's at the checkpoint."

"Good. Tell him I'm on my way."

Time had passed with incredible speed leading up to the day the hippodrome's gates would open to shelter the thoroughbred horses and their teams from all over the country. It was a rush to see the trucks and vans with animals arriving, everyone tired and thirsty, hasty to get out, stretch their legs, and settle. Doc was the first person to welcome the visitors as he checked their travel documents and instructed them about the local rules.

Recognizing the next newcomer as the chief trainer of the biggest state stud farm, Doc smiled and waved at the man arriving with two trucks and a dozen attendants.

"Hey, old boy. Don't forget to stop by for a drink at the restaurant tonight. First round will be on me, second and third on you," he said.

"Hi, Doc, long time no see!" the trainer said, waving in return. "Please hurry up—we're dying for some water!"

"Sure. Head straight, then right to the third stable over there." He pointed at the buildings behind the American restaurant, then handed the trainer a couple pieces of paper. "Please read this and pass it along to your staff."

The document was a list of the hippodrome's internal regulations. The directives were explained simply and clearly so even the kids could get them right.

"Those staying with us will be asked to sign an approval form," continued Doc. "It's mandatory for everyone—trainers, stable workers, owners, jockeys . . . everyone. You know how important the order is! It has to be established immediately, so as to prevent any possible obstructions or accidents."

"No worries. My guys are very well-behaved. They won't give you any headaches," the trainer said before moving on.

A white Mercedes limousine was waiting next in line, totally out of place in this context. But all the same, the locals knew it to be Ana's.

"Hi, Doc. How's it going?" Ana asked, poking her head out of the car as it stopped right next to him.

"Open the trunk please, lady. I have to check if you are smuggling a pony in it."

"Oh my, oh my, you got me." She smiled, then lowered her voice. "I have to talk to you. Come to the office as soon as possible."

"Okay, right after I'm done here."

*   *   *

Honesty and outspoken communication are at the core of every healthy relationship, including professional ones. Espousing that belief, so far Ana and Doc had managed to build a certain level of trust between them. After dealing with a couple of situations where colleagues or others tried to turn them against each other, their genuine communication saved their partnership and even transformed it into a new friendship.

"Everyone's set," Doc said when he entered the office later. "Now we just have to lock the doors and unlock them in two months."

"Well done, Doc. Now listen . . ." Ana was worried about financing the event. One of the sponsors she was relying on had recently declared a lower income than expected, and thus stepped back from the races. It was turning out to be damn difficult to engage companies for such an unfamiliar venture.

"It will be much easier next year, Doc, when we have videos, pictures, sales figures—a foundation to stand on. Right now it's like a mirage in the desert, and I'm trying to convince other potential partners that it's real. No evidence, just words."

"Yes, but don't forget the Collector has your back. He agreed to cover the budget if there aren't enough sponsors, right? Obviously you're working your ass off to save him money, but sometimes you have to play it by ear. Go and talk to him! He has to keep his word. He has to support us!"

"Ugh, it's gonna be tough. Even though he approved the budget, he hates to donate almost as much as he loves to collect."

"Oh, stop moaning! Look around. The season is about to start and we're totally out of choices. He's our only option now. Just do it!"

Clearly Ana had to make that call, and with a heavy heart she dialed the familiar number and asked for an appointment as soon as possible. Knowing her employer, she prepared a report about the current status of the arrangements and the reserve finances needed. She demonstrated that the facilities were in good condition; proper filming had been patched together with a professional production company; one of the leading TV channels had agreed to include the races on its most popular sports show, and a few cable ones, to broadcast it for free; the design and printing of the brochures had been organized; a few sponsors were still committed; the PR experts were mobilized; the attendants had arrived; and everyone was ready for action. Now Ana needed the Collector's help to fulfill the deficit, which was a moderate amount—far from millions, or even hundreds of thousands.

By the way, she had not a clue why he wasn't willing to announce the betting company a sponsor, since in her opinion, it should have been the biggest announcement. "Not yet" was his comment on that matter. Anyway, so far she had fulfilled all her obligations and promises, and now it was his turn to decide whether to keep his word or not.

She looks exhausted, the Collector noticed at once. *Maybe my protégés were right when they told me she works a lot.*

Of course, Ana's actions had been double-checked, sometimes triple-checked, as the hippodrome's administrator had assigned from headquarters an informant to file a monthly report behind her back. Everybody knew what he was up to, but so what? Let the dogs bark while the train moves ahead.

So the Collector listened to Ana's presentation, already aware of most of its content. Donating, though . . . did he really have to do it? Or maybe he could buy that exquisite antique for his collection instead . . . Ugh, it seemed he had to donate after all.

"Fine, continue operating. I'll figure this out somehow. The races will happen."

"Really? Oh, thank you, thank you!" Ana cheered, and literally ran out of his office.

On her way back, she called Turner Brown to tell him they were covered, but her celebration was short. He reported a problem. The main electrical transformer had crashed and the whole burg had lost power. Doc had already alerted the local emergency team, and everyone was relieved when after two hours the damage was fixed and the long, busy day was safely over.

At dusk the alley's lights started shining, and the hippodrome became quiet as the horses rested. From different directions three groups of people were walking toward the American restaurant, passionately discussing something about racing. When they all bumped into each other at the foot of the stairs, the relative silence was broken—they were saluting, laughing, and hugging. Apparently it had been awhile since they last met. The restaurant's door opened and the sounds of a merry fuss and country music snuck out from inside. Ana and Doc were there, too, shuffling around the tables. They had to be sure everybody felt welcome and comfortable.

"Guys, do you know what kinds of horses go out after dusk?" Doc was in his usual comic mood.

"What kind?"

"Well—the nightmares, of course."

It was a nice warm summer evening, the first evening of the racing season at the hippodrome.

*   *   *

The next day started as any other day at dawn, only this time there were many more souls to be awoken. As both locals and new arrivals had the same morning routine, it was very important to find the best way to cohabitate right away. Therefore Doc was waiting at the racetracks with the training schedule, ready to maintain order and discipline. It was drill time, and now he was the captain. As a proven veterinarian, he was aware that for the thoroughbred horses, morning practice was of a major importance. During the summer it had to be conducted as early as possible, when the air was still fresh and the sun was not blazing, so all the trainers and jockeys at the tracks were impatient to start.

"Okay, listen everybody: Let's do this the right way! Stick to the timetable and be tolerant with each other. Stallions and mares are allowed on the grass track only after I give them their individual go-ahead. Yes, I know how important it is to test the real capabilities of your teams on the correct racing surface, and I assure you that everyone will get an equal chance. Remember, we'll be together for the next two months, so please watch your manners. Otherwise we'll kick your asses out of here—no 'buts' about it."

And Doc was not joking at all. Of course there were some "buts," which he managed to deal with calmly. Hey, he was a good captain.

Naturally, it took a couple more weeks to adjust all the parts of the training routine, at which point Doc was no longer needed in the mornings. Thereafter, he was required only if something had to be changed.

CHAPTER 19

PARENTING DURING THE SEASON

The whole week before the first race day Ana was totally booked. From where she lived with Lilly in the central area near the Collector's headquarters, it took her at least thirty-five or forty minutes to get to the hippodrome because of traffic. Sometimes she had to travel back and forth twice in a single day. Hence her car turned into a mini office where she made most of her cell phone calls.

"How do you manage to juggle all those tasks?" her friends would ask her.

"I'm like a washing machine," she would answer with a smile, "though instead of 'rinse or 'spin,' my options are 'work,' 'sports,' 'have fun,' even 'make love.' Once the program is set I use my general capacity to deliver my best—just like a washer."

Of course, her manner of living was not that simple. She was first and foremost a mom—a mom in a slightly complicated situation with the word *single* stamped on her head. Ergo Lilly's growth was solely Ana's responsibility, including looking after her daughter's physical well-being as well as ensuring her mental enrichment. Ana was consciously creating a personality, and as many mothers do, she dreamed of being proud of her girl.

As it was the beginning of the summer and the end of the school year, Lilly had to finish her final exam and also attend her dance classes. However, Ana was now finding it impossible to have the time to drive her, so she called Vanessa. She met Vanessa and her son at a ballroom and Latin dance competition she had gone to with Lilly, and it happened to be quite a show! Diving into a world of grace and courtesy was amazing. The costumes were incredibly beautiful; the music—absorbing; and all those dancers performed with so much passion and artistry, it was simply captivating. Lilly was speechless, except for one phrase: "I want to be like them, Mummy." And Ana was glad to indulge her impulse. Dancing would build up her posture, manners, teamwork, and artistic skills, and at the same time she would overcome the fear of performing in public. Awesome! So Lilly found a nice partner in Vanessa's boy. Shortly the kids were enrolled in one of the best ballroom and Latin dancing clubs, cutely named "Tailcoat and Patent Shoes."

Classes were at least three times per week—two during the workdays and one (or sometimes two) over the weekends—and including travel time it took hours to facilitate the logistics. Neither mom had lots of free time, so very conveniently Ana and Vanessa found they could cooperate because they lived just seven minutes away from each other. One of the moms would take both kids to the dance studio, and the other would pick them up. As people say: "If there is a will there is a way"; and that was how the children made it to dance class.

Vanessa and Ana had many traits in common—both were single, attractive, and smart. Vanessa still had a husband on paper, but he was living thousands of miles away in Germany. Both women were hard workers—Ana as executive manager of her enterprise, and Vanessa as CFO of one of the commercial banks' leasing companies. So they had to be leaders, housekeepers, bill-payers, mothers and fathers, all at once. And one thing was for sure: It was not easy. It was not easy at all.

At that pace a year passed, and then another . . . Somewhere in between dinners after classes, supporting each other through the gusts of life while their kids learned to dance the cha-cha, rumba, and waltz, they became close friends. So Vanessa agreed without hesitation to shuttle Lilly back and forth from classes the whole week, and promised to attend the racing premiere at that.

With Lilly's engagements settled, Ana could focus fully on her job. The washing machine was running again. The to-do-list in her black notebook looked like this:

Forecast: perfect weather
Tracks: in good condition
Horses: properly listed
Timetable: punctual
TV shooting: arranged
Sound equipment: set
Music editor: ready
Commentator: steady
Photographer: booked
Posters: widely spread
Brochures: on the way
PR: well done
Media: properly informed
VIP invitations: handed out
The Collector: personally invited
Security: assured
Police: alarmed
Judge committee: selected
Start man: picked
Catering: provided
Decoration: lovely
Awards and bowls: ordered
Rosettes for the winners: delivered
Start bell: waiting to ding
Vet assistance: confirmed
Ambulance: . . .

The emergency center in the capital would have to be Ana's next step. Paramedics on the spot would be handy, though hopefully no one would need them. So first she arranged the details with the administrator downstairs, then climbed up to the executive's office on the second floor. She didn't have an appointment, so she needed to use her secret weapon—a small compliment and a big smile!

When she knocked, the secretary looked at her without recognition.

"Good afternoon, ma'am. I would like to leave something for you and for the director as well. Is now a convenient time?"

"For me?" The secretary was surprised.

"Yes, for you, madam." Ana fetched her envelope and said, "It's an invitation for the National Horse Races this Saturday at the hippodrome."

"Really! How wonderful. I will take my son. He loves horses so much. Thank you . . ."

"Ana. My name is Ana."

"And I guess you are the chief manager's assistant?"

"Well, actually, I'm the executive."

"Oh, I'm sorry. Let me notice the boss you're here."

Ana could hear voices coming from behind the director's door. Apparently he was not alone.

"Excuse me, sir, there's a nice lady here with me who wants to meet you concerning the horse races . . . Yes, sir . . . uh-huh . . . okay."

It seemed they were a good team.

"The boss will see you soon," the secretary said solemnly.

Within five minutes the previous visitor left and the director's head peeked out from around his door.

"And you are . . . ?"

"I'm the National Hippodrome's director."

"And you're asking for . . . ?"

"Nothing, sir. I just came to personally invite you to the first racing day this upcoming Saturday."

"Oh, that's kind. Come in. Let's have some coffee."

CHAPTER 20

THE FIRST RACE

Saturday morning, in the judges' tower located next to the tribunes, the officials were feverishly gearing up for the event. Ana was standing in the right corner talking to a man with headphones when Doc opened the door.

"Hey, guys. What do racehorses eat?" he asked, enthusiastically breaking up the conversation with a grin.

"Huh?" Ana looked at him with a questioning face.

"Enriched hay?" suggested the commentator as he made last-minute notes on the lineup.

"Nope, fast food," said Doc, staying true to his hilarious personality. He walked toward Ana and looked over the tracks. The tower provided a spectacular 180-degree view. He breathed in, knowing today would be a big test—and if they passed, they would prove to the whole community (and themselves) that they rocked. The goal was for others to recognize that the hippodrome was the top place for all kinds of racing occasions. May the force be with them!

Soon the members of the judges' committee—five men—took their seats in the middle of the tower. All of them were respected professionals known for their years of experience and high moral standing. It was about time to start, so Ana spoke.

"At last the moment we've dreamed about has come—right, Doc? Hopefully it will go off without accidents or drama."

"Ah, don't worry. I have a good feeling."

At eleven a.m. sharp, the music stopped and the sports commentator announced the beginning of the season.

"Good morning, ladies and gentlemen, dear guests . . . For me it's a great honor to welcome you to the first racing day at the National Hippodrome!"

He had a melodious voice. Ana noticed he sounded pretty confident, probably because of his broad background in the countryside's domestic competitions. The man continued.

"Luckily we're blessed with perfect sunny weather . . . Thank you, Lord! . . . So, what should you expect from us today, dear guests? Well, nothing less than an adrenaline boost that will raise you to the very peak of excitement. We'll present to you a show, a rivalry, a flurry . . . and much, much more. And now, please take your seats, and stay tuned. I bet your hearts will soon be galloping along with our steeds' hooves. And do you know why?" He paused and evened out the tone of his enthusiastic voice.

"Let me tell you something straight: It's scientifically proven that horse races are the purest form of gambling, and also the most addictive one. How come? Because of the duration. Each race takes an average of only two minutes each run—not fifteen, not thirty, not forty-five, but *two*. That's why the level of adrenaline in the human body increases so fast, and during the last seconds delivers to the brain an extraordinary amount of epinephrine. Simple biology, folks. It's in the books." He then reverted back to an excited state and continued. "Woohoo! Are you ready? I guess so. What a spectacular day we have coming up . . ."

The commentator switched the microphone off and sipped some water.

"Great introduction," Ana said. "Go on!"

"Yes," he said, switching the microphone back on. "Now, ladies and gentlemen, let me tell you more about today's agenda."

He then announced the categories of the competitions, starting every half hour and beginning with a mile-long flat run for the youngest, two-year-old thoroughbred stallions. Twelve of them were listed.

"Please don't be shy. For some of them it'll be their first time in front an audience. They will remember your goodwill and support!"

Dong dong dong! Exactly eight minutes before the start of the first race, the bell from the judges' tower rang—inviting the competitors to present themselves. The thoroughbreds came out of the paddock sequentially by number, then trotted in front of the tribunes. In the meantime the commentator guided the spectators through the racing brochure, announcing the horses' names and their pedigrees. He then introduced the jockeys and their achievements, distinguishing them by the color of their silks so they could be easily identified. Lastly he offered a few words about the trainers and the owners, sharing any intriguing facts he knew that were pertinent to the race. His remarks were punctual, clever, and amusing. Standing next to him in the judges' tower, Ana smiled. Those young stallions were so funny, marching briskly with their heads up—just like boys in a formal parade. Everybody loved them.

"They're so fascinating, Doc!"

"Shush! We should cross our fingers! They're totally unpredictable, those little horsy teenagers."

The start gate was situated at the left curve of the track, and they would be running clockwise. One by one the stallions were led into their separate boxes, equipped with two doors—one in front and one behind. Meanwhile the chronometer was ticking; according to the rules the task had to be completed within four minutes. A member of the judges' committee was regulating the race on the spot. He had the power to disqualify anyone not following the procedure, so the jockeys were strongly discouraged from messing with the start-man. Actually he was among the best trainers in the country, also having been an excellent jockey in his youth, as well as a domestic and international champion in his specialty of steeplechase, also known as jump racing.

"Half of them in," he reported over the radio.

"Roger, watch the timing," replied Ana before notifying the commentator beside her.

"Just a few moments more," the commentator said to the audience. "We are waiting for the horses to be settled in the gate." Now he spoke in a calm and relaxed voice, skillfully pacing the audience to focus on the upcoming start. "Dear guests, those are our fresh beginners, our best young thoroughbred stallions. They will be approaching from your right side. Please, pay attention to the finish line marked by a horseshoe, right in front of the judges' tower."

Ana concentrated deeply, seeing everything and hearing everything. She gripped the radio in her hands.

"Almost ready," confirmed the start-man, and everybody in the room heard him.

"Okay, let's roll, folks!" the commentator said off mic, stretching his neck as if getting ready to start his own sprint.

"Wait, wait, what's that?" Ana interrupted, pointing at the tracks. Two figures carrying huge cameras were sneaking to the opposite side of the runway in an attempt to take some pictures.

"What the hell are they doing? Tell them to get back immediately!" she instructed firmly.

The commentator grabbed the microphone. "Excuse me, gentlemen, crossing over the track is absolutely forbidden! Please evacuate immediately! Get off the tracks! It is extremely dangerous for both you and the contestants! I repeat: Evacuate immediately!"

Yet despite his insisting, the intruders did not register his appeal and kept moving on.

"Maybe they didn't hear me," shrugged the commentator. That was possible, as the speakers were pointed toward the tribunes, not the tracks.

"Tell the people we won't start until we resolve this!" decided Ana, who switched the radio on: "Hold the start!"

"Why? What's going on?" the start-man shouted amid the noise and adrenaline. "The horses are getting nervous, we can't keep them in the gate for long! There's no time!"

"I know, I know, just give us a moment!"

Fortunately, it took only a few seconds for the bodyguards to take care of the impudent photographers and escort them out. The audience roared.

"Situation's under control," one of the guards reported. "Very sorry about that, Ms. Ana. It won't happen again!"

"Okay." She took a deep breath and pressed the radio. "Start permitted!"

"Thank goodness. I'm barely holding it together here," the start-man said. Without even bothering to switch off his radio he then shouted, "Boys, boys, get ready! Remember: Fair play is our way! Ready? Ready? . . . Start!"

In that very moment, a spark of excitement ignited the scene, and the atmosphere energized.

"Here they gooooooo!" the commentator exclaimed. "A colorful mass shot out of the gray steel machine . . . Now the horses are moving in a pack."

The rules dictated they should run straight for the first fifty meters; afterward they could break apart. The jockeys' vivid, bright silks, decorated with lines, dots, or pentagrams, looked like Skittles spread across the opposite side of the runway. But in the monitors in the judges' tower, the picture was much clearer.

"Four stallions are galloping in front, led by Gagarin with the red jockey and Gently Light with the blue one, both following the champions' motto: Start strong, slowly increase speed, then accelerate through the final straight."

Soon the riders were going through the first curve and furiously approaching the tribunes.

"Two leaders ahead . . . Who will make it first, ladies and gents?"

The commentator was getting heated up. Most of the spectators stood up for a better view. The curve behind them, now the horses were madly spurring toward the homestretch.

"Come on, come on . . ." Doc was euphoric. He had a favorite among the leaders, while Ana—well, she was supporting everyone.

A phrase from a movie came to her mind: "It's not whether they think we won. It's whether *we* think we won!"

"Go, Gagarin, go!" Doc was hopping from one foot to the other.

Now the horses were running at maximum speed, taking huge strides with their right legs leading, stretching heads forward with every next gallop, all covered with sweat and slobber. Their nostrils and mouths were wide-open, providing more oxygen to the blood. Every contraction of their sinewy muscles was visible from a distance. They ran as if there were no tomorrow.

On the horses' backs, the jockeys made themselves as compact as possible above the saddles, squeezing the animals' bodies between their legs with superior authority and strength. With their left hands they held the bridles, and with their right hands they scourged the horses' hips, yelling "Ya, ya, ya!"

Ana's genuine reaction was amazement. This was her first race ever. That incredible mixture of humans screaming and horses snorting, galloping hooves and flapping whips, all those great ambitions, heat and sweat . . . It was truly amazing. If she had to describe the races in one word, it would be *energy*. No, two words: *biological energy*.

"Two are closing in, nose to nose, closely followed by four others, just a few gallops away from victory. Final yards, final yards, ladies and gents! What a remarkable race! Gagarin with the red jockey or Gently Light with the blue one? Who? Who will cross the finish line first? Who will be the winner?"

The commentator took a quick breath and continued talking even faster.

"Gagarin is pulling slightly ahead. His jockey is much more experienced. Will his background be the deciding factor in this race? Yes, yeeeeesssss! Gagarin is the winner, ladies and gentlemen. Gagarin is the winnerrrr!"

Outside there was a thunderous roar. That was it—the moment of the mass exaltation. And it was exuberant!

The commentator was lost in a trance for moment. When he returned to the present, he looked toward the judges for their approval of the race's outcome. The chief nodded; clearly everything was all right. He sighed with relief. Three steps from him Ana and Doc were embracing each other like children.

Eventually the excitement dimmed. The next race was up, so everyone had to get back to their personal obligations. On his way out to the paddock, Doc turned to Ana with a grin.

"A voice once said to me, 'Calm down. You're not the first doctor who wants to sleep with his patient!' Then another voice added, 'But you're a veterinarian, you idiot!'"

"Ha-ha, your jokes never end, don't they?" laughed Ana as he left.

Then, the judges' tower became quiet. Only the commentator remained. He removed his headphones and looked at Ana's glowing face, and seemed uneasy when Ana stepped toward him to speak.

"Thank you. Great job, buddy! We appreciate your passion very much. That was incredible commentating. Bravo!"

"And thank you!" he remarked with delight. "Usually people forget to express gratitude. I believe I'm gonna need a cup of hot coffee now. Do you want one?"

"Yes, sure. With honey, please."

Then Ana was left alone in the tower. And what was that strange feeling in her gut? Wasn't it pride?

CHAPTER 21

THE MAYOR COMES

Week after week, the days at the hippodrome followed the disciplined pace of their uniform routine. Every Saturday morning the commentator welcomed growing number of visitors at the tribunes. Usually there were six different competitions per day— flat races for English and Arabian thoroughbreds, jump races over movable obstacles, and harness races where horses would pull their drivers in two-wheeled carts called *sulkies*. The competitions had been mingled in order to make each day uniquely interesting, amusing, and memorable, like presenting different plays using the same stage scenery. Utilizing all five tracks, the common races had turned into a lovely spectacle, and naturally more and more people were willing to see them.

Every Saturday afternoon Ana rushed with her shooting director, Rozie, to the TV studio in the capital, where the raw footage had to be assembled. She met Rozie by chance during the first St. Theodore's Day celebration, and ever since they had been working together on all the hippodrome's events. Rozie was an energetic middle-aged woman with russet curly hair, a friendly temperament, and a great gift: She was blessed with an amazing voice, appropriate for folklore songs. In her youth she used to present world-wide, as far away as Japan. Nowadays Rozie only sang from time to time, though her passion for the native music remained. She had been producing a weekly folklore telecast, and besides, she had been consulting for projects like Ana's, bringing into play her various competencies and connections.

"We want to attract as many people as possible," Ana had declared to the TV company's director at their first meeting. "You'll have three main tasks: to interpret the spirit of the races; to clearly explain the rules; and to display the beauty of the show."

It turned out that Ana's ex-husband had helped the company get off its feet. Since he had disappeared before the director had a chance to thank him, the director insisted on offering his services to Ana at half price.

In the studio, the editors had to assemble an hour-long broadcast out of the raw footage, and Ana was exacting about the details. Often the efficient team had to stay up all night in order to have everything decently set for the next day's telecast. Sundays before noon, Ana would deliver the tapes to the TV station so their editors could watch and incorporate the material into a segment.

One day the producer invited her to be the special guest in the studio.

"Really?" At first Ana was hesitant. Was she competent enough? Yet for the cause she accepted, and the show went better than she expected. Even more, she liked being in the spotlight. Well, to be honest, she was a little vain.

Monday was the official registration day, when the start numbers for the next race had been defined; unofficially, the "quarrels" day. Jockeys and trainers let off steam from the previous matchup.

"Hey, why this retard was so late? My horse became nervous, so we missed the bronze."

"Your horse was nervous because you sucked!"

"He crossed me!"

"No, I didn't! The judges said there was no infringement!"

"Well, they were wrong. I don't want to run with him next to me!"

Meanwhile Ana silently observed all these adults acting like kids. She would look at Doc and, pointing at the watch, make a "running out of time" gesture.

"Guys, guys," he would interrupt, then tell one of his jokes. "Once the elephant asked the camel, 'Why do you have breasts on you back?' The camel replied, 'What a silly question from someone who has a dick on his face.'"

Tuesdays and Wednesdays Ana would meet with an army of people, starting with the chief commander—the Collector—then sponsors, associates, journalists, PR experts . . . The list seemed to be endless. Luckily her daughter was on summer holiday with her grandparents, otherwise Ana wouldn't have been able to do it all.

Thursdays included the final wrap of the race brochure, plus edit and design. It had to be printed twenty-four hours before the event, which was the next day.

Fridays featured the technical conference at the hippodrome, last-minute changes, and instructions. Primarily this was Doc's area of expertise, as he was in charge of the facilities. The range of topics was wide: condition of the tracks, veterinarian control, any discomforts, etc., and the conference usually ended with one of his jokes or anecdotes.

On Saturdays, before the event, every single soul on-site had to follow his or her own assignment. Punctuality was crucial. And so after the jockeys' medical exams in the morning, the whole cycle repeated again starting with the commentator's greeting: "Good day, ladies and gents, and welcome to the hippodrome!"

*   *   *

In the middle of that summer, the dynamics of the races created a vortex in the energy field of the entire district. The local population sensed it most. In the small town next to the hippodrome, all kinds of rumors swarmed about the Collector's future intentions and the interest of mysterious foreign investors, yet the most popular rumors concerned the prospective prices of land in the district. Everyone was hoping to get rich.

The mayor of the capital had been born in the same small town, and he still resided there. Over the last few years his career had been very successful, and he had become one of the most popular people in the country. Further on the astrologers were predicting a bright future for him and a string of great achievements. Who knew? Maybe they would be right.

Naturally the mayor longed for wealth and prosperity in his hometown, and he found the latest reports of revived events at the hippodrome quite admirable.

"I should look into that personally," he had said to one of his protégés, who was lodging horses in the burg.

By a coincidence or not, Ana had been intending to invite him that very same week. One day she entered the municipality with a nice bouquet of purple flowers to deliver the formal invitation especially for him. The woman in charge of his schedule promised that he would be informed as soon as possible. And so the next morning while having his coffee, the mayor opened one of his many envelopes to find the invitation. Awesome! He called in his assistant.

"Saturday we're going to the hippodrome. Though eleven a.m. is too early for me, I could make it at twelve. Put it on the schedule and notify them."

"Yes, sir," she said.

Then she dialed the woman who had brought the invitation.

"Hello, is this Ana? . . . I have good news. The Mayor will attend your event at twelve o'clock."

"Oh, thank you very much. We'll be expecting him, and you as well. There's one invitation for you waiting at the front desk. Please be our guest!"

"Lovely—thanks a lot." The assistant was flattered. She called her hairdresser to schedule an appointment for Saturday morning as she admired the beautiful the purple flowers on her desk.

*   *   *

On the sixth and most important day of the national competitions, three black limousines approached the tribunes and the judges' tower exactly ten minutes to twelve, just as the derby was about to begin.

Ana was already waiting outside. After the cordon stopped, the mayor stepped out of one of the cars and took in his surroundings. As a former firefighter and a former secretary general of the Ministry of Internal Affairs with a general's rank, he had the skills and the habits of a competent survivor. Ana noticed he was taller than she had thought. Moreover, he was a good-looking man with a sturdy body who set his feet firmly on the ground. No wonder he had a black belt in Karate—though nowadays he was more active in football and tennis.

The people immediately recognized him, and surrounded him chanting his first name. One after another his neighbors impatiently approached him to shake his hand and take photos, for which he posed like a world-famous celebrity. Clearly the mayor liked that kind of attention.

Once his fans had relaxed and stepped back to give him some personal space, Ana approached him.

"Welcome to the hippodrome, Mr. Mayor!" she said, maintaining eye contact. "We are delighted to have you with us."

"Who is responsible for this mess here?" he asked with fake reprehension and his hands in his pockets.

"Me," replied Ana.

"You?!" He seemed surprised.

"Yes, me. I'm the hippodrome's director."

"Huh?" It took him a second to judge whether she was joking or not.

"Would you like to reward the winners in the greatest race of the year, Mr. Mayor?" Ana said, smiling at him with a sparkle in her eyes.

"Sure, why not? What should I do?"

"Please, follow me," said Ana.

As she led him toward the tribunes, the commentator announced, "Dear ladies and gentlemen, today we have a special guest of honor: The mayor of the capital is among us. Welcome, sir! After the next race he will award the best horse of the year. Stay tuned. In just in a few minutes the derby will begin."

The rivalry was awesome! It would make such a great telecast. Everybody enjoyed it—the audience, the media, and the mayor himself. When the awards ceremony began, the jockeys were still trembling. The third-place jockey was saluted first by the guest of honor, and then by Ana. They repeated the salutes for the second-place jockey. When the winner stepped forward, the mayor shook his hand and skillfully covered the best horse with a beautiful red cloak. The music was solemn, and the victory was so sweet. More pictures were taken and many interviews took place. The derby was the hot news of the day.

The mayor stayed for the next competition, then excused himself for the rest of the day's urgent meetings.

Before getting back in his limo, he told Ana, "I'm impressed. Come to my office Monday at half past eight with a short draft of your main activities and plans. I want to know more."

"Okay, I'll be there," she confirmed.

Ana could still see the shapes of the limousines in the distance when a stable guy ran toward her with a panicked face.

"Ms. Ana, hurry up . . . Your daughter . . . she fell off a horse." The man could hardly breathe.

"What? Where?"

Anxiety clenched her heart. She looked in the direction where he was pointing and rushed toward the crowd that had gathered there. Among the group of people in the distance, she discerned Doc in the middle. He was holding Lilly as she cried. When he saw Ana's anguished face he swiftly reacted.

"Don't worry, don't worry! It's just a scratch."

On her daughter's shoulder and back Ana saw scratches . . . everywhere.

"Are you okay, love?" she asked. "Nothing's broken, right? How's your head? Have you hurt your head?"

Lilly was terrified. She could only explain that she had fallen off a galloping horse on the asphalt.

"Oh, my God! We have to examine her!"

"Hey, Ana, don't panic! I just did. She's okay! Don't you see? She's scared and you are making it worse."

Yes, Ana had to relax and pull herself together. Meanwhile Doc gently embraced the girl.

"Don't worry, sweetie," he said. "First we'll clean the wounds, and then I'll put some magical ointment on you so all the scars will disappear in a matter of days. We use it for our horses."

"What? You mean veterinarian stuff?" reacted Ana.

"Shush, both of you. Uncle Doc will deal with this." Then he turned to Lilly. "Do you know where the horses go when they get hurt?"

"No," replied the moaning girl.

"To the horse-pital, sweetie." Doc smiled.

Afterward he carefully took care of the scratches on her body and the fear in her soul, and suggested she get back on a horse as soon as possible so she would not become afraid. Ana disagreed, as did Lilly; but as promised, her wounds did quickly stop aching, and she began to feel much better.

"The golden hands of the mighty Doc," he peacocked later on. "And his mighty . . ."

Based on the sly look in his eye, Ana assumed he was about to add some "adults only" comment about another part of his body.

"Hold your thoughts 'til Monday, Doc. Now I have to make a draft for the mayor, remember?"

"Oh, yes, go, go . . . That's a major task. Break a leg!"

"Ugh, enough injuries for today," Ana said. Then she drove home with Lilly sleeping on the backseat.

*   *   *

On Monday morning rain was falling, and cars were hustling through a traffic jam. Ana parked her white car in front of the municipality and rushed up the stairs. Thirty seconds, fifteen seconds . . . at half past eight sharp she reached the mayor's office.

Oh, what a surprise—she was not alone. The capital's chief architect, a French delegation, and a famous singer were already present.

Ha! The early bird get the worm, thought Ana.

Once the architect finished meeting with the mayor, it was her turn.

"Good morning, sir." She saluted the tall man as she walked in.

"Morning. Coffee?"

"Yes, please."

The mayor asked some questions about the National Hippodrome's affairs, and within minutes he had the big picture: regular races, massive popularity, betting. It sounded simple the way she put it. However . . .

"How will you assure people that it's safe to invest in your endeavor?" he asked.

"Probably with a kind of union or public organization." Ana had been lately considering that option.

"And if you are not included in the bookmaking company's portfolio, how will you make money? You have many expenses, right?"

"I don't know yet, but it will come to us. Growing is a process, and we should proceed step by step." Then she raised her head. "And trust me, we have great ambitions—such as going international, providing better education for our jockeys and trainers, and in general, developing the global breeding and racing industry."

The mayor's head was bobbing. He liked that plan.

"I'm fond of your project and will support it in any way I can. Plus, I care about my hometown a lot, and your prosperity will benefit the whole district. To start, I'll move my own stallion from the countryside to the hippodrome. You'll take good care of him, I presume?"

"Absolutely! It'll be our privilege," said Ana, flattered.

The mayor continued. "A friend of mine has a couple of animals at the fourth stable of yours. Can you settle my black handsome stallion with them?"

"Consider it done."

"Fine, then my secretary will arrange the transfer." He handed Ana his business card. "Here's my number. Call me if you need anything. Or even better, text me, because I rarely pick up."

"Thank you. May I go now?" She had been in there for half an hour, and the French guys were probably cursing her outside.

"Yes, bye," he said as he picked up his ringing phone.

Walking out of the municipality, Ana looked left toward the Collector's headquarters, on the same street less than two blocks away. Was that a sign? What might spring up if those two giants united? The possibilities were endless.

At present the Collector was away. The destination and the date of his return as always was a secret. He was supposed to reach out to her when back from abroad. And a few days later he did.

"How did your meeting go?"

His office was unusually quiet that day.

"Well, the mayor said he'll support the project in any way he can." Ana then repeated the mayor's exact words.

"Really?" he asked in an even tone. Typical Collector again—pronouncing questions as if they were not.

"Yup," she confirmed.

"Sounds good. When did you meet him?" This, on the other hand, was a real question.

"Monday morning, eight thirty a.m."

"That early?"

"Uh huh." She smiled, as the Collector's workdays started slightly later—usually around eleven.

Ten minutes later, as she was leaving the headquarters, she looked right at the municipality. If only she and the Collector had known that in the near future the mayor would become the most powerful person in the country, that soon he would establish a political party with great influence, that as his party's leader he would win the elections three years later and rule the government as prime minister—not once but twice! Would it have made a difference?

Chapter 22

THE KISS OF DEATH

Right after the first season was over, Ana focused on measuring the outcomes. Would they please the Collector?

"There are not enough horses!" he said.

Unfortunately they hadn't.

The bookmaking company's experts monitoring the races had ably calculated the possibility of having predictable scores. Frauds, coincidences, and the losses they might incur should be avoided like deadly viruses. So in sum, the hippodrome's activities would be included as a betting option only if the number of horses was much bigger.

"Well, we might have an unusual solution." Ana reached for her bag, opened the black notebook, and glanced at her notes. "Since the mares' productivity is limited to a maximum of one colt per year, we'll have to increase importation of thoroughbreds. So either we'll have to invest in buying up animals, or we should define our long-term intentions so both the breeders and the traders rely upon us enough to get engaged, and thus put in their own money."

The Collector fancied the idea of others supporting his business. Ana continued.

"To this end I suggest we establish a Jockey Club like those in other countries. It will be a public organization with a significant role in the whole process, completing the cycle of relations between the hippodrome, the bookmaking company, and the official regulator.

Now is the perfect timing. Collaboration with a competent organization affiliated with the international authorities would guarantee the races' legitimacy. Then we could participate in worldwide events, and of course attract major sponsors."

The Collector did not react but did not look displeased. It was time for the last part of the argument.

"If we don't do it, somebody else could wedge themselves into the operation. Would you leave the supervision in random hands? Here." She handed him a piece of paper. "I've made a list of fellows likely to back us up in this initiative. We should act quickly and efficiently."

The Collector looked at the names. Ana forgot to mention that this plan would make him a total monopolist, though he had likely already calculated that.

"Fine. Let's sleep on it and decide tomorrow."

Apparently the Collector had slept well, because the next day, a team of lawyers was already at work on the organization chart. Meanwhile, Ana had to organize the constitutors' gathering and the first official meeting of the nonprofit organization to be called Jockey Club.

*   *   *

Ana read a funny anecdote about a setter puppy on the back page of the newspaper.

I should tell that joke to Lilly, she thought, and marked it for later. Now the work was waiting. She had to revise the Jockey Club's organizational chart, and it would be much better to do it from home. So she called Doc.

"Hello there, what's new?"

"Same old, same old."

It was late autumn and renovations were being done at the hippodrome.

"Hey, I'll be working from home the next few days, looking through the Jockey Club's issues."

"No worries. The workers have started repainting accommodations in the second stable. I'll personally watch over them so they don't mess with the colors you've chosen," said Doc. After a couple of "redo it" moments, he was becoming familiar with how touchy Ana was about aesthetics, which he was learning to accept as an inevitable aspect of female weirdness.

"Thanks, buddy. Robert Bloch said that friendship is like peeing on yourself—everyone can see it, but only you get the warm feeling that it brings."

Doc laughed. "Ha ha, good one, I'm buying it." Previously they had agreed that working with people who had good senses of humor was much easier; they made the problems seem smaller, and troubles—just temporary.

While Doc was on watch, Ana concentrated on business. But first she had to create the mood. So she took one gingko biloba pill—a kind of herb claiming to boost concentration—and then positioned the laptop comfortably in the middle of the living room table. Her cup of tea was steaming beside it, right next to the black notebook. There, everything was set. She started typing.

The next day she was repeating the same ritual when the phone rang. Her mom's name was on the caller ID display.

"Hi, Mom. What's up?" she answered with a merry tone. But on the other side, Mrs. K was not merry at all. Rather she was desperately crying.

"Anché, Larry is gone . . ." Larry had been their beloved pet for fifteen wonderful years.

"Oh, Mom, relax. He is probably out for a walk with dad," Ana said.

"No, no . . . When I woke up this morning, I found a note on the kitchen table . . . Saying, 'Dear Mom, I'm sorry, but I have to leave. I'm afraid you will not see me again. I won't be back this time.'" Mrs. K was sobbing while talking. "Your dad wrote it on Larry's behalf . . . His last good-bye note. Oh, Anché, our doggy left home as if he was human—with a note."

Now Ana was crying too. Neither spoke for a while. Only groans could be heard over the line.

Then Ana whispered, "Mom, I'm so sorry. He was such a good boy. We're gonna miss him forever."

"Oh my God! It hurts so much," said Mrs. K. The woman was wracked.

"Mom, please pull yourself together! Will you be able to pick up Lilly from school today?"

"Yes, should I tell her?"

"Ugh, she has to hear it, but be gentle, please."

"Okay, I will. So long . . ." Mrs. K hung the phone.

Lately Larry had been suffering from a severe form of cancer, and they had known his end might come soon—yet nobody could imagine living without him. He was not just a dog; he was a member of their family.

Ana recalled the day when she bought him. Back then she was in her second year at the university. It was late winter, and her parents had given her the privilege of picking the family's pet, but the peculiar fact was that actually he was the one who chose them. When Ana stepped into the seller's room, full of newborn puppies, one of the frisky setters scurried toward her and bit the string of her jacket as if saying, "Hey, let's play, sister!"

It was love at first sight. He was simply adorable! They named him Larry, after Sir Edward Laverack, a prominent breeder of English setters in the nineteenth century. Due to the breed's hunting nature, the dog need lots of exercise—and Mr. G had been in charge of the morning walks since day one. Their favorites were long weekend tours of the local meadows, where the doggy could run, run, run . . . Everybody in the neighborhood was familiar with their lovely duet—a white-haired man and his white-furred buddy, fond of each other very much. Was Larry gone for good? Was it too late?

Suddenly Doc called. Ana blew her nose and answered.

"Yes?"

"Ugh, Ana . . ." She could tell from his tone—bad news was pending.

"It's about Larry. Your dad brought him to the hippodrome early in the morning Actually, he woke me up. Because of the cancer, Larry was suffocating. He couldn't breathe and was suffering a lot. We called an expert in human cancers I used to work with, and the doctor came to examine Larry before work. Unfortunately, his diagnosis was . . . the worst one. He was dying. So to end his misery my colleague suggested euthanasia. I'm so sorry, Ana. The poor dog was agonizing, so we had to put him down . . . It was the most humane solution."

"Where's Dad?" she asked, sobbing with an aching heart.

"He is out, walking alone in the field, trying to hide his emotions. For him it was very tough to say good-bye to his friend. Mr. G was embracing Larry and kissing his head while the dog's eyes became dim. 'So long, buddy. One day we'll meet again,' he said, and closed his eyes. Dear Larry was loved 'til his last breath."

"Please, keep an eye on Dad, Doc! He must be devastated," wailed Ana.

"Of course, don't worry. I'll go find Mr. G right away. Oh, there's one more thing—we decided to bury Larry here at the hippodrome."

"Where exactly?"

"Under the little acacia tree," answered the vet.

"Oh, that's a beautiful, tranquil spot . . . I hope he'll rest in peace there. You are a good man, Doc. Thanks for everything."

"Hey, you can count on me."

Later that day Larry's remains were carefully buried under the little acacia tree at the hippodrome. Mr. G put a headstone down with his loyal buddy's name on it and swore never to get another pet. Nobody could replace Larry.

CHAPTER 23

THE JOCKEY CLUB

Ana had little time to properly grieve, as shortly the Jockey Club's establishment was officially announced, and she had to organize the first meeting. The event was held in the capital, and five dedicated people were chosen to be members of the board: one of the massive private breeders in the country; one entrepreneur with outlandish experience who used to successfully compete with his horses in France; one of the Collector's lawyers; the chairman of the existing Horse Breeding Association; and Ana herself. The fundamental goals of the new public association were to organize and to manage the country's horse races, according to the local laws and to international standards. Ana was appointed the club's leader, which flattered her but also came with more responsibilities and more exertions. Bye-bye private life, which had not been exactly plentiful anyway. Nevertheless, she gladly accepted the new assignment.

Shortly thereafter she met with the Collector in his headquarters.

"I got in touch with an English betting expert. Another Brit who met me last summer spoke highly of us to him. Maybe we should invite him over to examine the opportunities for international development on the site?"

"Hmm, how much will that cost?" asked the Collector's.

"Well, we agreed he'd be awarded only if his report is useful for us, so we'll only have to cover his expenses—a plane ticket and an accommodation here in the capital. We could afford it."

"And how long will he stay?"

"He said four days would be enough."

"And who will take care of him?"

"Me personally. Do you want to meet him?"

"No, I'm very busy as of late. You'll brief me later."

"Sure, no doubt." Ana was always doing it anyway.

The Collector continued. "About the report . . . what if we don't appreciate it?"

"Nothing."

"Ha! So you're telling me somebody will fly twenty-five hundred kilometers, work for four days, and write a statement without an advance? This guy might not be competent if he's not even flying first-class . . ."

"Yes, yes, and yes," Ana answered.

"Fine then, get him over. Let's see what he figures out. Who knows—something might come of it."

"Great, I'm on it," she confirmed, and afterward was quickly dismissed.

Two weeks later Ana, now the Jockey Club's chairman, was waiting at the airport. The plane from London had just landed. As she walked around the arrivals area, she was talking on the phone with a grin. Guess who was on the line?

"You wanna hear a dirty joke?" Doc said. "A boy in a white shirt fell in the mud. How about a dirtier one? He stood up and fell back down . . ."

Apparently there was more.

"And now a clean joke? He took a bath with bubbles."

"When should I laugh again?" asked Ana.

"Hey, you haven't heard the dirtiest one so far! Bubbles was the girl next door!"

Ana could imagine his jaunty face, and had finally started laughing when she saw the Brit.

"Listen, I gotta go. He's here," she said as she waved at the foreigner who had just walked out of the terminal.

Right away she intuited that the Brit was competent, even if not flying first-class, and also that he was committed to writing a worthy draft. Ergo, he would get his well-deserved remuneration. Moreover, he was a nice person familiar with international trends, and she gladly assisted him, showed him around, and thoroughly answered his questions.

Soon after his departure at the beginning of December he submitted his detailed report to Ana via email. The highlights included: The size of their stables was up to international code; the direction should be reversed, and the riders should run left-handed rather than right-handed; the new grandstands should be located at the point of the counterclockwise finish near the stables; and the most important one—Tote betting! If properly organized on the spot, it would guarantee the hippodrome's prosperity.

Margins would multiply unpredictably if the Collector's nationwide bookmaking company affiliates the races, Ana remarked to herself. Candidly, she was very optimistic about the future.

After spending New Year's Eve ice skating with Lilly, Vanessa, and her son, Ana sat down to distill the information from the Brit's report into an acceptable brief for the Collector. Of course, the key word as always was *money*. However, what if reinvesting the profits elsewhere was postponed for later? In Ana's imaginative vision the burg could be developed into a modern resort with perfectly groomed racetracks, new grandstands, a residential area, and lots of flowers— simply an adorable place with authentic charisma. Was there any chance at all to make it real? She shared the idea with Doc.

He was very excited. "It would be historical!"

Next Ana briefly discussed the idea with the Collector. As usual, he remained indifferent. Building castles in the air was a total waste of time to him, but he didn't stop her from digging further simply out of inquisitiveness. So together with Doc Ana turned to a shrewd lawyer for advice, then inquired a few real estate dinosaurs. After getting quite optimistic feedback from them, she texted the mayor to ask for a meeting.

"Friday," was his short response.

* * *

"I'm in a rush, so brief me on the highlights," said the major.

"Yes, sure," said Ana. "You once asked me how we're gonna make money if we're not one of the bookmaking company's options."

"Yes, I remember."

"Well, with the favor of the authorities, it could happen this way." Ana glanced at her notes. "There's a trend of rich Arab people looking to participate in European races with their own horses. As our country is situated at the border between the two continents, this advantage could be exploited. How? By turning the hippodrome into a major training center. Having in mind that racing animals are like professional athletes—they have to stay fit and to exercise daily, as well as acclimatize when they travel—we could offer them proper facilities for all main disciplines. Moreover, in our little country, everything is much cheaper than anywhere else in Europe—the labor, the rent, the food . . . everything. We could become the preferred location for foreign teams, and we could fully utilize our means for the whole year, not only during the racing season. It's all about the organization!"

The mayor was listening carefully. Ana continued talking with passion.

"So, with the municipality's permission, the hippodrome could become a modern resort for sports and leisure, including private apartments and a hotel with a recreational area at our mineral springs. We could even arrange a spa for horses in the lakes. It's possible! Plainly it could become an exceptional complex, the one and only in the whole region . . . maybe even beyond. What do you think about that?" She was red-hot for his answer.

"Well, I love it, but let me call the chief architect for his opinion."

Luckily the man was available to show up at once, and Ana was elated when he approved the project—yet she managed to suppress her emotions in front of the others. Hiding her feelings was a skill she learned in the Collector's academy, although she was still far from reaching perfection.

When the meeting had ended, she hurried home and started packing. Work would have to be put aside for the next few days as her daughter was attending the annual National Dance Competition in the countryside.

Because Vanessa's son had suffered a knee injury, Lilly was dancing with another boy. Such a pity, since she was not fond of her new partner at all. Nevertheless, she kept on practicing "New York" and "back to back" figures, waiting for the competition with a thrill. For costumes they had put their trust in a well-known local designer, who'd made Lilly a long satin peach dress for the ballroom dances and an extravagant short one for the Latin show in shades of white and purple. Ana put them in the luggage, along with all the shoes, accessories, and makeup needed. Everything was carefully packed in the car. As they drove, they sang along with the songs on their favorite CDs, and fortunately, nobody could hear them.

*   *   *

"Let the dances begin!"

They stepped into the bright, crowded hall right after the official announcement. Lilly was nervous, and so was her partner. The trainer tried to encourage them, but they were just eleven-year-old kids in a stressful position. And naturally they messed up the first round.

"He missed a whole figure," Lilly complained.

"She stepped on me," the boy countered.

"Hey, guys, cut the nonsense!" said the trainer. "It doesn't matter who made a mistake. You are a team, and you're meant to support each other. In the end nobody will ask what happened between you; only the score in your records will remain. So act like professionals and show them what you've got!"

Lilly looked at her mom with tears in her eyes.

"He's right, love. Work together, not despite each other," Ana said.

The commentator announced: "Next bracket: rumba."

The kids were barely breathing, exhausted from the last performance. But it was time for the second round, and they had to dance again no matter what. This was Lilly's preferred dance. Escorted by her partner she walked on the stage with a big smile and her head held high. Then they assumed the starting position. When the melody sounded and she made the first move, it seemed as though she had wings instead of arms. One, two, three, four . . . Lilly performed with such amazing grace and artistry, she seemed as if the judges had disappeared, and she was doing it for her own amusement. Dancing with passion was the key. At the same time her partner was keeping pace pretty well.

Ana could barely hold back her tears. Suddenly all those years of driving, waiting, and expenses made sense; all those efforts were paid being back in a moment of triumph.

"Bravo! Bravo!"

Ana applauded, overfilled with gladness. When Lilly came backstage she embraced her tight.

"Well done, my love. I'm so proud of you!"

Her daughter was glowing—because she had made it! She had reached new heights of excellence, and it was so uplifting. Because of the first bad round, they were rated the sixth couple in their division nationwide. Nevertheless, Lilly felt like a winner.

Driving home was a quiet journey—no music, no singing, no rush. Lilly was knackered, and her eyelids were drooping. At the same time Ana was quietly talking, partly to the girl and partly to herself.

"A friend of mine once told me that the soul gets enriched by the salty liquids—tears, sweat, or seawater. I would add that tears stand for emotions, sweat for knowledge and personal achievements, and the sea for a symbol of ultimate beauty. That's why I would mark today as a great day: We have experienced it all."

CHAPTER 24

THE VISION

Unfortunately the Collector was not in a good mood that day.

When Ana placed the papers on his desk, he asked firmly, "What's this?"

"This is my extended overview."

He didn't touch or even look at them. "What's it about?"

"The resort. Last week the mayor and the chief architect confirmed we'd be given twenty-two thousand square meters of building permission. It's more than enough. And there's a way to do it with no large loans, thought we might need a small one."

"Yeah, right." Obviously he was skeptical.

Ana unrolled the hippodrome's map on the desk between them.

"Look, once we reverse the running direction, the finish will be shifted closer to the stables and the new grandstands should be placed here." She pointed on the sketch to where the buildings were neatly located behind the Saloon. "This way we could assemble the horses on the right side, with a separate entrance near the American restaurant."

The Collector did not move a muscle. She continued.

"The main doorway in the middle could be used as the entrance to the grandstands, facilitating traffic from the nearby parking area."

The Collector looked at her with an expression that said, "Are you nuts? New grandstands? Do you know how much this will cost?" So she cut straight to the point.

"As for financing . . . let's look at the left side of the track. When the old tribunes are gone, there will be lots of empty space. We could reasonably build the residential area there, with apartments and a boutique hotel conveniently accessible from the left entrance." Ana outlined the designated territory with her finger. "The advantages of our complex would be: the super view over the racetracks and the fields outside; proximity to the stables and the rest of the amenities; the healthy climate; and the healing mineral water. In brief, it will be an exclusive resort: unique, ecologically friendly, and close to the capital. Once the paperwork is done, the sales could start, and this way we could fund the beginning of the project."

"Aha, the beginning . . ." The Collector was frowning.

"Wait, wait . . . According to the previous quote, the price of admission for accommodations fitted with special facilities such as ours would be three times higher than the cost of the construction work, and if well designed, it could be four times higher. We own the land already, so why not develop it?"

Then she broke down the figures based on the twenty-two thousand square meters available. The Collector was still frowning.

"Numbers, numbers . . . Who do you think would buy property at the hippodrome?"

"Anyone who's fond of horses or riding. See, it's similar to skiing fans. You do ski, right?"

"No, I snowboard."

"Passionate horsemen have the same mind-set. They would love to escape from the daily shackles, to dress up, to briskly walk to the stables, and to ride with the wind, free as mustangs. That's a pattern, and we could benefit from it. Believe me, this idea is absolutely convertible."

Finally, the Collector stopped frowning. From the humidor he took a Montecristo and lit it. Then he gestured for her to continue.

"Under the poplars along the hippodrome's borders we could easily make a riding alley—very convenient as the fences would protect the riders, especially the beginners. It would be long enough—a couple of miles. So we'll have enough options to meet various desires—fields, racetracks, alleys—and nobody else could offer that! The real estate experts are positive that with some good advertisement, it would sell like crazy."

"I don't trust them," remarked the Collector while exhaling.

"And here's the best part—if we declare the hippodrome a training center with veterinarians to horses coming from outside Europe, and from the Middle Eastern countries particularly, we could find a profitable application for the property year-round, though with a slightly packed schedule during the racing seasons. We can make it. And here"—Ana pointed at the area between the ovals on the map—"despite the recreational area in the hotel, we could arrange the horses' spa in the lakes, since we have two mineral water sources. Doing so would add more qualities to our complex and boost admission prices."

His cigar was half smoked when Ana wrapped up her final arguments.

"There are two important advantages to this project. Number one—massive financing would not be necessary, and two—by the end, the hippodrome would be independent, existing without anybody else's patronage. Our haunt would be appealing enough to attract people and to support local Tote betting. Though if someday the bookmaking company added horse racing to its portfolio, you would be the one to benefit the most."

There was a long pause . . . but no applause from the Collector. Instead he startled.

"I'm very late for my next meetings. Leave the papers. I'll check them later."

"But . . . do you like it?"

"I have to think about it. And regarding your priorities . . . well, you should focus on the upcoming season."

Obviously, Ana was not going to get resolution that day. So she left the office-museum with no map, no papers, and no clue about where her project was headed.

CHAPTER 25

THE GREAT DERBY

It was a busy spring. The next racing season was of vital importance to the whole enterprise, so everything had to be perfect. Based on its outcome, the Collector would be mapping out the future direction of the business.

"It has to be outstanding, Doc!" she said one day at the beginning of May.

"Damn yes, and we'll do everything possible to meet the challenge. Our community already trusts us, and the competitors are eager to run at the hippodrome again. They are calling me nonstop, asking for stables and hay. The equestrian tenants have to be transferred to other bases nearby during the season. Luckily this option was included in all the basic agreements. We're gonna need every box on site. Only this way will we be able to host thoroughbreds from all over the country."

"When will they start coming?" Ana wanted a specific date, and Doc answered.

"Great," she said. "When the thoroughbreds arrive, so shall me and Rozie. We want to shoot the morning practice and life backstage for the telecast."

"I see." He smiled. "Should I fix up my hair?" Then he made a gesture as if tossing his long hair back. It was funny because he was totally bald.

"Who knows? Rozie might decide to interview you."

Rozie—in addition to her role as the director of shooting on-site and Ana's trusted media and PR consultant—would play a key part this season, as Ana was to be an executive producer of a nationally broadcast TV show named *Jockey Club*.

"I love to work with people like you," Ana said to Rozie that morning. Rozie was sharp and punctual, and her word was reliable. As they drove together to the site, Rozie smiled, and replied, "Thank you." The traffic lights were red.

"Hey, I haven't heard your singing yet . . . I mean, I haven't heard you sing live," mentioned Ana.

"Come on, really?"

"Never ever. Would you please sing for me?"

"Now? Here?" Rozie was puzzled.

"Yeah, why not?"

"Why not indeed! Just a sec." She cleared her throat and announced, "This song is called 'Let's Forgive Each Other.'"

And then her melodious voice rang out:

"If at night the wind stops at your windows

And lowly taps gently waking you up

Listen to him, my uncos, he's whispering . . ."

All of a sudden the car turned into a music hall. Ana listened with her eyes closed, and for a few moments she was far away, somewhere where the wind was whispering a lullaby.

The sky was still dark when Ana and Rozie arrived at the hippodrome early in the morning along with the rest of the shooting team—a cameraman, an assistant, and a reporter. Doc was already waiting at the administrative office.

"Good morning, my ladies. The tea is served." He pointed at the table, where three steaming cups had been placed.

"Hey, Doc, long time no see," Rozie said, hugging him.

"Gee, you look even prettier when pregnant," he said, and yes, she was in her seventh month, as one could seem from her cute and quite big belly.

"Two more months to go. The big day is scheduled right after the races." And yet she was as vigorous as ever.

"Hey, have you heard that one?" Doc asked with a grin. "A man calls 911, saying, 'Please, come immediately, my little son has swallowed a condom.' In a minute the same man calls back. 'Oh, no worries, I found another one.'"

Rozie was still laughing when Ana urged them, "Come on! We have to go, guys. The horses are awake!"

They rushed into the dimness. The sun was rising, and it was time to work.

The purpose of the *Jockey Club* telecast was to educate the nation, to show every interesting aspect of orchestrating the glory of the races. At the core of every victory was repetition—day after day, month after month. Yes, hard work was definitely the key to all the rosettes and awards, and because of that it was decided the horses' daily training routines should be properly demonstrated on *Jockey Club*. So early that morning under the first rays of light, filming began. The cameraman shot the drills, the reporter interviewed trainers and jockeys, and Rozie masterminded their maneuvers. *Behind the Fame* was the initial material's working title, and everything in it was authentic, even the light.

Eight half-hour episodes of *Jockey Club* were contracted with the TV station, each part covering one of the racing days at the hippodrome. It sounded like plenty, yet it was not enough to show the relevant competitions, to clearly explain the rules and regulations, to cover the jockeys' and trainers' life stories, to present international news and highlights—and all in thirty minutes? Every second was precious. Nevertheless, the people involved with the project were committed to creating an engrossing, amusing, and enlightening show.

In the blink of an eye the summer came and the season started zippier than ever. And if working nights was necessary, then they worked nights. No complaints, no bargaining—they were chasing the dream of prosperity. It was the middle of the rush when the station's programing director, Roberta, called Ana asking for an unexpected meeting.

"Sure. Tomorrow morning?" Ana accepted, bewildered.

The next day she entered the TV director's office apprehensively.

"Hello, Ana, please take a seat," said Roberta as she took out some papers and smiled. "This is the latest ratings review. I don't have a clue how you do it, but look."

She pointed at the figures. *Jockey Club* was on the top, and its ratings were higher than the news'!

"Wow, that's fantastic!" Ana was amazed!

"We should do something more extensive next year," continued Roberta.

"Sure thing. Our team rocks, ma'am! Can I keep the ratings review?"

"It's all yours." Roberta smiled as she shook Ana's hand. "Congratulations!"

* * *

Meanwhile the general sponsor was waiting for Ana in his headquarters. He was a wealthy person, one of the local oligarchs. As an expensive hobby he bred racing horses, and competed with some of them in Europe. His lavish training center was based in Germany, and he also kept a separate residential facility near his hometown in the countryside. Admittedly the general sponsor was a genuine admirer of the races, having personally attended the Dubai Cup and the Royal Ascot more than once. His support was of significant importance to the whole event, and it was Ana's pleasure to show him the proof that their efforts had been awarded.

"I'm coming straight from the meeting with the programming director of the TV station. Look, sir. Our rating is higher than the news'!"

"Let me see!" He took the bulletin. The figures were clear, erasing any doubts he might have had. "Well done!"

Across the desk Ana stood as steady as a soldier reporting for duty. She added, "They want to collaborate with us on a more extensive telecast next year."

"Sure, and I have the feeling they won't be the only ones interested," said the sponsor, pleased that his donation had served a good cause.

"Here you are—the new brochure," Ana said, handing him a small colorful book. Its contents were diverse yet relevant to the races. It included an article explaining specific terminology; selected highlights from the national regulations; hot news about a world-famous jockey visiting the neighboring country; catchy details about America's Triple Crown; the traditional part with the commentator's analysis and forecasts; and of course overall information about the upcoming races. It was designed with pictures, style, and care. The general sponsor put the brochure on the table in the middle of the room, right next to the previous prints.

Aha, I expect he'll be showing them to his guests, thought Ana with a smug smile.

*   *   *

Oh, glorious day, it was the fifteenth of July, blessed with delightful summer weather—not too hot, not too humid—simply perfect. The tribunes were splendidly decorated with plenty of flowers and colorful ribbons in the spirit of celebration. Thousands of people were coming to watch the derby of the year, and many of Ana's friends were there too. Sis, Vanessa, Michelle, and Natalie were cheerfully chatting with their families beside Lilly, Mr. G, and Mrs. K in the first row. All the constitutors of the Jockey Club were presented, along with the local mayor, the director of the emergency hospital, Roberta, local celebrities, politicians, and even foreigners. The general sponsor was abroad, but he had warned Ana that he'd be watching it online. The mayor of the capital was going to join the ceremony later on to reward the winner as he had done the previous year. Only the Collector was missing.

As the visitors amassed at the grandstands, Ana and her fellows were on duty. She was in the judges' tower, Doc was with the vet committee, and Rosy was busy at the mobile TV station. The show was about to begin.

"How stunning! So many people are here, and more are coming," Ana said to the commentator while gazing at the tribunes.

"Cool, huh?" He gazed outside. All of the seats were taken, and the area around the tribunes was crowded too.

"I would love to hear one of Doc's jokes right now," Ana said, biting her nails. Frankly she was feeling a little tense about takeoff.

"Anybody longing for me?" Turner Brown said as he walked in.

"Me, I've got stage fright." Poor Ana was trembling with fever.

"Hey, hey, hey." Doc rubbed her back "Everything's gonna be tip-top. I have a good feeling about it."

"Sure?"

"Just look outside. Have you ever seen so many people at the hippodrome?" He chuckled. "Once a racehorse's owner took his very sick buddy to the vet. 'Will I be able to race with this horse again?' he asked. The vet replied, 'Of course, and you'll probably win!'"

"I get it . . . The man would outrun the sick horse. Thanks, Doc. You always find a way to cheer me up," said Ana. Her confidence was back. Apparently all she needed was a good joke, a back rub, and a bit of sincere empathy—nothing more.

The commentator, who had been laughing too, tried to calm himself as the clock approached eleven.

"It's showtime, folks," he affably announced, putting on his headphones.

Then his voice sounded from the loudspeakers.

"Today is not an ordinary day, ladies and gentlemen. It's the day of the great derby! And it's my pleasure to welcome you to the National Hippodrome! Also I would like to welcome Mr. Adrenaline and Mrs. Glory. They are about to tango for us in a few hours. Are you ready for that show?"

The uplifted audience reacted with a roar.

"Very well then," the commentator continued. "We shall start with a massive parade."

The jockeys and trainers then marched in front of the viewers on the grass track to the sounds of a live brass band. The spectators saluted them with enthusiasm. When the procession was over, he spoke again.

"While the competitors are getting ready for the first start, let me invite our patroness to speak on behalf of the organizers. Ms. Ana, please—the microphone is yours!"

Wearing a trendy milk-and-mint satin dress, Ana walked to the lawn in the middle of the track and faced the audience, secretly wondering how many eyes were staring at her right then. Her mouth was dry; her heart was thumping.

Come on, Anché, seize the moment! she said to herself, then spoke with a smile. "I would like to thank the sponsors for the generosity," she continued, "my colleagues for their devotion, the participants for the fair play, and all of you for trusting us!" It was a short emotional announcement met with plenty of applause. And she finally relaxed. Then Ana stepped back so the cheerleaders could perform a cheeky dance with their big yellow pom-poms.

"Let's thank these wonderful girls." The commentator invited the audience to make some noise before returning to the script. "Now let's look at the schedule for today. Six incredible contests are pending. First the two-year-old English thoroughbreds will run, then the sprinters. Third will be the great derby, fourth—the Arabian Thoroughbreds, fifth—the English marathons, and last will be the trot race. Terrific. Can't wait to see it all!"

The first start commenced on time, and the second one as well. Everything was going as planned when the mayor of the capital stepped onto the lawn to the accompaniment of the brass band's melody. Ana's fever was long gone and now she was heartedly celebrating the day.

"Nice dress," he complimented her.

"Thank you. Please follow me," she said, then settled him right next to a famous local pop star. At last the big race was about to begin. This time Ana remained in the audience beside the mayor instead of watching it from the judges' tower.

"Ladies and gentlemen," the commentator solemnly announced, "there are ten three year-old English thoroughbreds waiting in the starting gate. One of them will sign his name into history. Who was born with a champion's heart . . . and who was trained to win? Well, let's find out. Annnnd . . . staaart!"

Ana crossed her fingers. *May it all go well!*

Horses were spurring in the distance, raising the élan of the crowd with every gallop. It was a furious rivalry, strenuous and meteoric. Until the last two hundred yards, one mare was leading by more than a length when a stallion blew by her.

"Wow, what an unexpected overturn! Now Orange Way is slightly ahead. Will he keep his advantage? Just a few more yards, ladies and gentlemen, it looks he'll make it . . . Orange Way is madly spurring. Yes, yes, he crossed the finish line first!" The commentator's excitement was over the top. "He is the winner! Dear guests, the horse of the year is Orange Way! Woohoo, what a derby! I'll need a glass of water to cool down before the awards ceremony, yet not until after the final scales. The jockey's weight along with his equipment (saddle, helmet, and whip) is supposed to be less than fifty-eight kilograms. Don't go away, it will take only a while."

Meanwhile, Ana saw Doc heading to the judges' tower. He seemed happy as a lark. Shortly the race was confirmed as legitimate, and the awards ceremony began. Glowing with a big smile on his face, the winner was still trying to regulate his breathing as he approached the guest of honor. The mayor, Ana, and Orange Way waited for him, surrounded by reporters with cameras. Impulsively, he kissed the fabulous stallion.

"Ladies and gentlemen, I would like to underscore that this man is not only a jockey, but also Orange Way's trainer—so his prize is twofold. As we love to say here at the hippodrome: Hard work is the key to all the rosettes and awards. Well done, my friend! Congratulations to the champion!"

With massive applause the crowd greeted his dedication, while he waved at them with glee. After long years of experience in England and Germany, he had not only a European riding style, but also proper attitude. The mayor stepped forward, and firmly shook the winner's hand.

"The tougher the race is, the greater the victory! Congratulations!" he said.

"Thank you, sir, thank you very much! My stallion is amazing," the winner replied, and gently patted the horse on the neck. "Good boy, good boy."

Assisted by Ana, the mayor then covered the horse's back with a shining red mantle, stamped with the words "The Great National Derby."

"Bravo! Bravo!" some of the spectators shouted, while everyone else, in a state of euphoria, made all kinds of noise. It was such a clamor Ana could barely hear her own thoughts. The first notes of the national anthem sounded loudly from the speakers, and as one, the people stood in the grandstands, strengthened, and started chanting. The mayor sang too, and so did she.

"Camera six: Zoom in on the waving national flag," Rozie directed from the mobile command center. "Camera seven, I repeat, seven: Get a close-up of the winners. Great! Did you get that?"

"Yes ma'am," the operator confirmed, artfully capturing the tears on winner's face.

"Reporter and cameraman on the field, ready for interviews." Rozie was an arduous boss.

"Yes, on it."

The music stopped.

"How do you feel as a victor?" the reporter addressed the fortunate man.

"Well, I have no words to describe my feelings . . . I'm so proud that my horse was courageous. In my life I've attended lots of races, and actually today I've won my third derby in our country, yet for the first time I can say that the spirit of our local competitions is equal to that of the world-class ones."

"Thank you, buddy, and good luck to you and Orange Way," said the entertainer before shifting his attention to the mayor standing close by. "Would you like to say a few words, sir?"

"Sure, with pleasure. Hello, everyone."

When he spoke the audience immediately reacted warmly, greeting him with cheers. Gratified he carried on.

"What a wonderful event, huh? As you know I was raised in the neighborhood, and as a child I was keen on watching the races at the hippodrome. That was long time ago, wasn't it? Many of you recall it, right? And now . . . now I'm glad the tradition is back, and hopefully it will remain so in the future. To that end, on behalf of the municipality, I declare that we shall support the development of a modern resort here at the hippodrome, so even greater competitions will be able to take place in years to come."

That was a billion-dollar statement! And the mayor had made it not only in front of the couple of thousands at the grandstands, but also in front of the whole nation as Rozie's cameras were broadcasting. In silent triumph Ana stood beside him. He looked at her appraisingly. Wasn't she was just a chick with a beautiful vision?

Chapter 26

The Grief

Definitely that was a year of glory for the hippodrome. Due to the whole team's united efforts, the word *international* became commonly mentioned referring the next year's season. The last one had been well organized, spectacular, and widely covered, so the people's wonderment was finally awakened. Many reporters from all kinds of newspapers, magazines, television, and radio stations were eager for more information. Articles with titles like "Races with European Style" and "Hippodrome's Greatest Ambitions" had been published. Unexpectedly, though now clearly well earned, ratings for *Jockey Club* remained higher than those of the news through the rest of the season. And many sponsors, both present and future, had noticed. Ana's team was celebrating, though their greatest moment of recognition was still ahead—at the end of the year, the Horse Breeding Association announced a 30 percent increase in the number of thoroughbred horses in the country. Such an expansion had never been reported before! It seemed the nation was ready for regular horse races.

At the end of November, Ana and Doc were already making long-term plans.

"Next year we shall do internationals," Ana stressed.

"Well, that's another story, sister. For the internationals we'll have to double-check the doping tests. We should probably send samples abroad, either to the Turkish or German laboratories. I'll get in touch to check their terms and conditions."

"Why do you think our lab is not reliable enough?"

"It's not about the lab. It's about the human factor. Employees could easily fake the results in somebody's favor. I want everything to be sharp."

"You are my trusted veterinarian supervisor, counselor Doc! We'll humbly follow your advice."

He smiled. "Or otherwise it might happen like this: Right before the international races, a trainer could give his last-minute instructions to the jockey. Meanwhile he slips something into the horse's mouth just as the steward walks by. 'What was that?' inquires the steward. 'Oh, nothing,' answers the trainer. 'Just candy.' And then, to prove his innocence, the trainer offers one to the steward and takes one himself. After the suspicious steward leaves the stable, the trainer continues with his instructions. 'Just keep on the rail, dude, and you will be a certainty. The only thing that could possibly outrun you now is either the steward or me.'"

Ana laughed out loud at this. "That's one of your best. I'll try to remember it."

And she did, repeating it to her friends for days.

The next afternoon they agreed to meet with the Horse Breeding Association as soon as possible to determine the next year's racing calendar, so beforehand, they started putting together a strategy for the meeting. As usual during their creative conversations, she took the notes, only this time it was in a new blue notebook. The good thing about the meetings with the association was that with time the communication between them had transformed from arguing and contradictions to seminal teamwork, probably because now Ana's and Doc's reputations had improved. Whatever the reasons, the next year's calendar was smoothly determined within a couple of hour-long, constructive discussions, and subsequently was officially announced. By the time Ana was ready to travel home to help Lilly spend her winter break preparing for high-school testing, it was confirmed that the hippodrome was going to host almost the whole season.

"We'll have to tighten up the bridles," remarked Doc. And he was not kidding at all.

*   *   *

Doc was a dedicated person, who loved the hippodrome, the races, and teaming up with Ana. For him there was no difference between business hours and personal time. They had a cause. Therefore, it was not a surprise to Ana when the phone rang late one Sunday evening in December showing Doc's name on the display. She figured he was working on some issue and was looking for her opinion, as he had done many times before.

"Hey, Doc. This can't wait until tomorrow, can it?" she answered cheerfully.

But he didn't respond.

"Hello?"

Still nobody answered. In the silence, she could just detect some kind of noise resembling heavy breathing. What was going on? Was it a miscommunication or . . . ? Then she heard Doc's voice. He sounded as if he were speaking from outer space.

"Ana, I won't be able to come to work tomorrow . . . My daughter committed suicide this afternoon."

"What? What are you saying, Doc?" Ana was appalled.

"We lost her, Ana. We lost our girl . . ." the man uttered hollowly.

Then Ana realized that his voice was not coming from outer space; it was coming from hell.

"Oh my God!" The phrase dropped out of her mouth. She couldn't help but burst into tears. Doc's daughter was a lovely sixteen-year-old, only a couple of years older than Lilly. How was this possible? Why? Why?!

After a few seconds Ana finally spoke. "I can't find the right words, my friend. I'm so sorry . . . I'm so, so sorry . . . Is there anything I can do for you?"

"No, nobody can . . ."

"Oh, Jesus. I'll come over tomorrow morning."

"Okay," he said quietly, then hung up. The conversation ended without good-byes.

Urged by maternal instinct, Ana hurried to Lilly's room and tightly embraced her with tears in her eyes.

"Please sleep with me tonight, kiddo!"

The girl was startled. "Mom, what's going on?"

"I can't even say it," moaned Ana, letting her grief out.

*   *   *

For Doc's daughter's funeral, all the members of the community gathered for a last good-bye. Everyone mourned the one young, and people were soul stricken by death. It was so wrong! Doc and his wife were good people and caring parents, and they had been raising their girl to be a decent woman. Nobody blamed them for the tragedy—nobody except themselves. They knew it was because of teenage moods and wild hormones, and that now it was too late to avoid the worst. The devastating loss was already an irreversible fact, by which Ana was deeply shaken.

"May her soul rest in peace," uttered the priest, and with those words he sent Doc's daughter to a better world. The grief became the latest resident of the hippodrome.

After the funeral Ana went to her hairdresser and cut her hair short. Gazing into the reflection of her depressed face in the mirror, she made a fundamental decision to spend as much time as possible with Lilly. Nothing else mattered now.

"You are incredibly lucky to have her."

Those words of Doc's had been imprinted in her mind. And he was absolutely right.

It was December, and winter holidays were ahead, yet Ana uncharacteristically had not a clue what they would do or where would they go this year. Then an unusual plan came to her mind, which even at the last minute she managed to arrange. Because it had long been Lilly's dream to visit Egypt and the pyramids, Ana booked a trip for the two of them. And that was her daughter's Christmas gift.

"Wow, that's awesome!" Naturally the girl was beyond thrilled. That same evening she watched the movie *The Mummy* . . . again.

In Egypt they went camel riding, joined a dusty road trip around the desert, experienced an unforgettable day of scuba diving in the Red Sea reefs, and relaxed with an exclusive coconut spa treatment—which they thought of as strictly female stuff. On the trip, Lilly had her first period and became a woman. Life was almost the same as it was before the tragedy. They spent New Year's Eve in Hurghada by the sea. At midnight Ana had one and only one wish: *Our guardian angels up above, please look down on us with all your love, watch over us both day and night, and guide us with your precious light!*

For Lilly that trip was memorable; for Ana it was memorable and reviving. Her spirit started recovering little by little. Apparently, her daughter's love was the best therapy possible. Somewhere between the mighty pyramids of Cairo, or the mummies in the museum of antiquities, or the Red Sea beach, Ana rediscovered her lost optimism in Lilly's joy.

Flying home, Ana remembered the lesson of wisdom she had already learned in life: *Sometimes bad things happen to good people unexpectedly. Just like that.* She was feeling much stronger after the retreat, as if her courage had returned. However, organizing the racing season alone without the Doc's support . . . that was beyond her capabilities.

*   *   *

All the same, he would need time to recover, so Ana gathered their team for the season's first regular brief alone.

"It was a mournful December, and it's over. Happy New Year, everyone!"

People politely responded to her salute.

"Let's hope it will be a fortunate year," she continued, "and let's hope Doc can overcome his grief soon. Now it's a matter of survival for him. He'll need time, and he'll also need our backing as colleagues and friends. So let's unite to cover his absence in front of the tenants and headquarters. As a team we have to stand up for each other, right?"

Everybody agreed. Loyalty was not a stranger at the hippodrome.

"Perfect. Now let's distribute his obligations among us."

It took awhile before Doc got back to work. During the first months following the tragedy, Ana later learned he was trying to drown his sorrow in liquor. Of course, it was extremely hard for him to carry on after the loss. Mention of his daughter's name invariably filled his eyes with tears. People have said that the toughest thing in life is for a parent to live longer than his child. And regrettably, the humorous veterinarian with a big heart had to personally experience that doom.

When Doc realized that drinking was killing him, he quit alcohol for good. In search of answers and looking for faith, he found a mentor in the far former Soviet Republic of Kyrgyzstan. By following that wise man's advice, and by strictly practicing a personalized daily regime of physical and mental exercises, Doc came back to reality one step at a time. His "master," as he referred to his mentor, helped him tremendously, profoundly saving not only Doc's soul but also his wife's.

Ana was very happy to welcome her fellow colleague back to work.

"Good morning, my friend." She warmly hugged him. "Tea is served."

Two cups on his favorite selection were steaming on the table. Doc took one of them, smelled the fragrance of the herbs, and slowly sipped. Then he put the cup aside to speak.

"If you were a man, you would have such big balls," he said, making a gesture with both hands fisted.

For him "big balls" meant courage. In the past, Ana would have laughed at his comparison, though this time it wasn't funny at all. "I mean it," he added, reconfirming what both already knew.

Ana thanked him and uncomfortably changed the subject. "The Collector wants me to come to the headquarters tomorrow. I wonder what he has on his mind."

"This time I have a bad feeling," said Doc.

Chapter 27

THE GREED

The first signs of the global financial crisis took the world aback, and naturally the Collector was on alert. Led by his eagerness to cash out and collect as many personal benefits as possible before the collapse, he started reorganizing his companies like pieces on a chessboard. The human factor was of no importance to him; above all he had to outlast the crisis with as little personal damage as possible.

"By the way," he said nonchalantly when Ana came into his office. "We'll have to use the hippodrome's land as collateral for some bank loans."

"We? Why? We don't need loans. All we need is the resort," replied Ana. "Yet now's not the right time for expanding the complex. We'll lie low for a couple of years. The hippodrome can support itself without racing events."

"You don't get it. I said *as collateral*. We'll use the loans not for the hippodrome's matters; they will favor our"—and that meant his—"other companies. When they get over the cash flow difficulties, everything will be paid back. The property will be only an additional guarantee . . . for the bank management's assurance. Consider it helping others in need."

"But what if they fail to pay back?" asked Ana in alarm.

"I told you—it is just a temporary arrangement!" emphasized the Collector. Her persistence annoyed him. Once the money was within sight nothing could stand in his way, and explanations like these were simply a waste of time. However, she was still insisting.

"The hippodrome doesn't need all these complications. It's too dangerous. We might lose it if others are not careful or not able to cover their payments. I don't agree with actions like these."

"You don't agree?!" said the Collector with a look of disdain.

"Yes, this is not fair. We can survive a recession if you let us do it our way. Afterward we can follow through with the resort's project eventually. Yes, I know it might take years. So what? We'll cut the expenses until the uproar is over. The competitions will have to wait, and subsequently we'll lose the momentum of recent publicity. Yet this is not a big problem. If we did it once we can do it again. One day when the market levels out, we can catch up quickly. Please, don't jeopardize the whole project!"

Ugh, this no cooperative attitude was beginning to piss him off.

"We're using the land! Your father will have to sign the papers," the Collector stated firmly.

"No, this is not right!"

Her outrageous behavior was way too much. Her personal opinions would not abort the execution of his major plan.

"As you know I can replace him with the snap of my fingers!" he hissed.

"But this is not what we agreed on in the beginning of our project! You gave me your word!"

"Well, times have changed. The crisis is coming, and we need the land!" The Collector was demanding—no more explaining. Then he changed his tone to a calmer one. "Hey, you can stop overreacting. Nothing will happen. We'll keep the hippodrome, no worries."

Shortly thereafter Mr. G was quietly dismissed as chairman of the board of the National Hippodrome, and his position was assigned to a bookkeeper from the Collector's headquarters. Then the bookkeeper signed the documents permitting the hippodrome's property to be used as collateral for loans worth more than thirty million euros. The Collector stepped back from financing races, and ably the general sponsor took control over them, transferring the

Jockey Club's functions to his company. And with that swift swap, Ana was summarily isolated from the breeding community.

By the end of the year 2008 the financial crisis had furiously flooded the global markets. Ana's country was stricken too. The real estate market collapsed. Banks became neurotic. When after three months the Collector's companies' regular payments stopped, Ana got anxious about the hippodrome.

"What's going on? We've received a hostile letter from the bank asking for immediate covering of the loans."

"Yes, I was told as much," the Collector confirmed without emotion. Then he repeated as a mantra: "It's a provisional complication. We want to renegotiate the loan terms, that's all. Tell everybody to remain calm. We'll deal with the situation."

Ana considered his last words. Was he really going to find a solution? Based on his reputation among rich and influential people, the bank would likely prefer to keep him as a corporate client and to accept his conditions—or at least most of them. He was somebody, after all! So Ana chose to believe the bargain could go well. Moreover in her opinion, the hippodrome was a worthy cause, containing a realistic opportunity for him to make a lot more money from the project in the future.

Yet some doubts lingered in her mind: What about the timing? Was he willing to wait? Were his other companies solvent? So far she knew only that part of the loans had been applied to covering the new jets' mortgages, though the rest of the information was totally classified. Then the next question came to her.

"What about me?" she said aloud.

"What about you? Relax and do your job," answered the Collector.

"And what about my royalty? I believe I deserve some guarantees."

"Here we go again. What guarantees do you want, Ana?" He stared at her with genuine vexation.

"I don't know . . . Maybe you could give me assets in your last building endeavor, for example."

"Where, in Avalon?"

"Yes," confirmed Ana. She was a smart woman, asking not for cash but for square meters. Avalon was a new building complex that had just been launched in the suburbs of the capital; only a few apartments had been sold. Therefore, hers was a manageable, appropriate, and most importantly, cash-free solution. Ana watched the Collector quickly scaling the margins in his head: 3–4 percent of her royalty would be the equivalent of about . . . three apartments.

"Fine, fine," he said, clearly sick of listening and intent on making her shut up.

"Wonderful, thank you."

Ana cheered up as the Collector called the project's executive and conveyed to her the details of "Ana's guarantees." Even though the bargain was pretty complicated—requiring lots of calls to headquarters—in the end Ana was affirmed as the owner of three exclusive apartments. It was stated on paper, signed, and sealed. Now all she had to do was peacefully wait.

Chapter 28

THE PLAYBOY

Summertime at the seaside . . . So far it was a mélange of total relaxation, short skirts, and an around-the-clock lark. After the worries about the hippodrome, a vacation was exactly what Ana had needed to recharge her batteries. She was resting with Lilly and a lady friend in a small town located on a scenic bay along the southern coast of the country. It was such an idyllic place, distinguished by much historical significance. In the fifth century the old burg used to be protected by massive fortress walls, the remnants of which were still preserved at the southeastern end of the peninsula. At night they were picturesquely illuminated, together with the wall-walk along the parapet. Ana loved to have dinner with her friends at one charming restaurant there—just a few steps above the swashing waves, and under the star-spangled sky. Simply bliss!

Inside the fortress more than 180 monumental buildings, constructed in the middle of the eighteenth and the beginning of the nineteenth century, were nestled tight—all of them made of stone and wood, with narrow cobbled streets in between. The ambience of that authentic part was unique—artistic and sacred at the same time. It was declared to be a museum-reserve. In the very heart of it a small church from the tenth century hid. On a rainy day, when the beach was not one of their preferred destinations, Ana and her pals waited in a long pilgrims' queue so as to honor saints with a prayer and a candle. Afterward Lilly had the privilege of choosing a souvenir from the local art market. A few years before it would have been a ring, or a nacre necklace; however now, she was keener on a temporary tattoo. Certainly, she was thirteen.

One evening friends invited the two adults to dinner at an Italian-style restaurant called Arté, known for its exquisite cuisine. That night a famous touring chef was cooking. The restaurant was quite a romantic place, enchantingly decorated with statues and lots of flowers. When Ana walked inside, Connie Francis's "Stupid Cupid" was playing over the audio system.

"Welcome, guys. Listen to this," one of their friends said. "Once upon a time three brothers were living together with their father. When the father died, they decided to leave home in search of fortune. They made a solemn vow: Every one of them, when drinking, should drink for the three of them! Then they hit the road. Soon the eldest one found a decent job and a nice woman in a small town, and settled down. Every day after work he used to pop up at the local bar on his way home.

"'Three shots of vodka, please,' he would say.

"As every time he was making the same order, the bartender became curious.

"'Hey, why do you order three shots at once? Why don't you order one, and then another as others do?'

"'Well, I made a vow,' answered the eldest brother, then told him the reason why.

"Day after day he repeated the same ritual, until one day . . .

"'Two shots of vodka, please.'

"The bartender was surprised. 'Oh, I'm sorry, dude. Something bad must have happened to one of your brothers!'

"'Oh, no, not at all. I have just quit drinking.'"

Everyone laughed at that, as they ordered vodka themselves. At the next table two men were also snickering at the joke. One of them was familiar with Ana's host.

"Dude, we are going to the beach bar afterward. Come on over," he offered.

So later on the tipsy company arrived at the beach bar in good spirits and with a certain desire to dance. On a second glance Ana noted that one of the two men looked much the part of a classic middle-aged playboy—dressed stylishly, a little pretentious, and already drunk. His buddy was slightly younger, a sporty type of man with a dash of machismo.

"Girls, girls, over here," they said, swiftly offering Ana and her friend glasses.

"Those chicks over there have some designs on us," remarked the Playboy, pointing at some blondes on the left.

"Oh, really? Why would they?" Ana smiled.

"Isn't it obvious? Because we are supermen!" he replied. "With additional solid weapons."

He winked at Ana, carefully paying attention to her reaction. It was, she could tell, very important to him that she got the hint. Then the Playboy continued.

"One day Superman is flying around the city, feeling a bit horny. He suddenly sees Wonder Woman, spread-eagle and naked on top of a building. Superman thinks, *This is my chance!* He swoops down, faster than a speeding bullet, bangs her quick, and is gone in the blink of an eye. Wonder Woman sits up and says, 'What the hell was that!?' Then the invisible man rolls off her with the words, 'I have no idea, but it hurt like hell!'"

Ana laughed. This guy was behaving like a typical male moving full tilt through a middle-age crisis. What was his deal exactly? Well, as he soon explained, he was recently divorced and now enjoying his liberty "in every legal way."

The rest of the night was pleasant and amusing. Both supermen had great sense of humor, and the combination of their personalities was truly entertaining. After a dozen songs, one more shot, and lots of fun, it was time for Ana and her friend to go home.

"Will you give me your number, Ana? I want to see you again," said the Playboy.

For a second she considered the hazards. Secretly she had been observing his behavior the whole time, scanning for any sign of aggressiveness. After dealing with the Diplomat, she was very touchy about that. Luckily she had not detected a bit.

Why not? she thought, and dictated her digits to him.

The next day the Playboy called and invited her out for lunch, but Ana had other plans. So he insisted on dinner, and knowing she could leave Lilly with her friend, she accepted. Ana chose a lovely dress for the occasion—a white one with purple flowers, and a big belt enhancing her waist.

At eight p.m., the Playboy smoothly parked his cabriolet next to her.

"Get in, gorgeous," he said, opening the door for her. Yes, he was well-mannered.

Ana had a great time that evening, and so did he. The Playboy appeared to be clever, jocular, and a genuine gentleman—a quality she valued a lot. He was active in sports like skiing and golf, and he was the type of person who was always full of energy.

"Let's go dancing," he suggested after dinner.

"Okay, I love to dance," she said, and she really did.

When he brought her home early in the morning, he gently embraced her with candid affection. Ana responded in kind since. The attraction was mutual.

"I'm traveling next weekend. Will call you when I'm back," he said, then wished her sweet dreams.

The next Monday, he kept his word, and after a few more dates, lots of conversations, and hours of exploring, they became an item. "Have you heard the Playboy has a new girlfriend?" was the hot gossip circulating around. He was an appealing person, popular and well-connected, with tons of friends everywhere. According to his habitual life, they went out a lot, almost every night. Ana had never had such a high-speed social life before. She was well accepted in his circle, and she enjoyed meeting new, intriguing people and even creating friendships.

During her first visit to the Playboy's home, a random fact surfaced. He lived in the same suburbs as Avalon, right next to the plot where the new complex's construction had begun. Even though the noise and dust coming from there was irritating, deep inside Ana was celebrating. Her embattled apartments were rising right before her eyes. Standing by the window with a cup of hot coffee, she was already decorating her future home in her mind.

So far everything in their relationship was going without a hitch. They were fond of each other, and Lilly liked the Playboy as well. He had a cabriolet, and she was just a superficial teenager. Besides, she had never really spent time with her father, and interacting with somebody like him naturally spellbound her. On her behalf, Ana was satisfied. After the past few years of hard work and single parenting, now she was craving some sweet thrills in her life. Without the races she was finally able to invest her time and emotions in this auspicious affair. So day after day, the romance that had started after a couple of vodka shots grew into a love story.

It came with the territory that the Playboy was very open about sex. "A broad-minded person with no modesty whatsoever" was how he described himself. He was not afraid of experiments, and fortunately Ana kept pace with him pretty well. She was an ardent woman, with a body designed for sins. After fifteen years of working out in the gym she was as fit as a girl. Due to breastfeeding Lilly and losing lots of weight during the nightmare, she was unsatisfied with her breasts, but she quickly fixed that disadvantage with implants. The Playboy marked her body-tuning with a party.

Under his influence Ana started dressing extravagantly and even lustfully, boosting up her feminine luminance and style. All her friends commented she looked better than ever. And naturally the Playboy was cocky about it. Hey, he was suppose to be banging a wonder woman after all.

"Let's fly to London next week, darling. I wanna take you to a musical," he said one autumn morning, embracing her around the waist.

"Really?"

"Yup, and the rest of the time we'll go sightseeing and shopping—you need new garter belts for your legs—and we'll meet some friends. How about that plan?"

She gladly accepted with enthusiasm. Sharing the same passion for traveling was such a gift.

Their stay in England was incredible—enthralling and amorous. The Playboy was generous with gifts, compliments, and promises. He described their future full of joy and roses.

"Would you like to be my princess?" he asked.

Well, it would be a lie if someone claimed Ana had said no to that.

One evening they watched the musical *Wicked*. It was a wonderful performance. After the show, while crossing Piccadilly Circus, Ana consciously opened her heart to him. Tightly holding his hand, she let her guard down, and felt butterflies in her rib cage. She was elated! She was in love! Instantly Ana realized how much she had been missing that genuine sense of connection with a man.

"I hope we will last, darling," she whispered, and the Playboy agreed.

Later on they made love for the first time. It was not simply sex, but something more sensual and alluring.

For New Year's, the Playboy swept her away to the island of Koh Samui, and afterward Bangkok. Namaste, Ana was very excited to taste Asia for the first time in her life. The beautiful nature, amazing temples, and brilliant food fascinated her. Altogether it would have been the perfect vacation if only the Playboy had not being receiving dozens of calls from an unknown number that he was not willing to answer in her presence.

"Who's that?" she asked one day, looking at his silently vibrating phone.

"Oh, that? I don't care," he said.

But based on his reactions, Ana knew that he did. Yet she decided to give him time to deal with his "I don't care" situation.

*   *   *

Back at work in the middle of January, during their lunch break, Ana showed Doc photos from Thailand.

"It was about time to let somebody in your life, Ana," remarked the veterinarian. He was glad to see her pleased. Then he leaned closer and whispered, "I have splendid news. My wife is expecting a boy."

"Really, that's so . . . so . . . oh, Doc, I'm so happy for you." She hugged him very tight, and her eyes got misty. Hallelujah, her friend was blessed with hope. And then, Doc made a joke.

"He is going to have a big peepee like his dad. The echography was yesterday. I have proof!"

Ana smiled at him with glee. Finally, Doc was merry.

*   *   *

That year's traditional St. Theodore's races were bursting with horses, music, and acrobats. It was a celebration of life. And Ana had a special guest—the Playboy.

"Well done, darling. I'm very impressed."

"Thanks, we love what we do. Come on, let me introduce you to Doc," she said, taking his hand. It was a cold February day, and she wore a long fur coat in leopard print with a black belt.

"My lovely princess," the Playboy complimented.

Suddenly his phone rang. With half a glance he turned the sound off and put it back in his pocket as if nothing happened.

"Why don't you answer?" asked Ana.

"I don't want to talk right now," he replied and turned to Doc.

They exchanged courtesies, and then the Playboy excused himself. He had to rush home to pack for a weeklong trip in Turkey. As a passionate golfer, he was going to participate in the upcoming international Pro-Am in Belek. Due to her business and parenting duties, Ana would not be able to join him for a whole week. She could afford only a weekend away. And frankly, it was getting harder for her to roll along with him all the time.

When she arrived in Turkey, the Playboy met her at the airport with the question.

"Guess what?"

Evidently his buddy had met an amazing Russian woman; the tournament was going well; and he had arranged a golf lesson for Ana the next day. She was willing to learn the game, despite the fact that he had warned her it was very complicated.

"So what?" she said. "If others can do it, so can I."

The Playboy underlined that the Russian newcomer was not only beautiful, but also an excellent golfer. Oh, and she had five kids.

"Really?" Ana was impressed. "Can't wait to meet her!"

"Tonight, darling, we'll have dinner together."

With delight Ana saw for herself that the woman, Anastasia, had good looks but was also smart, positive, and proficient. She was about her age, and they talked a little, mingling Russian and English expressions. Ana appreciated Anastasia's personality a lot. When over time she got to know her better, Ana liked her even more. The Russian Anastasia quite fit the term "настоящий человек"—a saying that could not be translated in English with two words only. It meant an integrated person with a generous heart and high morals—a genuine one.

Soon after the Pro-Am, Anastasia arrived in their hometown. The Playboy's buddy was more than thrilled. Right away she was properly introduced to their many friends and taken to the most exclusive restaurants and bars in the capital. Thereafter they went skiing.

Ana was very glad to see her new friend Anastasia again, yet she had no spare time for lollygagging. Contrary to the Playboy, who was never very occupied, Ana was putting out fires left and right at home and work. Even though she cared about him and loved spending time with their friends, primarily she was a mother and the hippodrome's patroness. And there was heat on all fronts.

Firstly, her sweet Lilly had transformed into a fourteen-year-old demon Lilith. For Ana it was something new to witness her daughter's weird moods and rebellions, to personally taste how mean she could be when arguing. It hurt a lot. Since Ana had started dating the Playboy, her parents were supervising Lilly when she was abroad, which the girl didn't like at all. Actually, she no longer liked to be supervised by her mom either. When she switched saying "I don't like . . ." out for "I hate . . .," Ana was on alert. What was going on in her girl's head?

Now Lilly was in her first year of French high school. As she was an open and communicative kid, she quickly made lots of friends there. Fortunately there were no drugs or crimes at the school, yet most of the students were a bit nihilistic, hanging around and wasting their time. They shunned sports, hobbies, even ambition itself. Soon Lilly quit dancing and put on some weight. Moreover, studying dropped down in her list of priorities. Ana became worried—an empty soul was ruinous too. She had to spend more time with the girl! But how? The Playboy's agenda was consuming most of her free time. She knew she had to find a way, no matter what.

Secondly, the government's attention was focused on the hippodrome. The mayor of the capital had become prime minister of the country, and his hometown was to be equipped with a modern sewage system as a part of the global national project. So far so good, though the pipes had to go through the hippodrome's property, and Ana was in charge of dealing with the authorities. The Collector had assigned her to earn benefits for the burg. Fortunately, the authorities were very cooperative and accepted most of their terms. As usual nobody from the headquarters saluted Ana. Doc did.

As a result of the collaboration with the government, the bank was cautiously keeping her dogs tied up. Messing with a national project's execution was not a smart move.

And so, during the day, Ana sped between the hippodrome and the Collector's headquarters, and in the evenings she accompanied the Playboy to his activities. Lilly fit somewhere in between. It was difficult to juggle. Ana's presence was crucial both at home and at work, but instead she found herself packing all the time—and this time for Palma de Mallorca. While stowing her small black dress in her suitcase, a sense of guilt started growing in her mind like a weed.

You have to settle, Anché! You have to do it!

Therefore, when they returned, she declared to the Playboy, "I need to rest, and I need to spend more time with Lilly. Please, let's stay home more often."

"Okay, we'll stay home tomorrow. And we'll take Lilly with us next weekend to the countryside."

Apparently that was his idea of staying home more often, and of parenting a teenager.

*　　*　　*

Soon after a short trip to Vienna in May, they scheduled a proper voyage for Ana's birthday. They would cross southern Italy to Saint-Tropez in France, with a romantic stop in Venice. While driving his sports car, the Playboy's phone rang. He didn't pick up. It rang again, and again . . .

"Who's that? Why you don't answer? Why has this same number been calling you for months?" Ana was frustrated.

"It's not a he. It's a *she* . . . my ex-girlfriend," admitted the Playboy.

"Fine. I understand you have a past life, but why don't you answer?"

"It's complicated," said the Playboy before quickly changing the subject. "Isn't this seaside panorama magnificent?"

"Are you having an affair?" Ana asked outright.

"How can I have an affair if I'm always with you?"

But was the answer yes or no? Ana was perplexed.

At dusk, floating in a gondola through the canals of Venice with a bottle of champagne, Ana said, "I have to admit, that there's no other place like Venice. When I get old, I'll come here to write a book." It seemed the striking environment had awakened her imagination.

The Playboy just looked at her and superficially marked, "And me? I would like to grow old like Hugh Hefner, surrounded by young bunnies."

"You do?" Ana asked, baffled.

"Yes, why not?" Obviously, his princess was already out of the picture.

"And what about the real things in life?"

He didn't reply. This exchange remained recorded in Ana's head forever. What was happening with them? Was it in the secret calls? Or it was something else? She wanted to know the answers, and at the beginning of the autumn, Ana turned to their mutual friend, Sarah, for an opinion.

Sarah had known the Playboy longer, so she was familiar with his past relationships. It was about time for Ana to get some clarity.

"Something's wrong. He never stopped receiving calls from his ex-girlfriend. Is she really an 'ex'?"

They were drinking smoothies in the pastry shop near Sarah's office.

"I don't think so," was her unfortunate answer. "She is the one who ruined his family. That bitch used to call him in the same impudent way in his wife's presence, until the woman finally asked for a divorce. And now the same thing is happening to you . . ."

"I don't get it. Why is he letting her do this?"

"Well, they have something in common. And it's been going on for years," replied Sarah.

"What are you talking about?" asked Ana, not getting it at all.

"Ugh . . . They are both addicted to kinky sex, group experiences, stuff like that."

"What?!" Ana's brain jumped like a monkey from one branch to another, comparing facts, phrases, memories, suspicions . . . Blimey, they *were* still doing it. In her hands the strawberry smoothie's flavor turned into swill. That was the taste of indignation.

"Will he ever change?" she asked, though she knew the answer.

"I don't know, dear," Sarah responded tactfully, looking at her with compassion.

She had just diagnosed Ana's relationship with a severe form of cancer. The end was near.

CHAPTER 29

THE FORFEITURE

Before she even got a chance to properly talk with the Playboy about his affair, Ana was hit over the head with a change in circumstances at the hippodrome. With the sewage project complete, the bank was craving the land.

"Mobilize everyone, do not travel anywhere, notify me about every unusual letter or visit," instructed the Collector. It was a full alert situation.

"Roger!" confirmed Ana, who next dialed the Playboy. "I want to talk to you. It's very important!"

"Sure, I'll pick you up for dinner."

That evening Ana was not looking as fresh as usual. She was nervous and tense.

"It's about the hippodrome," she said between courses. At her request, they were left alone by the staff for a time. "You know how much I care about that project . . . and my team . . . Well, they are in great jeopardy. A tussle is coming, and it's going to be a tough one. We all have to become warriors to protect the burg. So I won't be able to travel, and if I may speak honestly, I'm afraid you will have to deal with the amazon part of me, which might cause you some troubles."

"What do you mean, darling?"

"Well, I'll be stressed, restless, and probably sometimes angry . . ."

"But I've told you I don't want troubles in my life," he said, if not a little indelicately. It was true, however; he had stated that many times.

174

"Nobody wants them, but sometimes they just come. And we have to react, right? I believe we should stand up for what we care about, don't you agree?" Ana was thinking out loud. Then she paused for a second and said, "Consider it a test—when troubles come, some people stay, some people leave."

She stared at him with a questioning look on her face, as if she was going to ask, "What will you do, darling?"

"But of course, you can count on me," replied the Playboy, who then hastily ordered dessert.

A week later he left.

Meanwhile, Lilly's attitude was worsening. She had dyed her hair bright red. Even though she had been the Playboy's sweetie before he left, obviously she was not pleased to be neglected by her mom due to Ana's relation with him. So Lilly invented an supreme way to gain Ana's attention straightaway: by pissing her off. It always worked, and she was getting better at it each day. Squabbles became more and more frequent, and despite how extremely unpleasant they were for both of them, it seemed that arguing had become an inevitable part of their communication. Lilly had become the embodiment of the Latin expression "spiritus contraria." With time her favorite word became *no*, her friends' opinions became supreme, and almost every conversation with her included the phrase "I'm not a kid anymore." Bloody hormones! But was that the only thing to blame? Where was Lilly's lovely sparkle? Ana started blaming herself for not being a good mom.

I have to fix this. I have to do something! And I have to do it soon, otherwise it might be too late! she thought.

The anxiety was disrupting her sleep, her mind, and her heart. Something had to change!

*   *   *

Soon, one gloomy November day in 2010, cloudy and cold, Ana was sent to the hippodrome on the most obnoxious assignment she had ever been forced to do. Exactly six years ago, she had driven here full of aspiration and ambition, and humbly introduced herself to the burg.

"Hello, dear land!" She would always remember her words spoken at the end of the alley.

Yet today . . . today she had to give up on everything. Instead of fixing the problems with the bank, the Collector had lost the case. Now the bailiff, his assistant, and the bank counselors were coming to do an inventory and to overtake the management of the property. As its director, it was Ana's obligation to let them in, to show them around, and to receive the forfeiture documents. Sad, sad November!

All dressed in black, she walked around the stables, paddocks, tribunes, and tracks with her head down, followed by the uninvited delegates. To her, she was not only giving away the land and the facilities, but also capitulating her dreams for the glamorous races, the vision of a beautiful riding resort, and Larry's grave. A cruel sacrifice she could barely bear!

After a few hours the immolation was complete, and one of the Collector's lawyers adopted the expropriation papers.

Totally spent, Ana dialed the Collector. "It's done."

"Come over here!" he commanded her.

Apparently she had to brief him. When Ana told him all the details of the forfeiture, his face turned gray. His eyes sparkled with anger.

"We won't give up! We'll appeal or we'll induce a new case. They might have won the battle, but the war is not over yet!"

Ana sat across the desk with no energy left.

"Can I go now?" she quietly asked.

"Sure, go, call me tomorrow."

Finally, she was able to hide somewhere in private. She locked the door to her home, took a hot shower, and made herself a cup of tea. Lilly was out with her friends.

What a cold day today, thought Ana. She was feverish. While sitting there alone in silence and dark, a conclusion just came to her: *Screw the Collector, and screw the Playboy! I'll take Lilly to meet her father!*

CHAPTER 30

SOMEWHERE IN LATIN AMERICA

Somewhere in Latin America, a man waited at the airport, eager to see his daughter after twelve long years of separation. His imagination was filled with overlapping pictures of a glowing baby face. Last time he saw Lilly she was a bit more than two. And now the little girl had grown to be fourteen years old.

I wonder what is she like now . . . he was thinking. He had seen photos of her and had spoken to her on the phone, yet to hold her in his arms . . . that hadn't had happened in more than a decade. Would she run toward him the way she used to when she was a kid? How would she address him now? It had been "Papsy" back then. He had many questions, though he would have to start with a basic one: Would they land on time? Air traffic was quite busy in December. The timetable clearly showed that their flight was going to be late.

Damn it, more waiting, as if twelve years was not enough, he thought. He frowned and went out for some fresh air.

Meanwhile, on the plane somewhere over the Atlantic Ocean, Ana was telling her daughter the unspoken facts of her father's life story. She had decided that Lilly was mature enough to face the truth. So Ana started from the very beginning, when Lilly's parents first met.

"Then he took me to the American restaurant."

"Really?" the girl marveled.

"Uh-huh," Ana said, smiling. "And he was driving a shining red BMW."

"Cool!" Lilly was at an age where she fancied cars.

Ana added more details about their marriage, the posh celebration in Paris. She recounted the peaceful months near the Eiffel Tower, before and after the happiest moment of her "Little Mermaid's" birth. Lilly listened carefully. During their previous visits to Paris they had dropped by all those significant places—their former home, Hôtel de Aigles, Champ de Mars . . . and now she could recall it all.

Ana shared her disappointment over the nasty environment she found in the motherland after her return; described the national catastrophe; then explained the dramatic changes that it brought to her father's business and reputation. She ended with the events during the nightmare, outlining the factors that had provoked Lilly's father to run away.

After a few seconds, the girl chimed in with typical teenage criticism: "So he abandoned us, huh?"

"Well, he had no other choice. He had to disappear in order to stay alive. Ever since, he has missed us a lot. Trust me, he cares about us, and about you especially."

"Yeah, right," remarked the girl sarcastically. "Don't forget that I live with you, Mom, and I know everything. I'm not a kid anymore.

He hasn't supported us financially or in any other way. If he missed us as much as you say, he could have sent us tickets to visit him at least once. But all I hear from him are excuses. Come on, Mom, really? He only phones from time to time, talking about the past or giving irrational advice nobody asks for. Is this what you call 'care'?"

"Oh, kiddo, haven't you ever missed him at all?"

"But how could I miss something I never had?"

"Okay, I understand you. Let me put it this way: Aren't you glad to meet him?"

"Well . . . it's kind of ridiculous. He's a stranger to me, claiming to be my loving dad. How am I supposed to act? Or to feel? I'm not even familiar with him. And frankly, I don't find him pally."

Ana remained silent. She had to admit that Lilly had some good reasons not to respect her father. Yet for the girl's welfare, she insisted.

"At least give him a chance. Be kind, please!"

"Fine, Mom, no worries," Lilly said, then put on her headphones.

The plane landed after more than an hour-long delay. It was hot and humid outside. When mother and daughter walked into the arrivals area with two big suitcases, the man standing in the corner recognized them immediately and ran toward them with a happy face. He first hugged Ana.

"Finally! I can't believe you came!"

"Good to see you, Papsy," Ana replied joyfully. Then she turned to the teenager on her left. "And this is Lilly."

"Wow, my big girl!" he exclaimed, warmly embracing his daughter.

Ana smiled. They looked like a bear holding a chicken. In her dad's arms, Lilly blinked in bewilderment, confused and at the same time tired from the extended travel. She acted friendly and politely, yet distant. Manifestly she was dealing with many mixed emotions.

"You'll have plenty of time to get to know each other," said Ana. "We better rest now."

Grabbing the luggage, Papsy led them outside to a silver Toyota and fit their bags in the trunk. Ana took the front seat, and Lilly shoved herself into the back. While driving home the man tried to cheer them up.

"Hey, a friend of mine told me a story the other day," he said, and he began reciting it with a lack of artistry. "Once an airplane was about to crash. A female passenger jumped up frantically and announced, 'If I'm gonna die, I wanna die feeling like a real woman.' Then she removed all her clothing, asking, 'Is there anyone on this plane who is man enough to make me feel like a real woman?' A nearby man stood up, removed his shirt, and said, 'Here, iron this!'"

From the backseat Lilly was silently observing him. While Ana was laughing, Lilly turned to her father humorlessly.

"And you find this amusing?"

"Yes, don't you?" he responded.

"Hmm," was her counter. Obviously she didn't. And it was not only this joke she was sullen about; later she told her mother that it was because she didn't like him in general—either his appearance or attitude. He was an average person, much fatter and much older than she expected. He drove an ordinary car, and on top of that, he was boring.

"From the pictures he seems fine, but in real life he is kind of bland," Lilly whispered to Ana before sleep. They were sharing a separate bedroom. "Actually he reminds me of Grandpa very much."

"Yes, I've noticed it too," whispered back Ana.

The similarity between Papsy and his father was clear, and it was not only physical. They both had an aged mind-set. Whilst the girls' life so far had been as hectic as a roller coaster, Papsy's long-term exile had naturally affected his whole personality. He had become an introvert, living in solitude day after day. For him time seemed to be moving in slow motion, and he was kind of stuck in the past. The Internet was his only salvation because he worked online from home. In Ana's opinion, such sustained ostracism was way too heavy a punishment for what he had done.

But what had he done precisely? Long ago the authorities had accused him of three charges, based on malfeasance and embezzlement. So far only the first one, for which he was arrested thirteen years ago, had reached a verdict: not guilty. However, the second and the third accusations were still in process. Who knew how long it would take for the tribunal to finalize them! Fifteen, twenty years, or more? At the end of that mess his life would be totally wasted.

By noon the next day, Ana was wondering what would happen before the end of the trip. Was Lilly going to let her father into her tender zone? Or would she keep the door to her inner world locked against him? So far she was reacting indifferently to all his attempts to hug or kiss her. Ana had never seen her holding her hands in her pockets so consistently. It was bizarre.

"Why are you acting like this?" Ana asked her in private.

"He's interfering with my comfort zone, Mom," answered the girl. Apparently to her, Papsy was still a stranger.

"You should interact with him more. No one can tell when you'll be able to meet him again," Ana encouraged her.

"But why should I?" Lilly was in a contrary mood. She was finding it more amusing to chat with friends on the Internet than talk to her father. Pity, the number of days with him was so limited.

"Hey, let's go hiking!" he tactically suggested one morning, hoping the teenager would loosen up a bit in the outdoors.

That strategy worked. They went into the mountains to a gorgeous wildlife sanctuary, where, in the heart of the rain forest, Lilly's mood lightened. She loved the giant trees, the hummingbirds, and all those bright colors. At the same time, the waterfalls fascinated Ana. She felt if there everything was connected, genuine, and mighty, as if they had been teleported into the movie *Avatar*.

"Holy moly, that was quite an adventure," Lilly said, much more jolly on the way back. She was holding a small souvenir bought as a keepsake—a plaque with the words "pura viva" limned onto it.

"I'm very tired," she then admitted when they returned to the house, so she grabbed a snack and went to bed early.

There were only the two adults when Ana commented, "The idea of 'pure life' is so tempting. But if I shared it with the Collector he would say I was going nuts."

"So tell me, what has actually happened to the hippodrome? Is it currently expropriated?" asked Papsy.

Then Ana told him everything about it.

"Hmm, that means the Collector cheated you," he concluded.

"It looks so," she confirmed with sorrow.

"Bastard!" fumed Papsy. "When I was tops he was asking me for favors." Then he dove into unnecessary explanations of how it used to be more than twenty years ago. The list of reasons his life had been stolen from him was long. He returned to bygone events again, blaming one or the other, but never himself. Words, words, words . . ."And now my daughter hates me," he said.

"Listen, why don't you go out, just the two of you?" suggested Ana. "Spend some quality time together. Try to treat her like an adult, don't patronize her. She's very sensitive to not being handled like a kid."

"But she's avoiding me!"

"I see it. But you are the mature one and you have to try to soften her. Be tolerant, that's it."

He sighed deeply. "Okay, I'll figure it out somehow."

Regrettably, he didn't.

The three of them spent Christmas at home strictly following their native traditions, and the next day they relaxed on the beach. After a little shopping and a little sightseeing, New Year's Eve came along. For their first time together in more than a decade, they went to the gala dinner at the nearby Intercontinental Hotel.

"Tell me, what do you like about your father most?" Ana asked her daughter just before midnight.

"I like that he listens to nice music," Lilly answered without hesitation.

"And . . . ?" There had to be more than this superficial statement. Ana was searching for some sentiment.

"That's it." The girl smiled, then promptly went to dance, leaving her mother to muse at the sparkling champagne in her glass.

Lilly's right, Ana thought. *Love is not granted by family name or chromosomes. It has to be earned. It's in mutuality, trust, concern, and tenderness. And we simply have to be present in order to provide all that. "Away from the eyes, apart from the heart," people say. And it's true.* She took a sip and looked at Papsy, a disappointed father.

A few days later it was time to go home. When Ana hugged him farewell at the airport, a few tears dropped on his collar.

"So long, Papsy," she whispered in his ear.

"Hey, thanks for coming . . . and for bringing Lilly with you. This was the best present I have ever received in my life."

The man spoke with a broken heart. Only God knew if he was going to ever see them again. Then he turned to his daughter.

"Bye, kiddo. Please take care of Mom. And behave!"

Well, the last part was questionable.

At the end he said to both of them, "You are always welcome here! Come again!"

"Maybe someday," replied Ana.

She waved at him for the last time before he faded away among the others.

*   *   *

On the plane Lilly was quiet.

"What's up, love?" asked Ana.

"Ugh, it's just . . . I carry his genes. Am I gonna become like him?"

"That would be up to you. DNA doesn't define one's identity. Rather, it comes from one's beliefs, one's life experiences, and one's brain evolution."

"You're sure?" Lilly saw the light at the end of the tunnel.

"One hundred percent positive, love! Sleep now—you're gonna be like me," said Ana, smiling. "Even better than me. I promise!"

CHAPTER 31

THE HOTEL

The Hotel was a ten-story building with simple architecture, not quite imposing or majestic, but at the same time one of the most significant edifices during the Socialist regime. Built in the heart of the capital over the expropriated land of a Jewish school, the Hotel became a supreme nest for the politburo of the Central Committee of the Communist Party. It opened its doors in 1962 under the superior surveillance of the government security services. Access to the building's premises, the first-class restaurant, and the luxury shop was restricted to the politburo's members and their families only. Rumors about the mysterious underground passages connecting the buildings of the Council of Ministers, the party's headquarters, and the Hotel itself circulated by word of mouth, and it was speculated that only a certain privileged group close to the superior leader had been allowed in those tunnels. He, of course, had a spacious personal suite at his disposal that took up almost half of the third floor. The word was that the leader had been visiting his chamber infrequently—only for unforeseen instances or an afternoon nap, and of course, always in total confidentiality.

Downstairs, in the vast plush restaurant on the ground floor, the best cooks of the time were installed to prepare all kinds of delights for the Communist Party elite. Only the highest quality, handpicked products were used. The Party's well-being and safety were of the highest priority. Thus, a modern laboratory had been equipped next to the kitchen area for agents to investigate the food's dependability. The Hotel was also chosen for the local senators to stay at during sessions of parliament. "Builders of the Socialist" was how they referred to themselves.

Later, alongside the local politicians (all of them party members), many foreign dignitaries and delegations also resided there. Names like the first astronauts Yuri Gagarin and Valentina Tereshkova, or the famous artists father and son Roerich, and many others were recorded in the long guest list. True, rumor had it that the Hotel's walls continued to keep many secrets.

After the end the Socialist regime, the local Jewish organization claimed restitution rights over the land. And according to the existing law the Supreme Court declared they should be compensated 49 percent of the Hotel, along with another building the next street over. The court had decided, yet the authorities did not budge. Standing on "the unclearness in the differentiation between the ideal parts and the real parts of the claim," the government offered neither monetary redress nor property returned. Instead the global auditing company KPMG, acting as mediator, offered the remaining 51 percent of the Hotel's state shares up for public privatization. And soon a new majority owner stepped into the game.

After years of waiting and complaining, the local Jewish community's patience had come to an end and the restitution offset turned into a serious international problem. In the year 2000 the Jewish lobby in the US had tied up the NATO invitation for the entire country in solving that Shalom casus. No more games; the heat was on. Immediately the other building was properly redressed. But what about the Hotel? That case remained in limbo. Naturally the lobby wasn't satisfied, and US President Clinton's special envoy on Holocaust issues got personally involved as a lawyer, though ultimately to no avail. Then in 2005 a journalist with a Jewish name wrote an article in the British *Telegraph* regarding the Hotel's case, quoting the same lawyer about the country: "Their inability to follow even their own court decisions indicates that they still have a long distance to travel before they reach the level of transparency and the rule of law."

In the same publication, the other councilor concluded: "If the rule of law is not applied, companies will not want to invest because they cannot be confident that their investments will be secure."

Well, what happened afterward would remind the world of an old story:

Once a rich Jewish family from New York went visiting relatives in a faraway country. The hosts acted kind and welcoming, and the guests had a great stay. When back in US, the family sent a courtesy telegram: "Dear relatives, everything was perfect. We would like to invite you over here." The relatives replied: "Thanks for the invitation. We would like to come. By the way, a teaspoon from grandma's precious set is missing. Do you have a clue?" "No," came back the short answer from New York. Half a year later the American Jewish family received another telegram from their relatives: "We have good news—the teaspoon was found. When can we come?" Yet in return the answer was: "You may have found the spoon, but the bad feeling remained!"

*   *   *

"You are exactly who we need for this task. Check the situation and give us your feedback: Can we save the Hotel or not?"

The executive from the headquarters stared sharply at Ana. She had hyena's eyes. Of course, the Collector was behind the assignment. Half an hour earlier he had personally instructed Ana to meet the executive, and she had. But what bewildered her was that no horses were involved. Rather, this was a hotel—*the* Hotel.

"Me?" Ana was surprised.

"Yes, you have the skills. We were impressed by the last St. Theodore's Day event."

Ana remembered that the executive had been among the audience. Even though the hippodrome was under the court's jurisdiction, Ana was still in charge of the events there.

"If there's any chance, we will fight for it," the executive continued. "Otherwise, we'll leave it to the wolves"—meaning the bank. "Ask for the chief accountant's assistance."

"Okay, I'll start this weekend," Ana said, accepting the mission.

As Ana's parents were not active Communists, she hadn't had the privilege of getting into the Hotel during its heyday. After the end of Socialism, she never had occasion to do it. So Saturday morning, a bit more than two months after her trip to Latin America with Lilly, she parked in front of the building and dialed the chief accountant's number with little idea of what to expect.

The landscaping outside was an assembly of weeds and bushes, as if never touched by human hands. Once upon a time the carpet on the main stairs had been vermillion. However, now it was frayed and dirty, with a kind of patchy camo effect probably achieved from the spilling of various fluids and smeared gums. Ana walked in. The entrance area inside was dark and worn-out, arranged with furniture probably leftover from Socialism. The wooden paneling on the walls was wounded in many places. Nearly half of the lights were missing.

The accountant came to the reception desk. She was a highly experienced, long-term employee temporarily in charge of the whole complex—including a casino, restaurant, cocktail bar, beauty salon, administrative building and, of course, the hotel itself. They walked around discussing the property's current state. Ana sensed some resistance concerning her competency—probably based on her age and looks—but business was business, and the employee was forthcoming with all the figures and information necessary.

Clearly the Hotel's finances were a mess. The company was drowning in various debts for taxes, insurances, heating, electricity, etc. The staff's wages were being paid with a six-month delay, and naturally people were demotivated. Ana was told that the former executive had literally run away after reaching retirement age, so now there was nobody in lead. It seemed bankruptcy was knocking at the door. They needed a recovery plan immediately!

*   *   *

"We can save the Hotel!" Ana said as she rushed into the Collector's office.

"You think so?" He was looking for her to make an argument.

"Yes, for sure! Here's the plan: in order to stabilize the hotel, we have to provide consistent cash flow, right? Therefore, we should rent out the first three floors as office space, as well as every other space available. And the restaurant—instead of managing it ourselves we could outsource also. This way we could accumulate enough income for the renovation, that we should begin during the summer, starting with the most visible area—the lobby and the reception desk. Afterward we should tackle the hotel rooms step-by-step. How about that?"

She was feeling very enthusiastic. Again!

"Hmm." The Collector was smoking as usual. It took him two seconds to reply. "Fine, do it!"

"Great! Meanwhile, they'll focus on all the Hotel's deferred payments starting next week. The chief accountant will make a full list."

"Uh-huh," he said, checking to see who else was waiting for him, which indicated Ana had to hurry up.

"As for me, I would like to have ten days off next month. I'm sorry, but I booked this school package a long time ago. I'll stay in touch with my colleagues the whole time."

"Well, if it's school, you may go," the Collector promptly allowed, as it seemed a significant person's name was pending among his visitors.

*　　*　　*

"I'll have to leave you for ten days. You can make it here, right?" Ana asked her new protégée. She had met Patricia, aka Patty, a few years ago when dealing with her car leasing documentation. Patty was active and law-abiding, and because Ana needed a person like that for the Hotel's matters, she properly introduced Patty to the Collector. Upon his approval, Patty was assigned as a commercial director under Ana's supervision. "You are my Doc here," was the common joke between them. By the way, Doc himself was visiting them in the Hotel from time to time. He was blessed with a son who looked just like him, as if the father's features had been copied and pasted onto the baby's face. Besides being supported by the European funds, Doc was building up his dream clinic.

"Where're you going? What's up?" Patty asked, as always willing to be aware of everything.

"School . . . in East Sussex, close to London," answered Ana.

"Cool, what will you study? Management? Leadership?"

"Well . . ." Ana smirked. "Actually, it's a golf school. I booked a package in January, and I really want to use it. Please don't tell anybody."

The Playboy might be out of her life, but the golf passion remained.

"You're such a naughty girl," Patty couldn't help but say with a smile.

While Ana was going to learn the secrets of the perfect swing in one of the best schools in Britain, Lilly was to stay with her grandparents. Soon Ana took her clubs, a medium-sized suitcase with mostly sports outfits, and flew to England with joy in her heart. She believed that the basics were of the greatest importance, and not only in golf. Building on a proper foundation was much faster and effective, right? After ten days in the sports camp, Ana came back fit and full of energy.

The next morning she woke up in good spirits. Life was so beautiful . . . then on her way to work she bumped into the neighbor who lived above her.

"Good morning," replied the neighbor with a fake smile, adding, "It was a hell of a party two nights ago, almost forty people . . . And it was tolerable until midnight, when somebody brought up the guitars and the amplifiers. I guess the whole neighborhood was awoken."

"Oh, it wasn't us. I was away. . . and Lilly was staying with my parents," refused Ana.

"Trust me, it was coming from your place."

Ana quickly dialed her mother's number.

"Mom, where was Lilly two nights ago?"

"She was watching a movie with her best friend at your place, Anché. I gave her permission because she was behaving so well . . . as a reward, you know. Trust me, they were chill. I called at nine to check on them, and everything seemed fine. Why asking?"

"I see!" Next Ana dialed Lilly's number. Somebody was going be grounded for sure.

On Mondays Ana had applied the hippodrome's routine to weekly eleven o'clock meetings at the Hotel. Yet that day she was late after dealing with Lilly's domestic mischief. When she entered the room, her staff was already seated. She briefly explained the reason for her delay with humor, and at the end passed along a favorite anecdote from East Sussex.

"Two guys are sitting in a bar. Suddenly one of then shouts, 'I slept with your mother!' The bar gets quiet. Everyone's nosy. Then the other guy replies, 'Go home, Dad, you're drunk.'"

After the meeting Ana's colleagues left her office in good mood. Only Patty stayed.

"I worry about Lilly a lot," Ana confessed. "She's at such a delicate age. She needs a father figure more than ever. He has to be the one who makes the rules, demands order, and maintains discipline—something of a 'bad cop' so I can be the friend-mom. I just have to be close to her to be aware of what she's doing and with whom. Genuine communication is of vital importance during puberty."

"Yes, you're absolutely right," agreed her colleague.

"We have to change her school," Ana thought out loud. "Yes—new environment, new friends, new values . . . It's probably the only way to deal with her father's absence. I have to replace him with a good college."

"Wait, I think I know the right person for this situation," said Patty as she nimbly found the number of a student counseling company.

Luckily Lilly was born under a fortunate star. Soon she was offered three superb possibilities, and one of them was truly a win. Based in Oxford, it was ranked the sixth best International Baccalaureate school in England, with a mission to advance international education and understanding.

Ana felt it was perfect, but Lilly was scared of the unknown. For the first time the girl had to make a significant decision, choosing between the comfort of a family life and an elite education.

"Gee, I really don't know what it will be like . . ." had been Lilly's initial reaction.

"Don't be afraid, love," said Ana. "We'll make it together. You'll come home every holiday and I'll fly to London as often as I can, and of course we'll talk each day. Think of it as an adventure."

Lilly remained silent, still hesitating. To leave her room and friends was bloody hair-raising. So Ana played the ace:

"And you will be independent."

That phrase encapsulated most teenagers' dreams, and of course her daughter was flattered. But the school was still so far—a mighty twenty-five hundred kilometers away from home. Ana sensed her apprehension.

"Lilly, don't worry. I promise to be there for you any time you need me!"

This worked better. To count on someone reliable was at the core of most people's courage. The girl looked at her mom with her big brown eyes and asked, "How do you manage to keep your promises, Mummy?"

"Simple. Above all I keep my word to myself," answered Ana. The virtue of self-respect was something she had recently been trying to pass on to Lilly, though with her "teenage glasses" the girl was seeing it more as being allowed to do what she liked out of self-respect. Well, for sure reality would adjust her reasoning soon enough.

Their discussion continued late that night and on through the next day, until—one drop at a time—the glass was finally full. "We'll go for it!" they decided, and Ana booked two tickets to London. At first they had to pass the introductory interview in person.

Two days later a well-dressed woman in high heels and an embarrassed redheaded teenager walked down one of the main Oxford roads as fast as they could to make Lilly's interview with the

Principal. The street appeared to be much longer than expected, and finally they got to the reception desk a little sweaty but with British punctuality.

"Please come in. He'll be with you right away," an assistant said.

The interview was extensive and all-encompassing. Initially the Principal talked mostly with Ana, and then he asked her to wait outside. It was Lilly's turn to show her knowledge, language skills, and morals. It took an hour, or maybe more. Finally the door opened and the principal smiled.

"It will be our privilege to have your daughter with us, madam."

Meanwhile, by the beginning of the summer, the Hotel's renovation had started off as planned. Somewhere in between choosing paint colors and carpet samples, Ana was elected chairman of the board of directors.

One hot afternoon, a maintenance guy brought her an old red hardcover book of recipes. When Ana flipped through the pages, she found little handwritten notes, and one, under the grilled lamb, was marked "for government security services." On the next page she discovered the former leader's preferences specified, then other names and marks. Holy cow, this was the original recipe book from the Hotel's heyday. Such a treasure!

Later that afternoon Ana rushed to the brand-new restaurant's tenant with the book in hand.

"We need to order a showcase for this book, to place it right next to the entrance so everyone coming in can see it. There's so much history in these pages. It would be a huge draw—the difference that makes us unique!"

"Let me see it." The guy reached for the relic.

"Be careful, please," warned Ana as she gave it to him.

"Whoa, that's what I call a bolt from the blue. A showcase, huh?"

"Correct. Also we should invite the supreme leader's favorite cook to work for us. He's retired now, but still active. I could talk him into it."

The tenant was a young aspiring person, and also very open-minded, so collaborating with him proved easy.

"Our slogan will be 'The Hotel keeps many secrets,'" decided Ana with a twinkle dancing in her eyes.

And so, by autumn the Hotel lobby was beautifully renovated, many offices were rented out (primarily by lawyers, as the building was located close to the courthouse), and the restaurant was ready to go. Many guests arrived on opening day, and the media too. It became immediately clear that the relic had brought them there.

"Is this the original?"

"Correct," Ana confirmed.

She gave an exclusive interview for the evening news about the book's discovery and the notes inside it. Beside her stood the famous cook, who had gladly agreed to work again in the kitchen where he had so many years before.

The Hotel's finances were getting stable and promising by each day, but the revival was not done yet. It would take Ana's team a year more to finally button up everything. Then she would write a personal letter to the Collector:

"Finally we've completed the renovation. All of the offices are rented out, the restaurant is going well, occupancy has increased twicefold, income has risen steadily, labor is reimbursed regularly, most debts have been covered, and the company is working smoothly and profitably. Sincerely, Ana."

CHAPTER 32

OXFORD

Oxford—students of all ages and divers nationalities buzzed around like bees in a garden.

Ana escorted Lilly at the welcome ceremony. After the motivational speech, all the children were allocated to different buildings, and Lilly was supposed to live in the "Baby House." Ana grinned.

"Hey, wasn't it obvious that you are not a baby anymore?"

"Oh, shush, Mom. One more joke and I'm gone!"

"Okay, okay, relax, let's look around," said Ana. She took Lilly's hand and they headed to the Baby House, which was a block away from the administration. The campus itself comprised twenty-seven redbrick Victorian and Edwardian buildings in the North Oxford conservation area. Students occupied some of the houses; classrooms, the library, the four science laboratories, the phenomenal art studio, and the music corner occupied others. It was a dream school.

"You will be in good hands, love. Please behave, and call me every day. I have to go now," said Ana, obeying the principal's invitation for the parents to leave.

"But of course." Lilly winked, kissed her twice with affection, and vanished. She was in a hurry to mingle with her new fellows.

With an aching heart Ana walked back to her hotel.

"Will you be alone tonight, madam?" asked the lady at the reception desk.

"Yes, I left my daughter at the college." Ana nearly choked on her words. Then she rushed to her room, locked the door, and burst into tears.

In the beginning of her studies, Lilly was preoccupied. Acclimatizing, adjusting to the new school standards, catching up with language gaps, socializing—it was not a breeze. For the first time she had to share her room with another person. The bathrooms were freezing. Even the food tasted different. But Lilly never complained and face her hurdles.

In the meantime, Ana tried to fill the hole in her life with work, work, and work. Her days were pretty busy; the Hotel and the whole complex were very consuming. Most evenings she spent out with friends to avoid the loneliness. Her home became quiet and empty without Lilly, only the cat roamed around. They both counted the days to the first holiday, scheduled at the end of October. Finally that day came, and Lilly was tasked with traveling back home alone.

"It's a piece of cake. Everybody does it. I'm fifteen," she said with such authority, as if she was thirty.

"Okay, I'll meet you at the airport."

"I miss you so much, Mom!" added Lilly. Her manners had softened.

Same flight Lilly missed twice in a row. She made it on the third try, learning the basic lesson to always be on time from now on.

Finally home—in between family dinners, chilling with friends, or simply hanging around with her mom—Lilly was invited to a local radio show to speak about the advantages of an Oxford education.

"Well, the environment at my college is very friendly," she said. "We call our teachers and even the principal by their first names— 'Hello, Tod!' for example. Our classes are more like discussions than lectures, and because we are sorted into small groups of ten to fifteen, everybody gets involved in the studies. It's very effective. Our teachers are strict, rigorous, and meticulous, requiring a high level of knowledge, and at the same time they do respect our personal opinions. I would say that they don't treat us like kids, but rather like adults. I love it!"

"Very interesting. And what else, Lilly?" asked the radioman.

"In addition to enriching the individualities of the students, they apply a CAS program."

"What's that?"

"Let me explain: *C* stands for creativity, *A* for activity, and *S* for service. Along with the mandatory subjects like mathematics and English, we have to gain a certain number of hours in creativity, including photography, drawing, visual arts, etc. Activity includes all kinds of sports; and service is about helping others. For example, I teach my classmates Latin dancing. For me it's service, but for them it's activity. Students can choose to help elderly people in the local nursing home, or they might participate in the student's committee, stuff like that . . . Basically all kinds of contribution."

"Whoa, that's awe-inspiring. My admirations," said the host.

"Good morals, indeed. Oh, and I would like to mention one more advantage: Everybody has classes in their native language. Yes, for real, I study my mother tongue even two thousand miles away from home. Isn't that great?"

"But how's that possible?"

"With tutors available for all international students," explained Lilly.

There was a short pause. It seemed the host was wordless. In a while he spoke up:

"Respect, ladies and gentlemen! That's all I can say. And thanks for sharing your experience with us, Lilly. Good luck to you!" Then he closed the session with the evergreen "Let It Be."

That break ended a few days later. Early morning before dawn, Ana drove Lilly to the airport. Sleepy and sad, they tried to act brave and to encourage each other by making plans for the upcoming Christmas holiday. But once they had to split again, the pain replaced their cheer.

Ouch, how am I supposed to make it for three more years? thought Ana. *For three long years to send my baby away?* She had not a clue. Would it always be this tough? If sending her daughter to Oxford was the best decision, why did it feel so devastating?

And poor Lilly, she was suffering too. In the beginning it was like an international camp to her, but now she fully understood she was actually living away from home—and spending time with her dearest ones on a daily basis was simply not possible.

During the flight Lilly snuggled by the window as a lonely sparrow, hiding her tears in a sleeve. With the headphones on, she played again and again that song about how danger and complicated this world is.

*   *   *

The second year in Oxford, Lilly was not staying at the Baby House anymore. Now she was a senior student, feeling much more comfortable and popular in her shoes. She had many friends.

Winter came, and unusually for the local weather it snowed. Lilly and her buddies had been freezing outside, when a senior student passed by:

"Hey, guys. What did one snowman say to the other snowman?" he asked.

"Nice carrot?" guessed Lilly.

"Looking cool!" the guy joked, and then announced:

"We're breaking out tonight clubbing. Do you wanna join us?"

"But . . . what about the wardens?" asked Lilly.

"You haven't done it yet?! We sneak out after midnight and come back before breakfast. They never had a clue we were out. Trust me, it's been proven throughout the years," he said, pointing at the crossroad nearby to specify the meeting point.

"Nah, I'll pass," said Lilly.

In February, the snow had gone in Oxford, yet for the rest of Europe it was the peak of the skiing season. Ana's friend booked a house in the Austrian Alps and invited her over. She accepted, fervent for some recreation. So far the Hotel was running well, Patty was going to manage it for a while, and Lilly was supposed to be pretty occupied with her midterm exams. So Ana packer her skis and boots.

That Monday Ana was in her usual good mood. The regular briefing had just ended when her phone notified her she'd received an email from Lilly. Why didn't she call instead of write? When Ana had called Lilly the previous day, she had said she was not feeling well, and would prefer to return the call later. Yet she didn't. Hmm . . . Ana clicked on the email.

"Mommy, I have bad news . . ."

What?! Ana thought, startled.

"Saturday night, I snuck out of the house because my friends (well, they are not my friends anymore) convinced me to. I was waiting for them on the street when a police car stopped, and the officers started questioning me. It was cold, and I was frightened, so I fainted. They called an ambulance, and a female officer to test me for drugs. No alcohol or drugs were found in my blood, Mom. But since my friends were still missing, the cops asked about my address to drive me there. I panicked, so I lied I was a tourist staying at the hotel nearby. They checked the registration list, and of course my name was not there. They threatened to take me to the immigration office, when finally my friends arrived and got me out of this mess. When I came back to my house it was three o'clock in the morning, and the warden was alerted. Afterward she reported the accident at school. Now I'm waiting for an audience with the principal, but don't worry, Mom. I won't be expelled." Ana couldn't believe her eyes.

What is Lilly talking about? Police, ambulance, the principal . . . And she expects not to be expelled? Ana was worried, mad, and disappointed. *That stupid girl of mine! She was too scared to talk to me yesterday, not sick.*

Lastly, Lilly apologized: "I'm very sorry for misleading you. I really am! I promise to behave better from now on. I'll start estimating the consequences of my actions in advance. I won't let you down again. I'm sorry for being such a selfish person. I love you, Mom. Please don't worry."

It was quite the email! Ana dialed her daughter for more details.

"Only the truth can save you now! Tell me everything!"

Weeping, Lilly confessed it all.

Ana's next conversation was with the principal. His voice sounded firm but polite. As a first penalty, Lilly would be dismissed from classes for three days next week until the college decided what their final judgment would be.

"Next week?!"

"Yes, madam, take her home! Or anywhere. She cannot be at school!"

"All right, I'll take her," Ana said with pity, thinking, *So long, slopes!*

So she managed to go skiing for two days only. Afterward she flew from Salzburg to London and took the train to Oxford. It is said that polar bears always come back for their babies, and Ana—also. Meanwhile, Lilly had been waiting for her at the previously booked hotel room—the same place she lied the cops about. Ana found her to be ashamed, guilty, and deeply sorry.

"Do you understand how serious this is, Lilith?! This wrongdoing might jeopardize your whole future! You could be expelled in the middle of IB," rebuked Ana. The girl remained mute with her head down. She had already considered her culpability, especially after the audience with the principal. Then, mother and daughter had a long discussion about responsibilities and obligations; meeting expectations; being grateful for what one has; and so on.

"Let's hope this accident will shake you up," concluded Ana. "It can change your mind-set for good. I'll ask for a meeting with the principal in order to properly apologize on your behalf. I'll ask him for a second chance for you, if it's not too late. May he be merciful!"

"I promise, I'll do my best if I stay," whispered Lilly.

The principal was surprised when Ana called for an appointment.

"You're here? Please come tomorrow," he said. Lilly's case was still hanging.

When the next day Ana appeared, he kindly saluted.

"Good morning, madam. Please come in."

"Hello, sir, nice to see you. I'm here to apologize for my daughter's behavior. I'm sorry for the troubles she caused you! I personally find her actions immature and outrageous. Yesterday I had an edifying conversation with Lilly, clearly expressing my disappointment and reflecting on the possible upshots. I believe she comprehends. She has to learn to obey the rules, not sabotage the discipline. And sir, I'll support you in your decision no matter what it is."

"Hmm, we won't support an attitude like hers here," firmly said the principal. "We haven't yet decided our definitive judgment. Expulsion is one of the options, and in this case no money would be refunded. I'm sorry."

"That would be a pity, sir." Ana shrugged. "I work hard to afford her education. I'm not an oligarch as some other parents here. However, money is only a part of the problem. If you exclude her in the middle of the second year it would damage her whole path and would tremendously affect her personality. She's very emotional kid. Believe me, in her core my daughter is a good girl. Please give her a second chance. She won't misbehave again!"

"Madam, I hope you'll get me right: if we decide to absolve her and let her stay, it will not be her second chance—it will be her last chance! One more sin, and we'll ask Lilly to leave immediately without refund. Do you agree?"

"Yes, I agree," Ana confirmed. "Thank you, sir! Thank you!"

A few days later the college stated: "Final warning" instead of "Expulsion"!

"Oh, thank goodness!" Ana could finally relax.

And in time it proved to be a good decision. Lilly put all the rebels aside, and focused on her studies. Lilith was gone.

CHAPTER 33

THE ITALIAN VOYAGE

At the end of her second year at the college, Lilly was positive she wanted to follow through with studying interior design. Great! She was creative, innovative, and sensitive to colors. Art was her passion. London or Milan were the two best locations for her further education. As the girl was already quite familiar with London, Ana decided they would explore Italy that summer. Afterward, Lilly could better choose where to continue her studies.

The Italian voyage was going to be one of the best journeys ever. Ana arranged everything with an appetite for accuracy. At the airport, the previously booked rental car was waiting for them—a cute Alfa Romeo Giulietta, their lovely Juliet. First stop: *La Finestra sul Fiume*, which meant "The window by the river," near Verona. Ana and Lilly sang freely the whole way there. And upon arrival they were even more exited. That friend who had highly recommended the place was absolutely right. It was as charming as its name. "For getting away, for being amazed, for losing yourself . . . and for finding yourself again!" was its slogan.

It was a rustic river house near a fourteenth-century castle in the picturesque area. Over the next few days they visited Juliet's terrace in Verona, the Gothic Duomo di Milano, the Stone-Age town of Sirmione at Lake Garda. They also spent a remarkable day taking in Venice's splendor, and then Ana drove a red Ferrari in Maranello while Lilly recorded video from the backseat. Afterward they tasted the delights of the *agriturismo* in a ranch in the Reggio Emilia hills, and traveled to Florence for the rest of the stay. There a friend, Beth, flew over to join, so they became three girls on the Italian journey. Beth, a few years younger than Ana, was a sensitive, gentle, and brokenhearted aesthete.

"Don't worry, we'll cheer you up," said Ana, embracing her with words. "The more the merrier."

The Duomo, Uffizi Gallery, Ponte Vecchio . . . beauty was all around them, and they wanted to see it all. Based in Florence they toured the area. The girls had lunch on the Piazza del Campo in Siena, and chilled on the grass beside the leaning tower in Pisa, capturing their memories in pictures. All around Tuscany they wholeheartedly enjoyed each other, the delicious food, and excellent wine.

The town of Livorno was also on their "must" list. Even though not as popular as their other stops, eighty years ago Ana's grandfather had studied in the Italian Naval Academy there. The Captain was Mrs. K's father, a noble man and a great patriot. He had passed away when Lilly was two, but his genes were still alive.

At noon they approached the Academy's imperial complex by the coast. As it was August, the huge metal doors were closed so they couldn't get in, but even from the outside its spirit could be detected: discipline, order, exactness. Ana had seen her grandfather's pictures of his tutors dressed in tails and top hats at the Japanese emperor's visit, inspiring reverence.

"Lilly, do you remember great-grandpa?"

"Nope, I don't, but I remember the photos of him."

"Did you know that he wrote an autobiography? You should read it! He's your ancestor."

"Sure, I would love to. What was he like, Mom?"

"Well, he was very popular in his hometown by the sea. Most of his life the Captain taught in the Naval Academy there, writing schoolbooks and manuals, heading up the 'Tactics of the Navy' department. Walking with him on the street was so boring for us kids.

His students and colleagues were everywhere. And he had to properly salute and talk to each of them. Ugh, the military courtesy sucked."

"But how did he make it to Livorno anyway?" asked Lilly, pointing at the buildings behind the fencing.

"With his brains and ambitions only," answered Ana, smiling. "In the year 1930 he won a scholarship for the Italian Naval Academy, and he came here on the third-class train. That was more than just a dream come true for a poor village boy; it was a miracle. So he seized the opportunity, learned as much as he could, and practiced on the two major sailing ships of the time."

"Sailing ships, like in the pirate movies?" asked Lilly.

"Exactly the same."

"Cool!" The girl's imagination drew astonishing pictures. "And then what?"

"After his third year of studies, as a junior officer and the chief navigator's assistant, grandpa sailed with the *Amerigo Vespucci* training ship from Europe to the United States. That was a long time ago, during prohibition. Now listen to this: In Washington he participated in the official delegation visiting the White House led by the Academy's admiral. President Roosevelt hosted them from his wheelchair. At the end of the meeting he personally shook hands with everyone, including your great-grandpa."

"Really? How old was he back then?"

"Let me calculate . . . I think he was twenty-four-ish. A junior officer, love. I've seen the photo taken on the White House's marble stairs right afterward. Now it's preserved in our Naval Museum by the sea. You should be proud of your origins!"

"Your mom's right. That is an empowering story," said Beth. So far she had been delicately listening.

"Let's walk down to the coast," suggested Lilly, taking Mom's and Beth's hands and pulling them away.

"On that journey to the States," Ana continued, "Grandpa visited New York, climbed all the way to the top of the Empire State Building, and walked on Wall Street. He was fascinated by the fast-paced life of Manhattan."

"Shall we visit the Big Apple someday, Mom?"

"Yup, definitely."

"But not before I turn twenty-one. I don't wanna be treated as a child," specified Lilly with a smirk.

"Deal." Ana laughed and kissed her girl on the cheek.

Meanwhile they reached the coast. There the three girls spent awhile just looking at the blue horizon. One was reminiscing about her grandfather, the other was dreaming of New York's clubs, and the third was dying for a glass of wine.

Lilly spoke first. "And what happened with the Captain afterward?"

"After his graduation from the Naval Academy? Well, he returned home. During the Second World War he became a fleet commander. Then he met your great-grandma and married her, and your granny was born in 1942. After the end of the war, the Captain was the first destroyers' commander in the country to be awarded several medals. They even put a bas-relief of him in the Naval Academy's lecture hall. That's all! Anyone hungry or thirsty?"

"Me, me," Beth admitted.

"Me too." Lilly smiled, already running backward.

Suddenly, on their way to the restaurant, a pair of stylish Armani boots caught Lilly's attention.

"Wow, they're so cool! Can we go in?"

And she snuck inside to ask for her size. Ana had to admit that she liked the boots, which were elegant and comfortable, but at the same time they were pretty expensive. When she heard the price, Lilly put them aside and apologized to the vendor.

"Oh, I'm sorry, that's way too much. We'll find something else."

Ana stopped her. "Wait, do you really like them?"

"I love them, but . . ."

"Will you swear that if we take them, you will earn at least one seven toward your diploma in return?"

Seven was the highest grade possible, and Lilly was already nodding with agreement.

"Remember: A promise is a promise! You'll have to keep it!" said Ana, positive for Lilly this would be a good lesson, a lesson of setting goals and meeting them.

The girl slowly swallowed, and then solemnly stated, "I swear on Armani that I'll have a seven!"

So they bought the boots.

Because of that vow or not, Lilly kept her promise. Her art portfolio was awarded the highest marks. Well done, and viva Armani!

CHAPTER 34

THE CONFLICT

Thirty million euros—the Collector had supplied his accounts with average that amount after using the hippodrome's land as a collateral. And he had promised Ana an adequate royalty. But every time she approached him for cash, he tried to weasel his way out of the commitment.

"Now is not the right moment, Ana," he would say. "The crisis was severe with heavy casualties. Some of our companies have gone bankrupt. We are still recovering, and income is very short right now. You have to wait for better days."

He then had required incontrovertible proof of any urgent expenses. She knew it was not only a matter of money shortage, but also his desire to exert domination over everything, including her life and finances.

"Incontrovertible like this? You've always said that kids are the priority, right?" asked Ana one day, conveniently presenting the invoice for her daughter's first-year tuition fee. Obviously the subject was pretty persuasive, and this time the Collector simply had to keep his word. He looked at her with annoyance because he hated unexpected costs. But Ana had been insistent, as she was the one responsible for Lilly's future.

"Can I count on you to make the payment before the deadline?" she wanted to know.

"Yes, yes," the Collector answered. "Give it to the secretary on your way out."

That day Ana used all her skills to distinguish the shades behind his "yes." Was he actually going to cover Lilly's education, or was he bluffing? As in fact, the Collector had the custom of rarely saying no. In the very beginning Ana kind of liked this oddity of his. For sure it was more appealing to her ego—and probably to everybody else's—to find her ideas approved. But soon Ana discovered that he was only occasionally following through and keeping his word; more often he wasn't. It was very confusing. Luckily this time the zoomed-in observation along with her female instincts had deducted empathy. After a couple of excuses and a dozen calls to remind him, the Collector had paid the fee nearly on time—in fact, two days before the deadline.

A year later, just before Lilly's second year in college, almost the same scenario repeated itself, only this time the Collector became suspiciously curious about her daughter's well-being. He asked, "How's your girl doing in England?" or "Does she have many friends there?" or "Does she go out to the nightclubs in London?" He had even offered his help as Lilly's custodian in front the college's authorities. As a person with a sophisticated house in Kensington and a business office in London, he was appropriate for this matter—but a self-stylized Collector wasn't. So Ana politely declined his proposal.

"We have it figured out already," she said.

"Well, you can give her my number just in case," he suggested.

"Thanks, but there's no need to bother you with our crap."

"Fine, whatever." He shrugged.

The word *alarm* had surfaced in Ana's mind. As a mother she did not trust his "goodwill intentions"; they were way too dubious based on his reputation. That year he paid the fee on the last day.

*　　*　　*

Now, right after the Italian voyage, it was time for the third payment, and unfortunately the sweetness of their romantic trip was salted by the Collector's aspirations.

That day the Hotel was overbooked by a number of foreign groups. The staff was quite busy. Seventeen-year-old Lilly was working as a housemaid there along with her best friend. It was early afternoon. At the reception desk a dozen tourists were checking in. The chief administrator was roundly giving instructions as bellhops ran up and down stairs with the guests' luggage. When the phone in Ana's office rang, she assumed the administrator was calling to summarize the daily figures. But no, it was the security guard from the lobby.

"Ms. Ana, you should hurry downstairs. The Collector is here. He is sitting at the outdoor bar."

"Yes, coming right away," Ana said, not surprised by this senior-level visit. From time to time he would come alone or with friends so as to personally supervise the property's management while having a drink. Outside Ana saw him sitting with companions at the VIP table in the middle of the bar, surrounded by bodyguards.

"Good afternoon. Nice to see you," she greeted him as usual.

The Collector nodded and invited her to join them for a coffee. After a short talk about the Hotel's affairs, in passing he asked, "What's your daughter doing? Is she in town?"

"Yes, actually, she's working here as a maid," answered Ana.

"Really? Can you ask her to come over? I would like to see her."

"Sure," agreed Ana. She texted Lilly, saying, "Can you come down to the outdoor bar, love? Somebody wants to see you."

Lilly soon arrived in short jeans, her hair up in a ponytail, and a big friendly smile on her face.

"What's up, Mummy?" she asked. Suddenly the smile disappeared. She froze as still as a statue when she saw the Collector scanning her from behind a screen of cigar smoke. Ana politely introduced him.

"Do you remember who this is? You were still a kid when you met him."

"Nuh-uh." Lilly seemed a little ashamed.

"Well, this is the Collector."

"Hello, sir." The girl waved.

Even though he appeared to be playing nice and was kind of smiling, his gaze remained sharp and cold as a knife.

"Well, Lilly, take a seat next to your mom. Tell me, how's life in Oxford going?"

The girl huddled beside her mother like a bird perched on a twig. Ana sensed her suspense; in fact, she had never seen her daughter so embarrassed before. Lilly was blushing, afraid to look the Collector in the eyes. Her body was tense, and she was sitting on her palms. Probably in that moment her very wish was to become invisible. So to his question, Lilly replied with the simplest and shortest answer she could find.

"Fine, thanks."

For a second there was an awkward silence. The Collector stared at Lilly from the opposite side of the table. It took only a moment for Ana to react.

"Oh, I forgot the last month's cash flow statement on my desk. Can you please bring it for me, kiddo?"

"Sure," Lilly said before vanishing immediately.

A few minutes later a bellhop brought the spreadsheet in Lilly's place.

Smart girl, thought Ana.

The Collector put the documents aside, took the last sip of his coffee, and puffed on his cigar. For his guards, that was an indication that they were about to leave. He stood up. On his way Ana reminded him:

"Please remember, we have to pay tuition by the end of August. Your secretary already has the invoice. It would be nice if we accurately kept the terms. This will be Lilly's last year at college, and the most important one. Exams and applying to universities . . ."

"Okay, call me tomorrow and we'll solve that issue," the Collector blurted out, looking toward the other side.

The next day at eleven o'clock, Ana dialed his number. Shortly after they exchanged pleasantries, he came right to the point.

"Listen, don't worry about the payment. It's a done deal. Meanwhile, why don't you send your daughter over to my office? I want to talk to her."

"To talk to her? What about?" asked Ana. This peculiar request was unexpected.

"Nothing in particular, just like . . . friends."

"Friends? But . . . but she's on duty today." It was the first stupid excuse that came to her mind.

"Well, give her a free day. I would like to see her!"

But Ana was anxious. Sending Lilly to his office would be an extremely dangerous act. He could corrupt her or even worse . . . She tried to handle the situation diplomatically.

"Come on, let's be rational. She's just a girl, and she definitely doesn't belong in your office."

"Hmm, that's your opinion," replied the Collector before demanding, "I want to see her today!"

Hell no, she wouldn't let him screw her masterpiece. "No, she will not come!" Ana said in frustration.

"We'll see about that!" he said, and hung up the phone.

Ana was hoping the Collector would change his mind. What kind of person would sabotage a young girl's education in her last year? He would probably reconsider. But then she received an email from the college saying that Lilly's installment was still standing and had to be covered at once.

Fine, I got the message. No millions can buy my daughter's soul! concluded Ana.

That day she and Lilly went to the bank and ordered the transfer out of their modest life savings. Thereafter Ana turned to her daughter with words.

"If you ever see him again, run! Run as fast and as far as you can. Don't look back! Just run!"

"Okay, Mom, I will," confirmed Lilly. "I'm glad that this absurdity has ended."

But had it? Ana was aware of the dramatic range of consequences their decision would bring in the future. Her career, finances, and certainty would be gone. If eventually she wanted to keep them, there was only one way: to obey the Collector's ultimatum.

That night Ana got drunk. Alone with the bottle she tried to calm her demons down—the ugly demons of insecurity, disappointment, and insult.

"That's impossible! I'll never do it! Burn in hell, outrageous, dirty bastard! I don't want to see your face again!" she muttered defiantly.

The next morning she had a terrible hangover. Even after the third aspirin her head was still as heavy as a boulder. While having her morning coffee, Ana tried to think. So far one thing she knew for certain: *I'll never dial his number again!*

And she never did. Neither did he try to reach her.

CHAPTER 35

CHANGES

Ana knew the Collector wouldn't tolerate her insubordination long.

Only until Lilly graduates. He has to compromise for only ten months, she hoped, counting on his clemency. But soon . . .

The week before Christmas without a call, notice, or admonition from the Collector, a Dutchman came to the Hotel.

"The boss sent me. I'm the new procurator," he said, showing Ana his affiliation documents signed and stamped in the headquarters.

"You?" She read the content. The newcomer was about to step in charge of the company; apparently the Collector's patience had expired. Should she call him? Nope, she had made a promise, although she texted him asking how to proceed. Nobody replied. So Ana dialed the hyena—the same lady who had allocated her at the Hotel years ago.

"What's going on? Who's the Dutchman?"

"Come over here. We have to talk," was the answer.

Shortly after, Ana arrived at the hyena's office, concerned, but not panicked.

"If the new management steps in charge—I'll leave," she declared. "I'm responsible for my actions and my decisions only. I won't split the leadership with a stranger."

"No, no, you don't have to leave, he'll operate temporarily. I swear I had not a clue about that," said the lady, trying to sound honest. But Ana was already a veteran, and she could smell the ambush from a mile away.

"Temporary? I'm aware of what's going on. Tell the boss I'm out of the Hotel!" stated Ana. And she meant it.

It was the last day before Christmas when Ana packed her belongings in a box, and so did Patty.

"I came here because of you," said Patty, "and I'll quit with you." She was loyal.

"You don't have to," objected Ana.

"But I want to! The Dutchman sucks. I won't be able to work with him."

"Fine then, let's do it together," agreed Ana, and they walked all the way through the renovated area, and then out of the main entrance.

Hail Ceasar, hail Ceasar, so many wars, crusades, and conquests, yet your name remained worldwide as a salad, thought Ana, leaving everything behind.

*   *   *

By New Year's Eve, things were not going in her favor. The hippodrome's land had been seized, the Hotel was behind her, and the Avalon complex had gone bankrupt along with her anticipated apartments. Her woes and her obscurity were snarling in the corner.

When her friends called to wish her a happy New Year, Ana couldn't think of any way to respond. "I hope so," she said, and then they invited her on a trip to Kenya.

She gladly accepted. "An escape. Count me in!" And so on January 3, as Lilly flew back to London, Ana headed to Mombasa. All the worries were behind her; ahead were only the jungles and the shoreless ocean.

The journey to Africa was kind of surreal—not planned, not expected, yet phenomenal—involving alligators, baboons, and Maasai people.

One gorgeous night beneath the starry African sky, her friend asked while having drinks, "What will you do from now on, Ana? Or should I call you Mama Maasai?" That day they had visited a native village.

In that very moment Ana realized that the Collector's era was over. She would refer to her background at his headquarters as graduating from the University of Life. True, from him she had learned many things, such as how to speak with authority and how to demand results. Ana looked at her friend slowly sipping the marvelous local Chardonnay, and replied that maybe she would step into life and business coaching, starting possibly with practical psychology trainings. A long time ago she had bough her first book on the subject in Russian. The language was not that complicated, as she had graduated from a Russian high school. She found the content captivating. It explained the basis of behavioral analysis, body language, and linguistic patterns. Shortly thereafter she had bought a second book, and then another one . . . The deeper she dug the more fascinated she became by the vast range of the lore's utility. It was universal!

And so, following that last desire, Ana chose the training course at her country's capital once back in the motherland. In those classes she learned the basic techniques, and at the same time she met many interesting people. It was both educational and fun. There she heard about a guy who'd had unforgettable, life-changing experiences at the summer course at the university of California. Calculating the price of plane tickets, accommodations, the training itself, and some sightseeing, Ana reasoned one would probably need ten thousand dollars and one month spare time to make it work.

"*Hey, who knows? Maybe someday . . .*" she marked for herself.

By the end of spring, Ana was absorbed by her new passion.

"What's that new hobby of yours?" Mrs. K, like many, was totally unfamiliar with the essence of coaching.

"It used to be a hobby, Mom, but now it's more than that. Basically it helps me understand people's behavior, gives me better communication skills, and fosters my dreams." Ana tried to explain it as simply as possible, but as a chemist, Mrs. K was looking for valence bonds in the context.

"I don't get it. How does it work?"

"You'll see if you join me at the certification. The trainer wants each of us to bring a person with no background in the field. You'd be perfect."

"Sure, I'd love to."

Mrs. K was flattered and curious. During that session she was open and interactive, humbly collaborating with enthusiasm.

"Do you get the essence now, mom?" Ana asked afterward.

"Well, it's a little complex, but for sure I better understand your zest for it."

"I'm glad you came . . . Listen, I have a wild idea that I can't shake from my mind . . . to study the next level at California."

"But why do you have to travel so far?" asked Mrs. K.

"Because they provide some of the best coaching trainings in the world. I want to drink from the fountain," explained Ana. She wanted to be true to her belief that if something had to be done, it should be accomplished in the best possible way.

"You keep surprising me all my life," admitted her mother.

"And I intend to continue." Ana beamed. "I'll text Stacy today. She keeps inviting me over since we ran into each other at the foreshore. I should visit them on my way since they live in the area."

Two years earlier her lost friendship with Stacy had been found in the most peculiar way. One summer day, Ana had been serenely reading a novel at the beach when she saw a man walking in the water, a man who reminded her of a person from her youth—Stacy's husband. The link between them had sunk somewhere in the Atlantic Ocean, after he and his wife had moved to California for his business shortly after Ana's marriage. She hadn't had seen or heard from them ever since. The couple's dog had been a pal to Larry once upon a time, and Ana's parents had once cherished Stacy as if she was their own daughter.

Then Mrs. K remembered.

"Stacy was with us at the cottage by the sea when you called to share the news that you were pregnant and getting married to Papsy in Paris." She laughed. "We were stunned with your dad, speechless, mainly because of the novelty that we were going to become grandparents soon. But Stacy, she was totally celebrating."

"When we reunited that day, we talked for hours—kids, parents, pets, relationships, work, lifestyle, experiences . . . lots of things had happened," said Ana. "At the end Stacy recapped my life wasn't smooth at all. Then I asked her if she had watched *The Game* with Michael Douglas and Sean Penn. Do you recall, Mom?"

"Sure."

"So I told Stacy, 'That's it, dear. I've been living in the game!'"

"Quite so," agreed Mrs. K. "And when do you think you'll visit California?"

"The training course is in August, after Lilly graduates. I could stay at Stacy's before or afterward. I'll have to discuss the precise dates with her," answered Ana.

"Please hug her for me," Mrs. K said sincerely. "I'm so happy that you've reunited."

The Prom

It was May. Ana's tiny family included two dedicated students at present—one in Oxford and the other at home. While Lilly prepared laboriously for her final exams, her mom caught up for the upcoming summer training. Meanwhile living in a distance had enriched the bond between them with tenderness and care. Now their regular conversations frequently ended with a warm "I love you" instead of the common "Bye."

"How's my little monkey doing?" Ana asked when she called her daughter to check in.

"Ugh, studying . . . This psychology survey is really tough. What about you?"

"Same thing, love, passing my tests step by step."

"Isn't it tedious?" said Lilly, cheering up.

"No, knowledge is very important," answered Ana.

"Hey, do you know the difference between knowledge and wisdom?"

"Huh?"

"Knowledge is the awareness the tomato is actually a fruit, while wisdom is not putting it in a fruit salad."

"Ha, who said that?"

"A British journalist, Miles Kington. He invented the Franglais language," explained Lilly.

"What language?" Ana marveled. Apparently Oxford's education was pretty broad.

"It's a fictional language, Mom, made up of French and English," said Lilly. Then she changed the subject. "My father called yesterday . . . to instruct me if eventually a war is coming we should evacuate to where he is . . . on a ship. He said, 'Flying will be too dangerous.'"

"Oh, boy, I'm afraid he's going nuts," said Ana, slightly irritated that he was disturbing their daughter right now, which reminded her: "And what about the universities? Any replies?"

Lilly had recently applied to her top picks.

"Not yet, unfortunately."

"It will come, don't worry," Ana assured her. "Okay, let's hit the books! I'll see you very soon at the prom."

"Yay, can't wait for it, Mummy! Love you."

"Love you too, kiddo."

The very next day Lilly called her mom with splendid news: The Marangoni Institute in Milan had accepted her application for interior design—exactly what she had longed for.

*   *   *

The big day was near. At the end of May, Ana packed her biggest suitcase with mostly elegant garments, sophisticated makeup, and high heels. On top she carefully stowed Lilly's dress.

Many lovely girls and boys had gathered in the courtyard on prom day, some dressed with style, others not so much. Yet for Ana one kid was shining bright as a morning star—her Lilly. She was astonishingly beautiful in her long royal blue dress, a combination of velvet and lace and decorated with a pinch of matching fur on the shoulders. Very stylish! She was accessorized with white gold, sapphires, and diamonds sparkling on her neck, ears, and finger—a graduation gift from Mrs. K. With an elegant bun and delicate makeup, Lilly looked like Princess Anastasia from her favorite childhood cartoon. And just like a real princess, she behaved with finesse, confidence, and kindness. Most of Lilly's classmates were amazed by her transformation. Without the jeans and the ponytail, she had become an appealing young lady, glowing from within.

Prom day was scheduled like this: first—a photo session. Then the kids would be transferred to London by bus, where a luxurious vessel would be expecting them. A vessel? Yes, while floating on the river Thames, the youngsters were going to celebrate their graduation with lots of music and fun, just like a contemporary fairy tale. Then after midnight Lilly and her best buddies would hit one of the most popular clubs in London. Wasn't the grown-up life wonderful?

Well done, Anché! Today you show off a lovely person to the world. May she always keep her sparkle alive! she thought to herself with delight.

"Hello, madam." The principal had approached Ana.

"Hi, sir, what a day!"

"Certainly. I'm very pleased Lilly has made it," said the man, smiling. He was candid.

"Thank you, sir. Not without your clemency," replied Ana with gratitude.

On the next day when the party was over, all the students had to move out of the college. So Ana and Lilly hastily packed her belongings and left. But when back in the motherland they found out the royal blue dress was missing. It seemed they had forgotten it in the rush and left it hanging on a tree outside the dormitory. Straightaway Lilly wrote an email to the warden asking for her assistance, but unfortunately the lady found nothing.

"Oh, such a pity, Mom." The girl was so sad—she loved that dress.

"Hey, let's think positive. It has served us already, and now maybe it will bring joy to somebody else who couldn't have afforded it," reframed Ana, though frankly she was sorry for the loss too.

CHAPTER 36

CALIFORNIA

"You're gonna love Cali!" Ana remembered Stacy's words. And her friend turned out to be right. Ana was spellbound, and not only because it was beautiful and so easy to live there, but also because creative fields were so ubiquitous. No doubt, Silicon Valley was the most innovative place in the world, bringing together giants like Apple, Google, Facebook, Yahoo, Amazon, and many others, just like progress's nursery. Most of the people Ana met were kind, dedicated, and peaceful. And they smiled a lot.

It must be the Redwoods' effect, she deduced one day after hiking in the forest.

The Californian Sequoias grew only there, and they were truly miraculous creatures. Ana was astounded by their size. She had never seen such huge plants, probably the largest and oldest things living on our planet. One of them was more than two thousand years old, and almost three hundred feet tall. Ana had wondered if it had sprung before the Anno Domini.

The Redwoods bore a mutual root system, which meant that their radixes were so shallow and wide that they could intertwine and even fuse together, giving them tremendous strength against the forces of nature. They could grow either by seed or by sprout, so if one were to be knocked over, its limbs could continue to grow into individuals of their own. And those family groups rising up from living remains of a fallen stump had carried identical genetic information in their cells. So, were they clones? No wonder the earliest Redwoods had showed up on Earth just after the dinosaurs, and before the flowers, birds, and humans!

The forest gave Ana a sense of sacredness; sacred like a church, where she felt connected to the collective consciousness, or to a global field of creativity, or to God . . . to something larger than the individual.

And so one night she dreamt the Redwoods. She was walking among the giant trees, touching them with her palms so as to feel something, and putting her ear on the bark so as to hear something. Then she suddenly started growing, as if she was Alice in Wonderland. Soon her head reached the top of the woods and bulged over it . . . in the distance a few pterodactyls were flying . . .

She was deeply grateful to have the opportunity to explore California. Since day one the Lovelands had shown her the sights from Stanford to San Francisco. She learned that the Golden Gate Bridge appeared to be red, not golden or yellow, and also that it was colossal—deservedly a wonder of the modern world. Lombard Street had such a cheerful spirit, and PIER 39 was an ideal spot for lunch.

"Tomorrow we're heading to Pebble Beach," Stacy announced.

"Woohoo, finally." Ana was red-hot to go there.

The famous links were an hour and a half drive from Loveland Court, so they left right after breakfast. Stacy's husband mentioned he knew a guy who worked at the golf academy in the area, but he appeared to be unfortunately absent that day.

"Never mind," commented Ana. With or without an insider, being there was exciting enough to her.

She asked for an hour of privacy, so the Lovelands went to grab a snack on their own.

Ana walked through the public area and bought some goods from the pro shop. Then headed the clubhouse's terrace. She chose one table with a mesmerizing view over the golf course and the ocean coast, and ensconced herself there. Everything was so green, so blue, so perfect . . .

Let's celebrate life, she said to herself, and ordered a glass of fine Chardonnay and a squid salad. She took a sip—the wine was excellent. Meanwhile a few carts approached the last hole in front of the terrace. Golfers were laughing. A sparrow perched on the roof nearby and looked at her kindly. Even the birds were friendly here.

But wasn't she overreacting a little? Yes, it was a famous course, one of the best three in the world. Yet why so much reverence? Well Ana believed that the ultimate prosperity was in the balance between work and free time, between duties and pleasure. True wealth was not in the expensive attributes or in the number of business trips, but rather in the quality of a person's lifestyle. And Pebble Beach was an accurate symbol of that. The ability to spend more time with loved ones or to fully enjoy one's hobbies—that was Ana's idea of affluence, not the new Porsche in the backyard . . . though she admired those convertible ones. Anyway, her point was that the highest reward for a person's efforts and achievements was the independence to celebrate life.

"I'm in heaven," she texted Lilly.

"I'm having a party," the girl replied.

"Oh, no, not again," typed Ana at once.

"Relax, Mom, I'm not a kid anymore," wrote Lilly, adding a smiley. Ana texted back: "Negative. You'll always be my kid. Love you."

"Love U2."

She then heard Stacy's voice. "Hey, it's time to go. The kids are bored, and I can't handle them anymore."

"Oh sorry, I got lost," said Ana, completely forgotten about them.

On the way home they took the scenic seventeen-mile drive along the coast. The whole area was prodigious! And that town of Carmel-by-the-Sea was simply adorable. Everything was made up with a flair, down to the smallest details. One cute cottage reminded her of Hansel and Gretel's house. On the small wooden fence in front a plate was nicely decorated with three simple words: "Living the dream!"

Chapter 37

EMOTIONS

"Hey, my buddy just texted back, the one who teaches golf... remember?" Stacy's husband announced a few days later, looking pleased. "Apparently he's staying with friends nearby, and he wants to invite you over for dinner. Would you mind if I give him your number?"

"Awesome, it might be good to have some social contacts before my classes. Is he a nice person?"

"Sure, he's super cool. I'll drive you there and pick you up, no worries."

"Ok, thanks."

The GPS in the car announced that the desired destination was just fourteen minutes from Loveland Court. When at the set hour, they arrived at a fancy house matching the corresponding address and parked in front, a short sporty man was talking on the phone in the doorway.

"That's him," said Stacy's husband.

"Hey, he looks better than I expected."

"Believe me, you look better than he expects too." Her companion added.

Ana was elegantly dressed in white patent high heels, white trousers, and a bright green top that made her face glow. Delicate makeup accented her eyes and features. She exuded comfort and confidence.

"Well, well, well. You *are* trying to match me with him."

"Let's just say we'd be happy to have you around more often." Stacy's husband blushed as they got out of the car.

The guy's call continued long enough for him to examine Ana from head to toe on the sly before they spoke. Then he hung up and introduced himself with a young boy's audacity. He was in good shape and had charming dimples when he smiled.

"Hey, nice to meet you, Ana."

The Golfer energetically shook her hand. He saluted Stacy's husband, and they briefly exchanged pleasantries. Afterward, Ana's friend arranged a time to pick her up and said good-bye.

"Please, come in," the Golfer invited, opening the door for her. The living room was quite big, but it was plenty occupied. There were five kids, five adults excluding Ana, a dog, and a nanny.

"Welcome to my house," one of the ladies greeted her. Apparently this was the hostess. And yes, her house was really impressive— spacious, luxurious, and well decorated. Outside, behind the French windows, a nice swimming pool and relaxation area were visible. Because it was a warm evening, the table was arranged al fresco with a bottle of white wine on ice.

Soon the party was in full swing. The food was delicious, all the people were friendly and nice. Ana was surprised to find out that the gathering was actually to celebrate Golfer's birthday, and she appeared to be his lady for tonight. Ha, it reminded her of a knock-knock joke:

"Hey, who's there?"

"Me, I'm your birthday present, so you won't be alone at your own party."

As the bachelor's guest, Ana was understandably in the spotlight. As she was both a foreigner and a newcomer, his friends were curious to know more about her.

"Would you tell us about your country?"

"And what about your life?"

"Oh, you have a daughter. Wonderful. How old is she? . . . Really? You look too young to have a daughter that age."

"And you came to the States for leisure?"

"Studying? What particularly?"

"Coaching, how fascinating!"

"Do you know that the kids call you 'Snow White'?"

Meanwhile, the Golfer was silently appraising Ana. The more she told about herself and her motivation in life, the more intrigued he seemed. Everyone was enjoying this amiable, humorous, and tipsy evening . . . until midnight, when it was time for Ana to go home.

"Please don't bother our friend. I'll send you over," the Golfer politely suggested, and Ana agreed.

*   *   *

When the taxi stopped at Loveland Court, all the inhabitants in the house were sleeping. It was quiet. The delicate light of the street lamps painted romantic scenery.

"You have a million-dollar smile, Ana," the Golfer said, kindly offering his hand to help her out of the car.

"Thanks, it was a wonderful evening." She took his hand and slowly stepped out.

"Would you like to have dinner with me tomorrow?"

"Yes, tomorrow will be okay, as my training begins the day after."

"Perfect, then I'll see you later, gorgeous." He smiled. His dimples were so cute.

"Fine, 'til tomorrow, birthday boy."

Ana hugged him, and walked into the house.

*   *   *

The next evening, on their first date, Ana planned to claim she had to be up really early in the morning if her date wasn't going well.

When sending her away, Stacy's husband had added earnestly, "And remember, a good way to get to know more about your date is to ask about their pets, favorite movies, and mom's maiden name. That way you can log in and read all their emails."

Later, in between the salad and the main dish, she learned that the Golfer was much more than a sportsman. After playing golf for a living in his youth, later on he had invented a robot to help people improve their swings. Because of that he was very busy and traveled a lot, with no weekends off or vacations. It was all about the work, no chilling! Despite the fact that he was a complete workaholic, Ana appreciated his good heart and big dreams. She concluded that the Golfer was a young boy inhabiting an adult's body, and he definitely had positive vibes. She liked him. There was merit in his being a visionary, and his progressiveness raised him up in her eyes. As a result, that night Ana completely forgot about "having to be up really early" and even told him her cat's name, Summer.

When the training started, Ana was glowing. She and the Golfer were texting all the time, and he asked repeatedly when he would see her again or when she could come over. So the only day she had off she spent not with her new colleagues, but with him. That night at dinner she asked every woman's most pressing question.

"Why are you still single?"

"Because I work too much," he admitted.

"Many people work too much but still have relationships and kids," Ana remarked disapprovingly. "Do you know how many divine moments you're missing?"

"How could I?" the Golfer answered simply.

Sure, how could he? Ana remembered Lilly saying of her father, "How could I miss something I have never had?" As he looked down at his plate, the Golfer continued.

"But I would love to have a family, especially kids. I adore them. It's just . . . I haven't met my soul mate yet. Hey, who knows? It might be you." The dimples appeared on his face.

"Me? I live on the other side of the globe. It would be a little complicated, don't you think?"

"Distance doesn't matter. Only feelings matter."

"Hmm, who said that?"

"Me, dummy," he joked.

"Well, I have had a slightly different life experience," said Ana, referring to her screwed-up marriage with Papsy.

The topic seemed to be getting way too serious, so the Golfer changed the subject. "When are you going back home?"

"Right after my training's over."

"Can you stay longer with me? I'll take a few days off so I can show you around. It would be fun."

Ana loved the idea. After all, she was there, the academic part of her journey would be over, and she didn't have to escort Lilly and settle her into Milan until the beginning of October.

"I think I can do it for a week or ten days. I'll have my agent check the flights. It would be great to spend some quality time together."

"Awesome. I'll introduce you to my parents. They're gonna love you. Let's drink to us!" He cheerfully raised his glass.

"Good one—to us, birthday boy!" she repeated, and blew him a kiss.

Ana spent the night with him, and early the morning she drove back to the university for class. Same day the Golfer texted her, "I love you." Well, later on she would discover that texting was the main way he communicated with the world, but in that moment, she replied: "No, it doesn't count. You have to say it in person." And he did. He said it many times regardless of the occasion.

Cupid was around! And so the best part of their romance, one of the most emotional ones in Ana's life, began after the end of her training when she brought over some of her luggage and stayed with him.

The Golfer was renting a small apartment in that lovely little town by the ocean, just five minutes away from his main occupation—the Golf Academy, where he was committed to spending two weeks each month teaching people in person. So they enjoyed a few wonderful days until his rotation was over. Then suitcases were readied for flight. First stop, Arizona; the second one, Chicago, where he was from; and then back to San Francisco.

On the plane Ana rested her head on his shoulder, while the Golfer caught up on emails. In the front row a father was trying to calm down his spoiled kid, who had been whining and sniveling since takeoff. With every minute the father got more and more embarrassed, because apparently his methods were not working well. In a while he turned around.

"I apologize, ma'am. I simply can't cope with my son. Do you have any idea how can I make him shut up?"

"I have one, sir. I'm from Chicago." The Golfer winked. He meant that the old-fashioned hard methods had been historically proven in his hometown. The little boy got him, huffed, and kept quiet for the rest of the flight.

In Arizona it was hot, both outside and in between the sheets. The Golfer was out on his duties during the days, and in the evening they chilled at the pool before having sushi at the hotel's fancy restaurant.

"Do you love me because I have a robot?" he asked at dinner out of the blue. His tone implied another question: "Do you love me because I might get rich one day?"

Ana considered her answer. "Yes, actually, I do love you because you have a robot. It demonstrates your creativity, consistency, and dependability."

And just like that she alleviated his suspicions.

The next morning they flew to Chicago—brisk, modern, and picturesque city. The shore of Lake Michigan was similar to that of the sea, as it was only four times smaller than the sea beside Ana's country. She took some pictures and sent a few to Lilly, who of course had already been informed about the love affair across the ocean.

"What do you think about him?" Ana texted her daughter, attaching a picture of her with the Golfer.

"He looks cool, and certainly you are a good-looking couple, but the most important thing is how you feel with him."

"I feel great. He's so gentle."

"Super, I'm happy for you, Mom. I gotta go now. Call me tomorrow?"

And the next day when Ana did call, she had news to share.

"I met his parents, love. They are such nice people. We had lots of fun, playing nine holes at a nearby course. And his mom, she was truly impressed by my appearance. She said, 'But she is a woman, son!'"

"She was surprised you're not a guy?" Lilly was lost.

"No, it was more like, 'She is a woman, son, while you are still a boy.'"

"A-ha-ha, gotcha. He's older than you, right?"

"Yes, two years… And afterward we had pizza at his favorite spot. It was the best ever. Tomorrow he's taking us to my first baseball game, the Chicago Cubs are playing."

"Awesome! When are you coming back? I can't wait to hear it all."

"Next week hopefully. I miss you very much," replied Ana.

"I miss you too, Mom. Love ya."

The baseball game was quite a show. Afterward, for their last night in Chicago, Ana and the Golfer went to the hotel's rooftop bar for a glass of wine while drafting plans to often visit each other when they were apart. Suddenly she felt woozy for no reason, and they had to leave before finishing their drinks. The Golfer put her in bed, carefully covered her with a blanket, and kissed her good night.

"Sweet dreams, my love."

"Sweet dreams, birthday boy. Thank you for all these wonderful memories. I love you!"

"Shush, you should rest now," he whispered.

Then he lay close by and tenderly cuddled her. They were happy . . .

*   *   *

The end of Ana's journey was coming soon, so they flew back to San Francisco a little sad, a little tired, and a little worried. What was it going to be like when they were away from each other?

"Are you sure you want to spend your last night at the Lovelands'?"

"Yes, I've promised them. Moreover, the rest of my luggage is still there. It will be more convenient for me to pack everything in the morning."

"Okay, but I would like to take you to the airport."

"Sweet," she agreed at once. Secretly she had been hoping for him to say that.

On her last night in California, Ana had a heart-to-heart dinner with her cherished friends, telling them about the places she had been and the emotions she had felt. Even though she was leaving the next day, the spirit in the Lovelands' home was quite optimistic. Hopefully this love affair was about to grow into something lasting, and they would be seeing each other more often. After a couple of hours laughing and daydreaming, it was bedtime.

"Gee, I'll rest well tonight. As you know, those who snore always fall asleep first," commented Ana, as the Golfer was the "prince" of snoring.

"Ha-ha, true." Stacy laughed, then they kissed and stepped into their separate rooms.

In the morning Ana woke up with a weird hunch that something was missing. She grabbed her phone and opened the app she used to track her period. The last date had been skipped.

How is this possible, Anché? You're not a teenager, she thought, and yet the gap was clear. She hastily packed her luggage and rushed to the nearby pharmacy. Blimey, the test was positive. She was officially pregnant. Knock-knock . . .

Her emotions were mixed. On one hand, it was a splendid opportunity for a new beginning with her beloved one, and Ana adored kids very much. Now that her daughter was grown, she missed those divine moments. On the other hand, she was aware of how tough parenting might be without a reliable partner. So far she'd had a great time with the Golfer, but it was too soon to predict if he would be, or would even willingly be, a good husband and a good father. She hoped he would embrace the unthought-of news. She didn't want to have to endeavor out on her own again.

Should I text him now? No, I'd better tell him in person when he comes later, she thought.

When Ana got ready to go, all the members of the Loveland family were out—the father was at work, the kids were at school, and the mother was on her way to pick them up. Soon the Golfer's car stopped out front. She was waiting for him downstairs with the door open.

"Hey, I missed you last night." He kissed her hello. "That outfit suits you very well, love. You are glowing."

"It's not the outfit, birthday boy. Have you wished for something more than me?"

"What do you mean?"

"Look," she said, showing him the sample with the two marks on it.

"Is this real? If I didn't fall asleep yesterday, I was going to ask you if you still can . . ."

Well, evidentially she could! The Golfer didn't seem to know what to say or to do as Ana, dressed in a vibrant yellow dress, stood beaming in front of him with her million-dollar smile.

"When did you find out?"

"Today, a few hours ago. I think it's a sign!"

"So you're pregnant with my baby for real?!"

He was still processing the news. It was possible, as he had not used protection when they were intimate; and also, she looked even happier than before. The test was positive, and . . . He had put together all the details—it was true!

"Come here. I wanna hold you so much. Let's make love right now."

"There's no time. The flight—remember?"

"No, stay!"

"I can't. I have to settle Lilly in Milan. No one else can do it. She has just me."

"I would like to text her. What's her number?"

"I'll give it to you in the car. Come on."

At the airport the Golfer was waving and sending his last "I love you" as the woman with the yellow dress disappeared into the crowd at the checkpoint area. He wished he could stop her, to beg her to stay, to even insist . . . She was carrying his baby, after all!

Soon Ana took her seat at the plane. Yes, it was time to get home. When forty days ago she flew over, even in her wildest dreams she couldn't have imagined that she would end up in love and pregnant. Life was such a mystery. Her journey to the States had awarded her with an incredible number of emotion, if they had been material objects, she could have filled the whole aircraft with them.

And now, now she had so many questions: Was the distance going to matter? How was the Golfer going to behave from now on? Was he going to take responsibility for Ana's pregnancy? Maybe this time everything would be just fine, and maybe she had finally found a decent man who would stay to enjoy parenting together. It would be so engrossing! In that very moment, Ana felt she was ready for that big step. But did the Golfer share in her true willingness to commit, or in his head was the case more like Ana versus the robot? Was he ready to start a family? And in general, was he brave enough to change his lifestyle in the name of love?

She had so many questions on her mind, questions with no answers . . .

CPSIA information can be obtained
at www.ICGtesting.com
Printed in the USA
LVHW09*1959050918
589239LV00012B/279/P